HOLD

HOLD

A NOVEL

RACHEL DAVIDSON LEIGH

interlude press • new york

To Michael. Sweet boy, this one's for you. ♫

*"In three words I can sum up everything
I've learned about life: It goes on."*
—Robert Frost

Sampson.
Gregory: A my word wee'l not carry Coales.
Greg. No, for then we should be Colliars.
Greg. Do you quarrell sir?
sir fir? no sir.
o sir, I am for you, I serue as goo
Abra. No better? Samp. Well

CHAPTER ONE

LUKE KEPT HIS HEAD DOWN.

As he pushed through the doors of North Grove Senior High and into the open foyer, he looked at the mock-marble floor and waited for everyone to fall into the dance he'd always known. He might have been away for more than a month, but some things never changed. Bodies moved, wrapped up in their own drama and, with any luck, they didn't notice him.

The hall clock outside the main office said first period would end any minute. Below the clock, where there had been a blank, white wall, someone had installed a mural made of tiny colored tiles. Luke had no idea who decided these things, but in the last two months they'd added hundreds of one-inch by one-inch tiles end to end until the wall shimmered with borrowed light. From far enough back, the tiles made an abstractly ethnic man with his wide, flat arms outstretched over a multicolored globe. Maybe he was supposed to be "Education" or "Possibility." He could have stood for God. It didn't matter. He hadn't been there in December. He was new.

Luke counted down in his head, but the bell never came. The hall was silent, and in the stillness the students swarmed into the hall, like hornets shaken from their nest.

He was slinking toward the side of the hallway with his eyes on the floor when a hand slapped hard across his back. Luke flinched.

"Ehhh, Punjab! Welcome back to the land of plenty!"

Perfect. He turned toward a pale face staring up at him with a guileless grin. *Wes.* He could always count on Wesley Corelli, with his long lacrosse-star limbs and his future-frat-brother smile, to make him feel like Indian Kid #2 out of central casting. He only came up to Luke's nose, but the ego added at least a foot. And, of course, he had half the lacrosse team trailing behind him.

Luke didn't know the first thing about India, but that didn't make a difference to Wes or any of the rest of them. He'd been *Punjab* since eighth grade. If you asked Wes, he'd say it was a compliment. Luke was his bro. Luke was cool enough for a nickname. He'd been elevated from mere nerd to honorary dudebro. Never mind that getting called the wrong name from down the hallway made him feel like a sideshow in someone else's circus.

If Dee were here she'd have torn him a new one, again. She'd have hollered, "His name isn't Punjab, you ingrate!" and threatened to tell their parents that "their son is a racist prick."

Not that she ever told on him; family is family. But the threat was usually enough to send Wes backing down the hall with his hands in the air as he muttered about crazy women. This time Dee wasn't here to tell her brother and his band of idiots where to shove it. He just had Wes and his boys, who leaned into Luke's space and laughed as if they were old friends. Luke's eyes snapped back down to the floor. What did he expect? He'd been out "recuperating" for almost a month and never told Dee he was coming back. She couldn't have known—

"Do you even still go here?" Wes's friend, Elliot, leaned over his shoulder and cocked his head in Luke's face. "Not to offend or anything, but I thought you, you know…" As he trailed off, he popped his fingers from a fist to an open hand above his head, as if to suggest that Luke had disappeared or spontaneously combusted.

The other guys whispered behind Luke's back. That was new. They never whispered before he left. Whispering implied shame and, until now, he could have considered that an improvement. Wes and the others stood in a tight pack near the wall, glancing back and forth with wide, worried eyes. For the first time in his three years at North Grove, his personal band of idiots seemed to care about his feelings, and he wished they'd go back to the nicknames.

Luke swallowed and scrambled at his backpack. His backpack hadn't changed. "This has been great. Really guys. But I have class, so if I could just go—"

He was two steps from the edge of the foyer when Elliot's voice echoed at his back. "Hey, Punj—I mean, hey, Luke?" His voice had nervous edges and Luke stopped in his tracks. "Jenny said you—she said—"

Elliot trailed off in the middle of the sentence. Luke wasn't sure if he was supposed to turn around and console the little thug for developing a conscience or keep walking because none of what they were thinking was any of their business. It didn't matter, because Luke couldn't make himself do anything. He stood, frozen and sick under North Grove's fluorescent lights, waiting for the hammer to fall.

Wes obliged. "God, you pussies." He laughed, and Luke could actually hear him roll his eyes. "Your girlfriend's probably full of shit anyways, El. Luke's cool. Just ask." He raised his voice. "Punjab?" he called. "Do you even have a sister?"

Luke closed his eyes.

He'd prepared answers to dozens of questions when he should have been sleeping. He'd invented answers to questions none of them were smart enough to ask, but he couldn't answer that one. He couldn't breathe. He couldn't take in enough air to move or speak, and if he fainted in the middle of the hallway—

"'Scuse me?" A voice sounded at Luke's back. "Is this a bad time? I just need to speak with—" A finger tapped at Luke's shoulder. "Excuse me, are you Lucas? I've been told I have to talk to a Lucas Aday."

A bad time? Luke was living the textbook definition of a bad time and he was about to say so when the owner of the voice emerged. Luke's answer died in his throat. It was a guy, a not-horribly-unattractive guy, all rich brown skin and thick, furrowed brows. He blocked Luke's view down the hall, and Luke didn't entirely mind. The guy just needed to stop smiling and explain himself. He didn't belong at North Grove. For one thing, he was too well-dressed. Even the former Catholic school kids didn't show up in button-downs and khakis and they never showed up in light *pink*.

"Hey. Sorry to interrupt." The guy held up a slip of paper and waved it toward the others, but he didn't sound sorry. "I've just got this *thing*," he said. His voice was too loud, and, as he brandished the paper, Luke might as well have been onstage in a play without his lines. This guy caught his eye and said *thing* as if it was supposed to be their inside joke, as if he expected Luke to look away from his clump of idiots and laugh.

"The hell?" Luke said, under his breath. "What do you think you're doing?"

The preppy guy's smile grew. It was a good look, but unnerving. "I'm doing a good deed. Is that a problem?"

Luke blinked. The kid wasn't tall. They were almost the same height. He might have been wider and more solid around the shoulders, but that didn't explain how he could lay claim to half the hallway. His left hand was tapping away at his side, but his eyes weren't impatient. They were calm, and he was definitely new.

"Eddie, by the way," the guy said. "That's who I am." He held out his hand, the one that wasn't tapping against his leg. Luke didn't take it. "Mrs. Danes told me to find you and gave me a sense of what to look for. I started here a couple weeks ago?"

Luke stared at his outstretched hand. What could his English teacher have said: *Keep an eye out for a bony Indian kid with big ears, but don't move too fast, he's twitchy*? That would have worked. He looked up the hallway and then to the cracked tiles at his feet. Why hadn't he told Dee he was coming back? She could have been waiting for him. He couldn't breathe.

Eddie followed his gaze and his smile faded into a grimace. "I really do have to talk to you, just to be clear, but the timing was—" He jerked his head back as Wes and the others peered around his back. "You needed help. I didn't mean to hold you up, but I know those guys a little and I thought if you were new and I wasn't quite as new we could—I don't know—be new together?" His hand wavered, still held out and waiting. Luke could have taken it.

"No," he said, so quietly he almost didn't hear himself. Luke wanted—he didn't know what he wanted, but he didn't want to be new. Everything else was already new. "I don't know you," he said, his voice tight in his throat. "I don't know if Mrs. Danes actually sent you or if you made that up to be a good guy, but stop. I know those idiots."

"Idiots? Bro, that was uncalled for," Wes called from the wall. They all waited there, watching like vultures. "I'm not the one with *the thing*."

"I already know all of this," Luke went on, "because I'm not like you." Eddie leaned away, his eyes wide. "You've known them for the five minutes you've been at this school. Congratulations. I've had them on my back for eleven years." Luke's stomach seized and he clenched the straps of his bag as he yelled to the boys huddled against the wall. "Hey, Elliot? Your girlfriend was right. I had a sister, and now she's dead, so now I have a dead sister."

Eddie's shock felt like victory.

"Welcome," he bit out between his teeth, low enough only for Eddie's ears. "I don't know what you're trying to do, but I don't need it. Not today. Thanks. Have a great day."

His mouth slack, Eddie looked as though he'd taken a sucker punch in the solar plexus. Maybe he couldn't breathe either.

Good.

Luke turned and stalked toward the commons as Wes whistled at his back. His chest—there was a vise around his chest and it wouldn't come off. If he put one foot in front of the other, he could maybe reach his locker before he froze or cried or passed out on the floor. He hated this place from the ground up, but everything needed to go back to an awful he could understand.

After two months of hospital corridors, hospice and a tasteful funeral, he'd have turned down a million dollars for one week when no one stared or waited for him to fall apart. He hadn't cried in front of the grandparents he hardly knew or the family friends he couldn't stand. He wouldn't fall apart for them, and he certainly wasn't going to fall apart for Wes Corelli.

Luke hurried past the sophomore hallways and toward the junior commons with eyes on his back. They watched his steps and burnt holes in his sweatshirt. He wore layers—a too-large sweatshirt over a T-shirt, and both under a jacket—but it wasn't enough. They could still see him and make him small. Two years ago when he'd "officially" come out as the little queer kid he'd been since preschool, he might as well have been a bug in a Mason jar. For days, he'd known everyone was watching him, until Dee had said that the world didn't care. She'd been wrong about that. They'd cared when he got pushed down in the hallway—again, but he'd pretended she was right. They hadn't cared about him, so he hadn't cared about them. *Easy.*

Dee would have said the same thing now, and this time, she would have been right. He was being ridiculous. He dragged his feet and let the squeak of his soles carry him down the hallway. The kids didn't really know about "the kid whose sister died;" if they stared it was probably because he just made an ass of himself.

And he couldn't breathe. A lead weight sat in his gut and squeezed the air from his lungs.

"Watch out, asshole!"

As he entered the junior commons, Luke almost stepped on a pair of shoes. The girl wearing them found her way around him and scowled under her breath as Luke leaned against the nearest wall. He was going to look teary-eyed and breakable no matter what. Along the edges he couldn't do more damage, and that's where he caught the flash of blue. It was on the wall next to the boy's bathroom.

The poster, held up by Scotch tape, announced the theater department's Spring Review in the same color and font they'd used when Luke was nine. Ten years from now they would probably still perform Shakespearian tragedies and *Oklahoma*. This year, they were doing *25th Annual Putnam County Spelling Bee,* but he didn't care about that. He cared about the names of the tech crew written across the bottom of the poster. That was their spot, his and Marcos Aldama's and Dee's. For a year and a half, since they'd been trusted to not to electrocute themselves, they'd run tech for every production this school had bothered to stage. Dee was supposed to be the stage manager, Marcos was supposed to be on sound and he was supposed to be on sets.

But he wasn't there.

He found Dee's and Marcos's names right where they were supposed to be, and then there was a third name. He'd been replaced by Neil Vargassi. *Vargassi?* Luke had last heard that name when he'd found out that "that Vargassi kid" had fallen off the stage during warm ups and had had to be sent to the emergency room.

Luke read the poster three times with his hand pressed against the wall beside it. The wall wasn't going anywhere. He wasn't sure about anything else.

They wouldn't—he read it again. But of course, they would. He'd been gone a month at the beginning of the spring semester with no explanation. Of course they would have found someone to take his place, and he'd had the easiest tech job in the world. He wasn't irreplaceable, but he'd never thought—

He turned away from the poster and made himself move, as the sickness slid into his gut. It pooled in a sludge below his navel, like a toxic spill, and his body wanted it gone, but there were people going in and out of the bathroom. There were people everywhere.

Luke clasped his hand over his mouth. On his right, the door to a dark classroom sat ajar. He threw himself inside, grabbed the trashcan by the door and gagged until his eyes watered. Nothing came up. He couldn't even make himself puke. He couldn't do anything but make people feel sorry for him.

Luke crouched at the closed door with his back flat against the metal kick plate and pressed his fingers against his temples until pain blossomed under his skin. His stomach turned.

I can't make it stop, because I shouldn't be here anymore.

He closed his eyes against the empty classroom, the dirty book jackets and the kick marks on the legs of the chairs.

I should be gone. It should have been me.

Luke pushed himself to his feet and tasted tears. His phone rang in his backpack again and again. He had to answer it because it could have been his mom, but his hands couldn't remember how. He pulled at the zipper on the front of his bag, but it wouldn't give. He couldn't make it move. He tried again and, before he knew what he was doing, he hit it. He hit the bag over and over again until it crunched under his fists. He punched grooves into the plastic lining and ripped holes in the straps.

The holes were real. He made them. The fabric tore under his hands. He made that happen. But the phone wouldn't stop ringing—four, five, six—and, as he gasped for air, he lifted the backpack and heaved it across the room like a grenade.

Luke turned away, closed his eyes and waited for it to smash against the far wall. He waited and listened for the crunch and the snap, but it never came. His bag never hit the floor.

CHAPTER TWO

When Luke thought of his sister, Luke remembered her tongue.

It seemed like an obscene thing to say, so he'd never said it, not even to the friends who had come to the funeral and watched all the *Marvel* movies afterward. He'd let them pet his hair and hand him sandwiches he wouldn't eat, but he hadn't talked about that. It was too intimate for words.

He'd been in the room when Lizzy died. They'd all known it was coming, but he had been the person in the room when she'd gone from being Lizzy-the-sister to Lizzy-the-body. His aunts and uncles had asked about his favorite memories "of your dear sister," but Luke hadn't been able to stop thinking about her open mouth and the tongue that stopped looking like a human tongue. It had looked like a prop, like a plastic thing they might have put on the props table backstage, outlined in Masking tape so it wouldn't get lost. Her hands and her hair and even her eyes had still been human, but her tongue had said she wasn't real anymore.

He had seen her death coming for months. They all had. As long as he could remember, Luke had known Lizzy wasn't supposed to still be alive. Her condition—they only ever said *condition*—with seizures and septicemia, was supposed to be too much for little girls, at least when she'd been born. For a long time, Luke hadn't known if that was true or just something fathers say to little boys who don't know better. First, the doctors had said that she would die before age three, and then before five. By the time Luke had arrived, seven years later, they had given up predicting what would happen next. Lizzy hadn't been following their timelines, so they'd stopped making them. She'd lived to see her twenties, and Luke had liked to think of her existence as a constant *screw you* to the medical system. They were so bad at being wrong.

In the end, it had been bronchitis, not her *condition*. He wanted to write that on a sign. She hadn't died because she was disabled, and it wasn't a blessing. It just was. He hadn't been able to put his dad's tears into words.

It hadn't helped that the doctors had never stopped wondering what he was doing there. They couldn't get it through their thick, educated skulls that he could be related to the little white girl in the hospital bed and her white parents. When his mother had politely reminded them that Luke was their son too, the shock was momentary, but the admiration went on for days. His parents were an "inspiration." When his mother had heard them, she'd told them where they could shove their inspiration, but she hadn't always heard.

Even at the end, Lizzy had laughed hardest when Luke hurt himself. He'd say "ouch" and she'd giggle through sixteen different kinds of medication. Luke had liked to think that she was actually a ninety-year-old asshole, because, not so deep inside, so was he. She had died on a Thursday, while Luke was sitting on the hard couch in the corner of the hospital room. He'd been drawing superheroes for Dee, lost in the captions around Hawkeye's head, and when he'd looked up—

He'd kept on breathing and he hadn't cried.

His parents had stopped. The stillness had started before Lizzy died. As soon as she was checked into hospice care, back in December, the entire Aday family had taken up residence in her room and never left. The couch had been Luke's ground, the way the recliner in the corner "belonged" to his dad. He could have kept going to school, but after one week turned into two, his parents had stopped. Unread back issues of *Newsweek* had piled up on the hospital end table, as though one day his dad might read them, and, back home, mail had built up on the kitchen table.

By the time Lizzy was gone, the kitchen pile had slid onto the floor, but Luke wasn't sure his parents could still notice. His mom kept reorganizing family photo albums, moving a picture of the whole family before and then after a shot of Lizzy's first birthday party, as though there were some way to get it right.

"It was a beautiful cake," she murmured. Luke didn't respond.

His dad disappeared into the kitchen; he'd cooked for the wake and then for the visitors who showed up on their doorstep and then for the rest of the family until spoiled hotdish piled up in the fridge. Then they ate take-out on the floor.

Luke lived in his room, painting and drawing and spiraling circles into circles until he'd run out of space for curves. He'd started a collage of drawings above his bed on the last day of seventh grade, but after Lizzy died it had grown from five pictures to more than fifteen. Mostly, they were superheroes. Spider-Man and Miss Marvel, in all of their masked glory, bled into a picture of five-year-old Luke and twelve-year-old Lizzy at his first Concert in the Park. The drawing had him weaving strands of crepe paper through the spokes of her wheelchair while she giggled to The Rich Lewis Band. He hadn't included the part after the show when it had rained and he'd cried over bits of soggy red and green. She'd loved her chair. It had meant freedom and he'd made it beautiful.

The day Luke had gone back to school, he woke up alone. While the light had been still dim between the shades, he made a lunch in the stale air and forced himself to open the front door. The February wind hit him like an accusation, but he stepped into the chill and kept walking. The house was still asleep and the traffic moved too quickly for seven-thirty in the morning, but he was unable to wait any longer. The phone calls from the school had turned into threatening letters and even his mother had noticed he wasn't supposed to be still at home. As she had pasted "Lizzy at her sixth birthday" next to their trip to Quebec, she'd asked if he was going back to school the next day, and Luke hadn't had a reason not to say yes.

Being at home in the quiet wasn't reason enough not to say yes.

CHAPTER THREE

THE BAG DIDN'T LAND.

Luke waited for the splintering plastic and metal as his bag broke the smartboard or sent markers flying, but it didn't come. The room was silent. Even the heater had gone silent, leaving just the sound of Luke's shallow breath. He turned with his hand braced against the doorframe, and his knuckles went white.

He never heard his backpack slam or break because it never hit the ground. It was still in the air, hanging over the teacher's desk as if suspended by invisible strings. The bag must have opened as it flew and before it stopped, because the front pocket gaped and what had been inside was in the air. His pens, pencils and phone trailed in the bag's wake, suspended as if held by invisible hands. His calculator, a bottle of Tylenol and a wad of cash led back to his hands in a wide arc of debris, all frozen in the moment they'd tumbled out of his bag and some cosmic entity hit the pause button on the world. Except, it forgot to stop him.

Luke inched forward with his hands tight at his sides. He passed under his wallet, pencils and pens, all of them static as frozen angels. Finally, he stopped as his blood beat in his ears and stared up at the bottom of his own backpack. His mom had written his name on the underside when he'd started freshman year and there it was, over his head, in faded black. He opened his hand and reached up until the bag was only inches above his palm. He could have touched it, but he let its shadow ghost back and forth over his skin. The bag could have a shadow, but it couldn't fall. The room held its pose, like a dancer en pointe, and he wanted so badly for it to be real.

It wasn't though. Of the two of them, the world wasn't the one that cracked. Part of him wanted to sit under his bag, with his back against the front of the teacher's desk, and wait to see how long the hallucination could last. It couldn't be long. His brain would eventually kick him out of the silence and back to the spinning nausea of the day.

At the same time, Luke knew, the way he knew his favorite color, that waiting wouldn't do any good. He squinted at the pens above his head. They weren't moving. Maybe the pieces of the world wouldn't go back where they belonged. Maybe they liked it this way, too. Luke moved to the door and slid it open to peek into the hall. He didn't know what he expected, maybe other people freaking out about gravity-defying school supplies. That would have been better than what he found.

The hall was still. As he cracked open the door, Luke stared into the frozen face of his chemistry teacher, Dr. Ayalote, rounding the corner toward the junior commons. A minute ago she might have been talking or singing to herself, but now she stared, her mouth open mid-word. Nothing suggested that she saw him. Maybe she only saw whatever she'd looked at before her world stopped, like a movie frozen in front of her face. Past her static smile, walking legs, swinging arms and turning heads filled the hallway. Every single body stood suspended mid-motion. Jenny—Elliot's Jenny—laughed down at her phone, except that she didn't anymore. She just held her hand over her silent mouth and stared at the screen.

It wasn't just this room. It was everywhere, except him. He could move.

How—? How did *he*—? Luke mentally slapped himself. *Stupid.* It was stupid to think that, somehow, his selfishness stopped the world. This couldn't possibly be his fault, but—

Luke took one last look at Dr. Ayalote's frozen face, slammed the door behind him and slumped against the frosted glass. Pretending to have superpowers was bad—really, really bad—but it was better than hallucinations. If he'd made the world stop he could make it go again. He just needed the right words.

"Go," he whispered. "Go. Go. Go. Go." Each time, he got louder until he yelled into the silence at a backpack that was still in the air. "Damn it." He couldn't be stuck like this forever. He had to go back to Dee and Marcos. He had to go back to his parents.

Oh God, his parents.

He couldn't be crazy. He couldn't. His parents couldn't take that, too. "Don't do this," he said through clenched teeth. "Please, come back. Please. Please. Please. Please. Unfreeze. Unhold. *Come back.*"

He squeezed his eyes shut, and the world came back.

The late bell rang as his bag hit the board with a dull smack. His cell phone screen cracked as it hit the floor, and spider webs rippled across the glass. He picked it up, turned it over and let the heaviness sit in the palm of his hand. The calculator and the pens all landed and broke, as they were supposed to, and, if he believed the clock, no time had passed. Something had made the whole world stop around him, like his own bubble in time, but it was gone. He couldn't crawl back inside. *I'm sorry. I don't understand.* He curled around his backpack with his things scattered like debris and willed the silence to come back.

CHAPTER FOUR

MR. EDELHEIT WAS ALREADY IN the middle of announcements when Luke crept into the back of the room. His seat behind Dee sat empty, and Luke breathed out a tiny, embarrassing, sigh of relief.

Mine. That seat was his and it was where he'd left it. It wasn't back in the empty classroom hanging in the air.

Luke's hands shook as he closed the door, but the room helped. Nothing ever changed here. He could come back to Mr. E's room in ten years, and one wall would be filled with information on World War One poets and another with the ways to get a paper dumped in the trash. Luke wasn't sure if the guy was serious about the vital difference between "alot" and "a lot," but it was safer to assume he meant every word.

"Okay, and number two." Mr. Edelheit raised an eyebrow at Luke's entrance and kept reading from a book in hands. "The narrator says, quote, that 'Dominicans are Caribbean and therefore have an extraordinary tolerance for extreme phenomena. How else could we have survived what we survived?'" He looked over the top of the book with his significant face, which meant everything was *very significant.* "What does he mean by that? What do you think 'tolerance' has to do with Oscar's love of science fiction?" He sing-songed through questions on the smartboard and his words rang clear as gibberish. Mr. Edelheit spoke, everyone else wrote and Luke might as well have been on the moon.

"Take out your copies of *The Brief Wondrous Life of Oscar Wao* and use the next ten minutes to write out your thoughts on both questions. You will be turning these in, people."

Luke pretended he had his book. Luke pretended he could focus on words. Luke pretended.

Dee didn't turn when he sat down. Even after Mr. E's announcement, as the class shuffled to find books and pens, she had her chin resting on the heel of one hand and her eyes locked forward. He sank down at the desk and pulled his cracked phone into his lap. When he blinked, he still saw his backpack hanging over his head, like a ghost behind his eyelids.

He opened his eyes again and typed.

[From Luke to Dee] You got Vargassi for set construction? What kind of a budget do you have for hospital bills?

He reread the text to Dee, with half an eye on the back of her head. The words sounded normal, or at least, as normal as they got. When she texted back, he was so relieved he almost dropped the phone.

[From Dee] hello to you too.

Normal. That was normal.

[From Dee] where the hell are you? Kazakhstan?

Luke kicked the back of her chair, and she whipped around; her eyes grew wide, and her mouth dropped in a silent *holy mother of God.* Her hair was shorter than when he'd last seen her, but it was still the same dirty blonde wreck.

[From Luke] You have no chill.
[From Dee] YOURE BAKC!!!!!!
[From Dee] HIIIIIII WHEN DID YOU GET BACK?!

She wasn't even pretending to hide her phone anymore, and Luke loved her, even from his spot on the moon.

[From Luke] :P
[From Dee] I CAN'T HUG YOU RIGHT NOW BUT ALSO I HATE YOU. You fell off the face of the earth you asshole.
[From Luke] Yeah. Sorry.
[From Dee] I forgive you *is magnanimous* *is an angel* *is better than you* And now I can fire Vargassi.

She peeked over her shoulder with a tight smile. Anyone else might think she was mad, but if they weren't in the middle of class, she'd have him wrapped up in the kind of hug reserved for veterans returning from war. What Dee lacked in height, she made up for in energy.

Luke was about to poke her in the back when a crumpled piece of notebook paper landed in his lap. He unfolded it without looking. He was not going to get in trouble on his first day back. When the page fell open, he bit his lip to keep from laughing. He'd loved that chicken scratch since seventh grade.

!!!! And also!!!!!!! I want to ask how you're doing, but that's a *stupid question.* Pretend I asked it because I had to and you already answered it so that we don't have to do all of that in real life. I like Vargassi, but it's good to have you back.
—You know who (<3 Voldemort)

On the other side of the room, Luke found the author exactly where he was supposed to be. Along the far wall, Marcos Aldama grinned like an idiot and waved under the desk. His dark hair twitched each time he moved his hand. *Subtle*, Luke thought. *Marcos is nothing if not subtle*, but he grinned back. He couldn't stop. That's how it had been since Marcos had walked into his life in seventh grade, like a human ray of sunshine who made Luke forget how to spell his own name.

Luke took a deep breath and willed the heat that crept up his neck to get back down where it belonged. *Not now.* He could deal with the crush that would not die another day.

He slipped the note onto the edge of Dee's desk and went back to his phone.

[From Luke] ??
[From Dee] Marcos lost his phone. He's been trying to communicate with sign language all day.

[From Luke] ... cool?

[From Dee] He doesn't know sign language. I think he offended several people that do.

Luke looked over as Marcos tapped one open palm over top of his closed fist, as if he was giving it a little hat, and didn't doubt that for a second. He watched Marcos pretend to build a tower—or kill a very small man—across a crowded classroom and imagined these people and the unchanging them-ness in this room were all that mattered. He could pretend he'd walked into class without Wes, Eddie or flying backpacks getting in the way.

Almost.

He steadied his hand against his leg and typed.

[From Luke] What are you doing after school?

Sampfon. **CHAPTER FIVE** *Greg.* Do you quarrell ſir?
Regory : A my word wee'l n...	...quarrell ſir? no ſir.
Greg. No, for then we ſhould be Coliars.	...u do ſir, I am for you, I ſerue as g
Abra. No better?	*Samp.* W

CHAPTER FIVE

THEY DIDN'T HAVE TO SAY where or when they would find each other after school. Dee, Luke and Marcos met outside the south entrance by the wobbly picnic table, because that's what they'd been doing since they were thirteen. Luke let Dee hug him, twice, and they walked toward her house as though nothing had changed in a month of absences and ignored calls.

They fell into step along the side of the road with the February wind at their backs. Neither of them said anything about the funeral, and, after days of flowers and cards promising Lizzy's arrival in heaven with all the pretty angels, Luke was so grateful he would have let them hug him all over again. It was the kindest silence.

Five years ago, in seventh grade, the walk had begun as a two-some. Back then, Dee and Luke had bonded, in hushed, embarrassed giggles, over their shared crush on the new boy with the soft brown skin and the big, toothy smile. *He was so sweet.* She'd been the first person to get how the pieces of Luke fit together, before his parents and long before anyone else at school. She'd glommed onto his side like sticky tape and it all should have been a mess. By rights at least one of them should have ended up heartbroken and in tears, but by luck they'd both fallen for a boy who liked neither of them and was too dense to understand the problem.

It wasn't until freshman year, when all three of them were connected at the hip, that Dee finally had broken down and told Marcos why she and Luke had both suddenly become obsessed with *Ender's Game*. Of course it was a good book, but it was also his favorite book and at the time that's what had mattered. They'd created a Marcos Aldama book club, for God's sake, and they might have started on *The Song of Ice and Fire* series if Dee hadn't gotten up the courage to ask if *hewantedtowalkhomewiththemsometime.*

When she'd explained, he'd just stared at her over the top of his ham sandwich. "But how?" He'd asked. "I looked like Manny from *Modern Family*."

He hadn't, not really. Except maybe a little in the face.

Most of all, even when he'd awkwardly clarified that *no*, he didn't want to date Luke or Dee and asked if that was cool, Marcos had never said a thing about Luke being a boy. It had probably never occurred to him to care.

They walked out of the school parking lot and down West Thirty-third toward Dee's house. As always, she marched ahead while the boys trailed behind. Marcos's arm was slung around Luke's neck, as if to make sure that Luke was actually, physically, there. Their hips knocked together in an uneven beat when Luke stepped forward on one side and Marcos stepped forward on the other. They couldn't find a rhythm, but neither pulled away. Luke used to imagine that this was what a first kiss would feel like: all awkward limbs and too much feeling.

Neither of them asked questions. Instead, Dee chattered about one show she'd convinced Marcos to watch and another, which she hadn't. Luke hadn't heard of either of them, but that wasn't new. Lizzy liked old TV shows, so that's what he knew best. Luke caught every other word as she ran through the plots, but the rest flowed together like music. By the time he focused back in, she'd moved on to the fall play.

"I didn't think it would be a problem using Vargassi in your place for *25th Annual Putnam County Spelling Bee* set construction," she said to the open road, her shoulders tight and high. "There's literally no way to screw up that set. We need bleachers, a microphone and a teacher's desk. That's it. At some point, there might be a piano. If Ms. Danes wants to get all fancy, she could make us do something for the flashbacks, but that's some next-level shit."

Marcos mouthed, "next-level shit," and they giggled in Dee's wake.

"Vargassi could have literally put a bunch of chairs on the stage, but can he do that?" She turned back over her shoulder, and Marcos took the hint.

"Nope," he called. "No, he can't."

She huffed. "Not even a little bit. He would have found a way to screw it up, and that's if Danes didn't switch to *Little Shop of Horrors* three days before auditions. *Little Shop.* My God." She spun around and walked backward into the sun. "Did you know he's never used a power drill? He just told me, as if it was a joke.

At this point, I'll be happy if he's had actual, physical interactions with a two-by-four that didn't make him cry."

Luke snorted until she glared, but there was no heat behind her eyes. "Yes, dumbass, the theater department would fall apart without you, but that doesn't mean you're not getting it the minute that you come back."

"I wouldn't expect anything less," Luke said softly and pretended not to notice them staring. They threw glances Luke's way, as if he might explode, and he didn't blame them. He'd been a fidgety mess in every class. Not that he was usually a model student, but he'd spent the day staring into space as if he were expecting space to start staring back. Everyone else might have written it off as grief mixed with awkward nerd, but Marcos and Dee knew better. Or, at least, they wanted to.

As the day had gone on, Luke hadn't been able to decide if he was more worried about what would happen if he had secret powers or what would happen if he didn't. There was always the off chance that it was real. He might have actually stopped time, but what if it never happened again? He'd spend the rest of his life remembering one hallucination about his chemistry teacher and a backpack. *Fantastic.*

He had tried making it happen again. Between classes, he'd tried to make stuff stop moving. Once, in the hall, a pencil had been rolling down the hallway toward the front doors, and he'd stared it down until he was almost bent in half. *I want you to stop right where you are,* he'd thought, with his face a foot away from the floor, and when that had failed he'd screamed *no, no, no, no, no* in his head, as if he could scare the pencil into submission. It hadn't worked. The pencil hadn't stopped, but people had stopped to watch him mentally screaming at the floor.

He'd tried stopping papers and doors and people until he was cross-eyed with concentration, but it hadn't happened again.

Hallucination one. Superhero zilch.

So Dee and Marcos stared, and Luke sighed under his breath. He'd figured that by the end of last period he'd have come up with something better to say than "I'm worried I might not be able to stop time with my mind," but that was the only way he could put it into words. If he'd gone all *Marvel Comics* overnight, that was scary, but not nearly as scary as any other option. Either way, they were almost at Dee's house, and, if he waited any longer, the words might never come out.

He grabbed Marcos's sleeve and stopped in the middle of the sidewalk. "Guys? I—" He scuffed the ground with the toe of one shoe. If he couldn't tell them, he could show them and, for that, he needed something to throw. "I need to try something. Can I use your duct tape?" Dee was a self-respecting stage manager; she always had duct tape. Eyes narrowed, she fished it out and dropped it into his hand. The roll was heavy in his palm and tacky around the edges, like not-quite-dry paint.

He needed a flat surface, in case the tape didn't stop. He couldn't explain himself out loud, but Marcos found what he needed anyway. It was just a brown garage door, but it didn't look as if anyone was home, and Marcos held up his hands, as though presenting it for their approval.

"Just—just a minute," Luke said, and tried to feel his run into the empty classroom all over again. He'd been pissed at Wes. There was that, right at the fore. And then there was the new kid, who'd smiled at him as if they had something in common, as if they were the same. It had been a gut-punch of nausea when he lived through it, but he couldn't make that sickness come back. In its place was only an open space and the dull echo of pain.

Luke stared at the image of the kid's face behind his eyelids until he could almost make it real again. If he focused on the stranger, on *Eddie*, the confusion and the embarrassment rushed back, almost like new. When the sickness was strong enough to taste, he squeezed his eyes shut and threw the roll of tape toward the garage with his whole weight behind its flight.

And nothing happened.

Luke blinked as the roll of tape smacked against the garage door and rolled to land in the flowerbed along the front walk.

For a long moment, he stared at the silver roll in the bushes. *What did I do wrong?* As he'd released the roll from his hand, he'd thought, *Stop. Please stop, stop, stop, stop*, as if they were the only words he'd ever known. He was more focused than he had been all day and yet—

"What are you waiting for?"

Luke turned to find Marcos sitting cross-legged on the frozen ground with his backpack propped up in his lap like a portable desk. There was no accusation in his voice, just curiosity. "It didn't work, right? We didn't miss anything?" Luke slowly shook his head. "Then you should probably try again." He leaned his elbows against his backpack and propped his head up on his hands. Luke wanted to kiss him. Luke always wanted to kiss him, but this time he had reasons.

"But—" he began, and Dee tossed the roll back into his hand.

"Here you go, crazy boy. Toss away." When he opened his mouth to protest, she held up a hand. "You remember when I had a crush on Alex and then I *had* to go to the anti-prom with Michael? I was the worst. First, she was gorgeous, and then he was the cutest thing I had ever seen." She smiled. "You put up with my little queer ass. There was roleplaying, and I never even asked her out." Luke had wanted to throttle her at the time, but that was half the fun of being her friend. "I don't know what you're waiting for, but if you need to chuck tape at a wall to get your yayas out, then chuck away, Babycakes." She jerked her head back at Marcos. "He's just a pushover."

"Lucky me," Luke said softly. Dee squatted in the gravel next to Marcos. There wasn't any snow on the ground, but sitting on the dead grass must have felt like squatting on an iceberg. Luke squared his shoulders to the garage door and wound up to throw again.

Still nothing.

For four, five and six throws, time moved through every pathetic *thunk* against the aluminum door. Each time, Luke tried a different variation on the silent scream. He whispered, "stop," then "no" and, finally, "for God's sake, please don't, don't, don't, don't. Goddammit." By the sixth toss, he gave up on the anger because it made him want to stop throwing things and curl up in a ball on the concrete.

The sound effects didn't help, but they didn't hurt either. After toss number four, Dee and Marcos made up stories for each throw. The most recent was Air Captain McSticky going in for a dangerous landing. It was Dee's idea, but the voice of the doomed pilot was all Marcos. "He's not going to make it back to base camp," he said through his cupped hands. "Tell his mother that he loves her!"

Dee made explosion noises and directed Luke like an amateur extra. "Give it a little more arc this time! I've got an idea, but I need more air time."

"Oh! Do the same thing on my turn! I want to try something with a flying nun." Like a puppy, Marcos gestured for Luke to throw the tape again, and Luke couldn't take it anymore.

He laughed. He looked at the bruised roll of tape in his hand and bleated like a cartoon character with a speech bubble over his head. Usually Dee was the only one who laughed like a dying goat, but neither of them had been this slaphappy since tech week last spring when poor Abdi Saladin set fire to the curtains.

He closed his eyes and giggled until he choked on his own breath and his stomach muscles cramped. Dee told him he'd lost it. He'd gone nuts, but she was laughing too when she hoisted herself from the ground, turned him around and made him throw the roll again. When he wound up, her hand pushed against his shoulder, and Marcos hooted at his back. *Maybe I am crazy. Maybe I'm hallucinating.* But the idea didn't sound so bad anymore. He could go crazy as long as they came too. They could stay right there forever, in the gravel and the dead grass, telling tales of "Marty the asshole sky diving instructor" in the dying light.

He didn't think about anything when he threw. And the tape stopped.

At the top of its arc, before it should have come down to the ground, the tape stopped moving and, with it, everything on West Thirty-third.

I did it. Luke threw his fists in the air and punched the sky with a wordless howl of joy. The tape hung in the air as it was supposed to, but as he celebrated Luke turned around and his smile dropped. He'd almost forgotten that people froze too. Marcos could have been meditating, but Dee was frozen motion. Her mouth hung open mid-word, and her body had pitched so far forward Luke almost ran to catch her fall.

I actually did it.

Dee's tape hung in mid-air. If Luke backed himself up against the garage door, he could release the Hold and let the tape drop into his hands, like playing catch all by himself. Dee would flip. She'd smack his arm until it went blue. But what if he didn't want to wait for the tape to come to him?

Luke inched forward until the tape hung over his head like demented mistletoe. Slowly, he reached up with one hand, wrapped his fingers around the tape and plucked it out of the air, as easily as picking an apple from a tree. It didn't resist. As much as gravity didn't want to pull the tape down to the ground, it also didn't want it to stay where it was. The roll gave way under his hand, as though it had been waiting to be placed where it was actually supposed to be: in the palm of his hand.

Luke turned the tape over. For the first time since he'd walked into school that morning, his hands didn't shake. Was he supposed to be upset? Falling leaves hung in the air, his friends stared into space and he didn't know what he felt. In the classroom, he'd been half lost to panic, but not now. A tug, like a dozen helium balloons, pulled at the back of his mind, and if he let go of the strings, he knew time would rush back into place. He could put it back. Then again, if he held on, it would wait. He could wait.

The peace wasn't totally new. He'd felt something like it before. When he was eight, North Grove had had its largest blizzard in decades. After a night of howling winds against the windows, he'd stepped outside into a new world. Icicles had hung from the edge of the roof like the daggers in storybooks, and the snowdrifts had sat higher than his head. Even his breath had stayed in front of his face. He'd run back inside, to Lizzy, and the only way he could explain was to get ahold of his mother's snow globe from the office desk, hold it in front of Lizzy's face and say it was "just like that, except without the shaking."

He'd had zero control that day, none, but he'd had awe, awe at the silence and awe at the busy, too-big world forced to shut up and hold still. He hadn't known that in very special times, Mother Nature could make everything stop. That had been his favorite memory for years, but it was about time he made something better.

He smiled, closed his eyes and let them go.

The first gust of wind was glorious.

"How in the hell?!"

Luke opened his eyes to find Dee glaring up from the dirt. She'd rocked back onto her hands and looked ready to kick his ass.

"You were right there," she said as she pointed to the ground in front of her feet. "Now you're over there." She raised her finger in an accusation and fell back into the grass. "I'm not going to ask how you did that, because I won't believe you."

"You won't?" Luke didn't want to laugh, but he hadn't seen her this mad since Mrs. Danes had suggested *Cats* for the spring musical. He raised an eyebrow. Marcos said raised eyebrows were mysterious; her glare said otherwise.

"Of course I won't," she snapped. "I'm not an idiot. I should probably look for wherever you hid the magic mirrors, right?"

"Right." He shrugged and tossed the roll of tape back and forth from hand to hand.

"Luke!"

"I don't know what to say, because it's going to sound crazy and you won't believe me."

"You were worried." Luke almost forgot Marcos was there, but he was looking up with his chin resting on his hands and his eyes squinted. "What were you worried about?"

"Mostly, that I wouldn't be able to stop time." It sounded even weirder out loud, but better too.

Marcos pursed his lips, and Dee looked at him as if he'd grown a third head. "Oh, my God, you're in on it too." She pushed herself off the ground and grimaced at the dirt on her hands. "I hate you guys."

"You were worried," Marcos said again, "but you're not worried any more, are you?"

"Nope." Luke said with a smile. "I'm not." That was it, exactly. He wasn't worried at all.

"You really—?" Marcos cocked his head, and his eyes grew as the puzzle snapped into place. "What made it happen?"

"I don't know!" Luke clutched the tape to his stomach. "The last time I tried, it just stopped." He leaned into the word, as though he could make Marcos feel the intent with the force of his whole body. "I threw the tape, and everything froze."

Marcos gasped. "No way." His face split into a grin. He got it. It was impossible, but Marcos got it.

"The last time?" Dee said, faintly. "*The last time?*"

Luke nodded like a bobblehead doll. "It was right here. The tape, I mean. I walked underneath it like—like I was walking through this model of my own life. And you were right there, but you were looking through me, as if I weren't there."

Marcos followed the line of his finger, as he pointed at the ground. "Maybe you weren't," he said, slowly. "If everyone and everything else in the world has stopped being aware of its own existence, do you still exist?" He wrinkled his nose in concentration. "If nothing corroborates your presence in the world, are you really alive?"

"Do it again." Dee shook herself out of her disbelief and wore the glare she usually saved for freshmen.

Luke blanched. "Excuse me?"

"I think we were all kind of dead." Marcos said with his eyes fixed on the sky. "Cool."

"You heard me." Dee crossed her arms over her chest. "If you, Lucas Aday, can make life come to a standstill with the power of your mind, then please honor us *mere mortals* with a second display of your powers."

Luke rubbed the back of his neck. "When you say it like that—"

Dee rolled her eyes. "There's no other way to say it without taking you home and putting you to bed." Luke just glared back until she raised her hands in self-defense. "Don't be like that. I just—" She broke off. "Look, you've never gotten a higher than a C in physics. What am I supposed to think?"

"Think whatever you want." Luke sounded petulant even to his own ears, but it had been a long day. "For the record, neither have you."

"Okay, so we're both bad at science, but I'm not the one making DC Comics sound realistic." She stretched out her hand, and it took him a second to realize she wanted the tape. Her eyes softened as she wiggled her fingers: a moment of silliness and a plea.

He sighed and dropped the roll into her hand. He might not like it, but she had a point. "What do you want me to do?"

"Um." She scanned the space in front of the garage, and the mental wheels turned. "I want you to move me. Freeze everything just like you *apparently* did before and then—I don't know—move my hand or turn my head. Do something."

Luke stared. She seemed excited about the idea. She almost vibrated with pride, but— "You want me to move your body while you're not aware I'm doing it?"

Marcus raised a hand from his seat on the ground. "I'm sensing some consent issues."

"Boys!" Dee threw up her hands. "I hereby give you consent to non-sexually move the non-sexual parts of my person in order to prove we have not all gone insane."

"Most people would consider the head and the hands at least moderately sexual."

"Marcos!"

This time starting and stopping came more easily, or at least it did until Luke had to follow through. It was creepy. Even walking toward Dee when he knew perfectly well she couldn't see him coming was all kinds of wrong. Thank God Marcos didn't want Luke to do the same to him, because he never could have gone through with it. Touching Marcos always featured extra levels of "don't be a creep."

Her eyes were closed because he'd practically ordered her not to look. He wouldn't have been able to stand her staring through him while he was manhandling her like a living doll. After counting down from three, he grabbed the end of her sleeve, and, when he tugged, the arm moved as easily as the roll of tape had. It floated through the air, as though it had become an extension of his body. He pulled her arm—gently—until it was extended as far as it could go toward the garage and, for just a second, he wondered what might happen if he kept pulling. Would she fall over, like a statue, or would the arm keep following, regardless of whether the rest of the person wanted it to go? He shuddered and just stopped pulling. He wasn't ready for the answer to that question. Instead, he gripped her hand between his thumb and forefinger and turned it out, until her palm lay open toward his chest, and folded each finger down toward her palm, until only her pointer finger extended toward the sky.

He bit his lip and smothered a giggle. Dee could have auditioned to play animatronic Abraham Lincoln in the Disney World Hall of Presidents, but this was what she'd asked for, and he was, for once, happy to oblige. This time, when he closed his eyes and let the Hold go, he didn't step back. He and Dee opened their eyes together; their faces were hardly a foot apart.

She blinked up into his eyes, looked at her pointing hand and laughed loud enough to wake the dead.

CHAPTER SIX

IT TOOK HOURS FOR DEE and Marcos to decide what he should do next. By the time they got anywhere, the sun had set, and Luke knew he wasn't cut out to be part of a super-team.

The Hold was real. His friends had seen it too, and that lifted a weight from his chest that had been sitting there since November. One day he could hardly get out of bed and the next he could stop the world. He could run through silent streets and control the sun. Dee and Marcos wanted to fit him for a cape and tights, but after months of just his parents, his sister and the nurses for company, their enthusiasm was more than a little overwhelming.

First they needed data, and Luke became their superpowered lab rat. Dee's part of the neighborhood didn't have sidewalks, so they hugged the curb, balancing on the raised edge and tossing things into the air like incompetent jugglers. An hour after Dee's howl of joy in front of the garage, Luke had tossed, rolled or moved everything in her backpack, including three pens, a highlighter and a package of tampons. Each time, Dee and Marcos burst into applause when their stuff disappeared into thin air and reappeared in Luke's hands. It was like playing a game of peekaboo with adults.

When Dee ran out of stuff to throw, the ideas got interesting.

"Did you try stopping things in class this afternoon?" Dee asked. "Because you could absolutely do this in class."

Luke crouched to pick up Marcos's chemistry notes he'd just chucked into the air. It was almost too dark to see what was on the page. The streetlights had long since come on, and Luke's toes ached from the cold. "Why would I want to do that? Is there some top-secret reason you want to make a calculus class even longer?"

She shrugged. "What about tests? You could take a potentially infinite amount of time on all of your tests, and no one would ever know."

Marcos's eyebrows shot skyward as Luke dropped the notes back into his hand. "Wow! And here Luke was planning to misuse his powers to save the universe. Thank goodness you reminded him to cheat on tests."

"I can hear sixty years of superheroes crying into their capes." Luke said, his hand to his ear.

"I dunno, Luke. She might be right. They are worth forty percent of your grade."

"Oh, shut up." Dee made a grab for Luke's backpack and was about to pull him back when she stopped with her hand on the strap.

"There must be a name for someone who lets down the entire heroic legacy," Luke said, with a grin.

"No seriously, Luke. Shut up." She worried her lower lip between her teeth, and her eyes peered into the distance. "Oh, my God," she said, as her eyes locked back on Luke's face. "You can go anywhere."

Luke frowned. "Do you mean anywhere in the world? I think I could do that before."

"You could stop time and walk somewhere really far away, like Alaska," Marcos said and bounced on his toes. "That would be cool."

"No! I don't mean Alaska!" Dee snapped and tugged on her hair. She'd been pulling at her own hair all night. She did that when she was stressed, and, as they waited for her to find her words, her hair stood out in angry, blond spikes. "If you stop time, you can break into any building in the world, take whatever you want and walk out again without anyone knowing a thing."

Luke thought about the nicest way to tell Dee she wasn't making sense. He'd just about decided to pretend he hadn't heard when Marcos let out a sound halfway between a cough and a laugh. "Holy crap," he said. "She's right."

Dee's face split into a grin. "Right? How could they suspect Luke? If they notice anything's gone, he could never get arrested because he would have been outside the building or the house or whatever the entire time!"

She smacked Luke on the arm between every sentence until he swatted her away. "How are you taking this seriously? One minute you've got me acing Harvard with my test-foo and now I'm, what, stealing from the Smithsonian in my free time?"

"No. I'm not suggesting a life of crime. Jesus. For one thing, you would be awful at it. But, if you were the kind of person who got off on petty larceny you could walk into any house on this street right now and no one would ever know that you had been there." She clapped her hands. "Boom."

"From the homeowner's perspective, I'm not sure it would count as breaking and entering," Marcos said as he considered the sky over the thirty-three-hundred block of Brownlow Ave. "This is, of course, assuming they don't have locks and that security systems don't work in Luke-space. The homeowner would only move before and after you went in, so if you weren't in the house while they were aware of the movement of time, were you ever really in the house at all?" He shrugged. "I don't know if it would count."

Dee nodded, and Marcos echoed the nod as though Luke's problem was a lack of consensus. He'd created monsters.

Luke sputtered. Of course it would *count*. He hadn't really followed the Marcos-speak, but this wasn't a philosophical question. "I'd be in some stranger's house!"

"And they would never know or care," Dee said with a smile. "But we get that it doesn't matter, because—well, you know." She trailed off, much to Luke's frustration. He didn't know.

He said as much, and she rolled her eyes. "Oh, don't look at me like that. Jeez. I just mean that randomly breaking the rules isn't your thing. You never wrote your name on the wall backstage because the whole graffiti thing makes you feel weird, and that's okay." She patted his hand. "We love your moral compass. It's sweet. So, you're our moral compass guy, and really, Luke, it was just a stupid idea."

She turned away, and the words sank in. *Moral compass guy. Wow.* Luke hadn't been trying to find a superhero alter ego, but if he had, that might be the saddest description he'd ever heard.

"Which house?" As soon as the words were out of Luke's mouth, he didn't want to take them back. Dee turned back, a question in her eyes. "I'm not kidding. Which house do you want me to try? If you're both right, they won't know anyway." He tried for a casual, I don't care about breaking-and-entering, shrug, but it turned into an insecure shimmy. "I can do this," he said, but his voice was too high, and even he didn't believe himself.

He worried the inside of his cheek and watched Dee and Marcos as they had a long conversation using only their eyes. Luke expected one of them to veto the experiment, just to let him off the hook, but Dee just pointed to the house across the street.

"None of the lights are on, and it's so big you probably won't even run into creepy frozen people in the dark." She looked at her watch and groaned. "Speaking of which, my mom's going to think I fell off the planet."

She was right about the size. The tall, rickety house wasn't much bigger than the other Victorian types on the street, but they all had the look of almost-mansions that had gone slowly to seed. Slats were missing from the porch railing, and, even in the darkness, he made out cracks beside the third-story windows. Judging from the number of times he'd gotten lost in Dee and Wes's big old house, he probably could have walked into any of the houses on the block without running into people, whether time was stopped or not.

If anyone was in there, they had no idea he was coming and, if it worked, they'd never know he'd been there. Luke swallowed. "If the door is unlocked, and I can actually get in, what do you want me to do, take a selfie?"

"Oh, man," Marcos gasped, "we never figured out if you could take pictures! We should try that when you get back."

"Just take something worthless, like a rubber band or a safety pin or something. We'll believe you," Dee insisted, with a grin. "But bring something out anyway. It will be like your own teeny, tiny worthless trophy!"

Marcos nodded and said, "I promise to frame it, and we can give it a name that won't mean anything to anyone else, like, I don't know—"

"Number thirty-three sixty?" Luke read the number from the mailbox.

"Exactly," Marcos said, as he read off of his imaginary frame, and Luke stared up at the white, shuttered doors. "This is house number thirty-three sixty, and we were here."

DEE AND MARCOS COUNTED DOWN to the Hold as though Luke were taking off for a walk on the moon.

He didn't have the heart to tell them that the noise made it harder to focus. Since his demo outside the garage, Dee had made him stop time sixteen times, and he'd gotten faster. He'd even figured out how to make it look easy, but on the inside he was frantic. Every time he'd screamed different words in his head, first "stop," and then "freeze," and finally a litany of "no, no, no, no, no, no." If one didn't work, he'd switched to another, rapid-fire, until something did the trick. In the end, it always seemed as though he'd gotten ahold of the strings that held the universe together, and no one could take them away. But until he had the strings in hand—or in brain—it was a mad scramble to make the universe pay attention.

So far, he'd been effective or lucky, but he had no idea how long the time-stop might last. For all he knew, he could find himself on the second floor of number thirty-three sixty and watch the Hold slip between his fingers. More importantly, other people might find him standing on the second floor of their house with no explanation for how he got there.

It wasn't hard to imagine the next day's headlines: "Weird Indian Boy Wanders into Stranger's Home: Police Investigating Substance Abuse and Grief-driven Psychosis."

With a whisper and his eyes squeezed shut in a wish, Luke pulled the world to a stop. Dee and Marcos had closed their eyes, too, and Marcos had his hands squeezed into fists at his sides, as though he'd help Luke stop the world with the force of how much he wanted it. Luke patted Marcos's frozen fist. If only he could bring other people back to life, one by one. Then he could tap Dee and Marcos into the game. They'd be better all together as a band of time marauders. On his own, he wasn't a compass. Mostly, he was lost.

The stones on the front walk were uneven, so Luke's stride up to the front porch became more of a wobble. When the wooden steps squeaked, he froze, his heartbeat in his ears, and it took a breathless second to remember that no one could hear him. He could have screamed the national anthem out into the night, and no one would notice.

The door wasn't locked.

When he turned the knob and it gave way, he wasn't sure he was happy, but maybe it was a sign someone wanted him to step inside. Granted, in Dee's neighborhood, almost no one locked their doors when they were home, but still. It passed for kismet.

The front entryway was darker than he expected for an evening in the middle of the week, and that was a blessing, too. Lights meant people and the chance he could run into a frozen face around any corner. He could turn, and there it would be, eyes wide and seeing nothing. On the other hand, lights on also meant he wouldn't land on his ass after he tripped over crap he couldn't avoid.

If possible, the house seemed even bigger on the inside. It might have been a trick of the darkness or a side effect of the mess. From the entryway, a room with a wicker chair and a leather stool stretched to the left, the entrance to a kitchen opened to the right and a broad flight of stairs led upstairs. The owners didn't seem to believe in putting things away. Half-empty (or full) cardboard packing boxes stood as high as Luke's head along blank walls. The owners seemed to have stopped mid-way through either packing or unpacking. Scattered masks, glass plates and neatly folded piles of clothing clumped around open boxes and spilled into the hall.

The people who lived here could be moving in or moving out. Either way, no one would notice Luke was here. He could swipe the ottoman and walk out the way he came in, but a tug at the back of his mind made him walk past the living room. If he didn't know any better, he'd say the Hold liked it here.

He felt his way up the stairs on tiptoe and inched down the dimly lit hall on the second floor. Closed doors dotted the hallway, and at the far end, light slid from under a closed door in a thin line that snaked up the wall. Luke stopped in front of the line of light; his breath was tight in his chest. On the left side of the hall, beside the lit door, was another door, as dark as the rest. Luke ran a hand down the beveled wood, and paint flaked off in his hand. Where the other doors sat blank and white, this one's owner had put up a three inch by five inch picture from *Monty Python and the Holy Grail* with King Arthur up against the Black Knight, who was already down an arm. The text below read, "I've had worse."

Luke's laugh echoed in the silence. Why anyone would choose that picture and those words for a door was beyond him, but anyone who would—

Luke turned the knob. The door squeaked as he pushed it open, stepped inside and almost tripped over a pile of books. Under a single, uncovered window, lit by streetlights, a twin bed sat surround by piles of half-folded clothes. For a second, Luke wondered if the owner of the room would have neatened up if they'd known he was coming. *Would they have straightened the sheets or left everything undone? Was the owner as open as their dresser drawers?* The bed, as small as it was, took up almost the entire room. A few steps forward, and Luke would have fallen face-first into the mattress.

Still, this room was owned and loved. Luke knew it. Maybe it was the hand-lettered sign inside the door that read "Abandon Hope All Ye Who Enter Here." He'd made one like it, when he was thirteen and desperate to demonstrate that his bedroom was his castle. It had stayed on his wall for years, just under the picture of Jesse Williams. He wished that he'd been clever enough, like the door owner, to add, "If you already abandoned hope, please disregard this notice."

Luke ran a finger over the bookshelf as he walked along the right side of the bed: *Ender's Game*, *Calvin and Hobbes*. He considered flipping through the pages, but there was a script book on the floor at his feet, and he stopped to smile at the black outline on the cover, the hand raised toward the sky. He had one just like it, a gift from a relative who didn't understand the appeal. The other books could have been sitting on the shelf for weeks or years, but this one must have been loved. Even in the dark, the corners were clearly worn and a broad, red stain spread across one corner. Someone must have loved this book. It was surprisingly easy to imagine a faceless boy or girl as they hummed under their breath late at night and dropped the book to the side of the bed when they had to sleep.

As he crouched to touch the binding, Luke caught a flash of gray-green in the darkness. He turned to peer into the shadows under the bed and went as still as the room. Under the bed sat dozens of rolls, each no larger than a clenched fist. After squinting into the darkness for a long, slow breath, he realized each roll was made of bills. He couldn't see the amounts, but Luke was pretty sure, based on nothing more than gangster movies, that no one made rolls of one-dollar bills. They made rolls of twenties, fifties and hundreds, amounts that added up fast. He pushed a roll to the side with one finger and found another behind it and then another. They were stuffed under the bed like animals in hibernation, and Luke worried that, if he moved the wrong ones, they might all come pouring out at his feet.

With his thumb and forefinger, Luke picked up a single roll and held it up to the beam of light from between the blinds. He peered into the face of Andrew Jackson, whose waves of hair curved around the roll of bills. He'd never seen so much money in one place, and it couldn't possibly be real, not the pile, not the hazy, speckled light, and—*God*—not the silver muzzle visible in the gap where the roll in his hand used to be.

Luke didn't have to touch it. He knew what a gun looked like. It looked hard and bright and perfectly at home tucked in with piles of money that had no business being in this room. Those books and that sign made sense. He could imagine that person, but this—

He needed to go. He'd needed to go ages ago, before he got pulled into this room. But now he had to run. He had to find a stupid thing to bring out to his waiting friends, who weren't really waiting, and go before any of this started to make sense. Luke wedged the roll of twenties back into its place over the flash of silver, and as he stood he thought for second that the door had closed when he wasn't looking.

He couldn't see into the hallway anymore. When he'd come in, he could see out, but he couldn't now, and the door wasn't blocking his vision. There was a boy, with a round face and wide open eyes that Luke already knew.

Eddie. The boy in the doorway, who stared frozen and blank into what had to be his own room, was the kid who'd stopped him in the hallway, the kid who'd made him into a stranger in his own school, and Luke couldn't comprehend how he got into the doorway. Luke would have noticed a body when he'd walked in. He wouldn't have come in the room if there had been a person standing there, and there's no way Eddie could have moved while Luke was in the house. Unless—

Luke swallowed hard and stared up into Eddie's surprised eyes. He could have let the Hold falter. He didn't feel a change, but maybe when he saw the money, he let it go and didn't notice when a boy he almost knew stepped into the room.

Eddie stared from the doorway past the bed onto the floor at Luke's feet, and Luke couldn't un-see what was there. The money. If he was in Eddie's home and Eddie's room—because this had to be Eddie's room—that meant the money under the bed was probably his, and with it the glint of silver lodged in the back of his mind. Somehow, Eddie had to be four people at the same time:

1. The boy who protected Luke in his own hallway.
2. Some guy who robbed banks in his spare time.
3. A person who walked through Luke's hold on time like so much tissue paper.

Most of all,

4. He was the boy who saw Luke crouched at the side of his bed and staring at his gun.

His gun.

Maybe that was where Eddie got his wide-eyed surprise. His jaw was slack, and his left hand gripped the doorframe as if it were the only thing keeping him from landing on the floor. Luke pressed a hand over his own mouth and sucked in the will to scream. Eddie was in a light T-shirt and dark pajama pants that hung from his hips. He could have been getting ready for bed when Luke came in.

No, when I broke into his house.

He could have found Luke staring under his bed, looking, for all intents and purposes, as though he came to rob someone who could defend himself just fine. If the gun was his—but—

Luke inched forward with his eyes trained on Eddie's frozen stare. He walked until they were face to face and the shock around Eddie's mouth and between his eyebrows was level with his own. *How did you get here?* Luke peered into Eddie's frozen eyes. *How did you move?* Eddie didn't respond, but when Luke blinked, he could have sworn Eddie flinched.

He got back down the stairs at a run.

It was too fast. On his way up the stairs, he'd been careful. He didn't move the stacks of books and clothing. On his way out he didn't care what he kicked over. He couldn't breathe. He hadn't been able to breath since he knelt at the side of that bed—Eddie's bed. The house itself might as well have been caving in, and he had to get out before he passed out on the stairs.

He shoved through the front door and stumbled down the walk with his heart beating in his throat. Marcos and Dee were exactly where he had left them. They stared, expectant, into the empty space where he had been. After the half-light of the house, his eyes couldn't remember how to see outside, and his friends were just an echo in the darkness. When he dropped the Hold, the release hit him like a kick in the chest.

"You did it?" Dee slapped at his side, and it took him a moment to remember that, for her, no time had passed. He could say he hadn't gone into the house at all, and she'd never know.

But Marcos would know. "Of course he did. Look at him," he said, as if Luke were his favorite book. He couldn't lie to Marcos.

Then again, he'd never really tried. When Marcos asked what he had to show for his adventure, Luke balked.

"Nothing. I—I forgot." The truth rolled from his tongue. He had forgotten. In the nether-space between the money and Eddie's face, he'd forgotten his own name.

"How?" Dee's laugh echoed over his head. "How did you forget? What did you do, take a nap in there, Goldilocks? Did you curl up on one of the beds and try out the porridge?"

"I—" Luke had a sudden vision of telling them everything, about the money, the gun and Eddie's eyes, but somehow that idea was even worse than walking into a stranger's house and rifling through his things. Eddie'd stood there in his pajamas, and that was already a kind of intimacy Eddie hadn't been able to refuse, but talking about it to his friends seemed like the real violation. "I think I'm just tired." He avoided Marcos's gaze and turned toward home; the others followed in his wake.

"'Course you're zonked," Marcos said to his back. "You reordered space and time at least twelve times. Plus, you did stuff while the rest of us just hung around, being statues."

When Luke glanced back, Marcos grimaced gargoyle-style and threw his hands up in frozen claws. "We lived one day, and you lived at least four," he said, with an intense nod. "By the time we hit graduation, you'll be ancient."

"Yeah." Luke coughed out a laugh that rang hollow in his ears. "Maybe I will be."

CHAPTER SEVEN

A DAY LATER, LUKE STILL hadn't said anything about Eddie's bedroom.

In fact, for Dee and Marcos, he might as well have fallen off the planet. He didn't respond to any of Marcos's texts before he went to bed—even the one that was just a string of question marks—and at school he ducked into the bathroom to avoid Dee. He had faith that they would not worry. Stressed-Luke tended to go radio silent. Dee liked to call it his "reboot." They knew to let it ride; he might fall off the map, but he wouldn't stay gone for long.

He kept telling himself that this was the most usual part of his week; going AWOL was a completely normal reaction to an ass-backward life. But this time, when he ducked and hid from his best friends, it seemed like a big lie. Dee and Marcos assumed he was processing his new "skills," when he was really watching for Eddie.

Luke had been in the guy's bedroom, seen him in his pajamas and snooped through his things, and it was stunning to realize just how little he knew about the boy who may have seen Luke rob his house. After hours of ignoring Marcos, he'd lain awake, stared at the drawings on his ceiling and waited for the cops to bang on his door. What Eddie would have told them, he couldn't imagine:

"Officer, I offered to help this kid at school and the next thing I know he showed up in my room."

Okay, so maybe he could imagine. Less than one day with time-stopping mojo and he'd already turned into a crappy villain. He'd discovered Boris-and-Natasha levels of incompetence and he could only think, *Please, universe, don't do this to my parents. Please don't do this. They've had enough.* He didn't know who or what he hoped would listen, but he repeated it until he heard his dad make breakfast downstairs. *They don't need me to screw up. They've had enough.*

At school, through the fog of exhaustion, he watched for Eddie, and it turned out he wasn't hard to find. For a guy who'd only been at the school for a month, he'd already carved out a home between the faded stone welcome sign at the front entrance and the broken locker doors. Luke couldn't pin down exactly why, but Eddie belonged, as though there had always been a gap at North Grove just waiting for him.

For one thing, he smiled a lot. At the cafeteria, talking to students from the African and Middle Eastern Association and at his locker, talking to the lacrosse team captain, he always looked right into people's eyes and beamed as if they'd given him an extra year of life. It was exhausting watching him, and he never broke. Even when he tripped over his own feet, he came up laughing. He was "such a klutz" and "it's amazing his parents even let him leave the house," he said as he fixed his shirt. By the time he walked away, even teachers beamed at him. He was self-deprecating, joyful, funny, charismatic and probably completely full of it. But, if so, Luke might be the only one who'd know.

He lost Eddie, or Eddie lost him, after lunch and with him, the purpose of the day, and so Luke stared into his locker. He moved books back and forth from his bag to the shelf and then back to the bag. When he closed his eyes, the hovering backpack had been replaced with flashes of green money and silver metal that glinted in the darkness. He shuddered. Eddie was different, pure and simple, especially if he really was from Somalia or Ghana, as Luke's chem partner said. That, in and of itself, was perfectly normal; it was Eddie who was odd.

North Grove liked to think of itself as a liberal la-la land. It celebrated Eid al-Fitr and Rosh Hashanah so loudly, they could probably hear the self-congratulation in the next district, but that didn't mean kids born outside of the United States got to be prom queen or student council president. Lots of students came from Laos, South Korea, Somalia or somewhere else. Either that, or their parents did, or their parents' parents, or they just weren't white, but somehow there were always more white kids in AP classes and in charge of the honor society. If a teacher could say, "You know, I'm not sure if she's ready for that challenge," a white kid was probably in charge. If it weren't for the day before, Luke might have liked seeing a kid from Africa taking the school by storm.

But he'd had that day. He'd had two whole moments, one in a hallway and one in a bedroom, and no matter how he turned them over in his mind, they wouldn't add up to a single, logical human being.

"Are you going to live in there?"

Luke's head snapped up. *No. It couldn't be. I only lost track of him for a minute—*

"Clearly, you need a second to commune with the locker, so I'll be right back." Eddie stood behind him, human evidence that the world had a screwed-up sense of humor, and if his eyes were anything but amused, Luke couldn't tell. Despite what he said, he didn't seem to be going anywhere. Luke dropped the chemistry book onto the bottom of the locker with a metallic *thunk,* and Eddie watched it go. "Got a second?"

He leaned against the locker at Luke's left, and Luke stared, which, for Eddie, must have translated into a yes. "First," he said, as he clasped his hands in front of his body, "I have to apologize for yesterday."

"Yesterday?" Oh, there was the voice, and so nice and squeaky too. Luke wrapped his arms around his waist and tried not to hug himself into submission.

"Yes." Eddie said, and his smile softened into something with fewer teeth. "I shouldn't have gotten mixed up in your business. I get that. It was your issue, and I shouldn't have tried to play the hero. I'm sorry if, I mean, *when* I overstepped." He bowed his head in something like contrition. "You know, I generally like to make a better first impression." His smile widened to the grin Luke remembered from following him all day. It was blinding and all wrong for the moment, like fireworks at a funeral. Luke could have sworn Eddie was delighted to see him, but that wasn't possible, not after Luke's giant, public "screw you." "So, if I can start again, my name is Edward Sankawulo, and I understand that you have some interest in theater."

"Huh?" Luke tried with everything that he had, but he couldn't finish the damn thought. "What are you—?"

"That's what Mrs. Danes wanted me to talk to you about. I'm not actually stalking you."

No, Luke thought, *that's my job.*

Eddie explained slowly. He was in Ms. Danes's theater class. He'd missed the chance to pair up with someone for the final, because he was in Chicago at the beginning of the semester. He needed a partner to be his director, and would Luke be cool with stepping in? When Luke stared, Eddie just talked, as though folks usually related to him like human puffer fish. Luke could direct a few monologues, he'd get extra credit and, yes, Eddie knew he wasn't a director.

"You do tech," he said, with a shrug, as if the two jobs were interchangeable and, more importantly, as if that were something everyone just knew.

When Luke forced out a "How?" Eddie smiled.

"I checked."

"You checked. After I told you to go fuck yourself."

Eddie laughed and focused at the ceiling, as though the argument was up there to review. "I heard it as 'have a good day.'"

You would. Eddie could probably convince himself that Voldemort was just rough around the edges.

He insisted, too quickly to follow, that it wouldn't be much work. Eddie had to pick six scenes, but Danes already had a whole folder full of options. Luke just had to show up, and there was no way in hell he could say yes. If Eddie might have seen Luke in his room, with his gun, then Luke had to stay far, far away, ideally in another state. If he were smart he would have turned around the moment he saw Eddie's face and walked until he was in Michigan.

Apparently, Luke wasn't smart.

"Sure," he said with a nod. "That's fine." His mouth stretched into something between a grimace and a grin. *Fine? Fine? On what planet was that fine?* Luke couldn't tell if his mouth was going AWOL because of curiosity or because Eddie had a really, really nice smile, but there was no way any part of this was fine.

"For real?" Eddie clapped his hands over his head as if he won the lotto. It didn't make any sense. All he got was Luke. "Excellent! That is just—that is excellent! I'll, ah, meet me right here after class tomorrow, and we'll find a place to practice." Eddie spun on his heel and strode down the hallway toward the cafeteria. As the hallway merged with the senior commons, he turned to point back and his eyes were crinkled with joy. "You won't regret this!"

Nope. I definitely don't regret this already.

Luke pointed back with a queasy smile, but Eddie didn't pay attention. He'd already grabbed someone halfway down the hall and started talking away as if they'd known each other all their lives. They laughed as Luke turned back to his locker.

It was a friend, then. Of course. Edward Sankawulo had nothing but friends.

After last hour, Luke told Dee he had to go home. He couldn't be at practice the next day to take over for Vargassi because his parents needed him at home. He felt a twinge at the lie, but he had to go to Eddie's rehearsal and he couldn't pinpoint exactly why. She didn't ask what he had to do and he was grateful. He could have made up something about having to sort through another room and bring another box or twelve to the Goodwill, but he didn't feel like going to hell.

The lie would have been based on truth, though. They needed to go through room after room of Lizzy's clothes, music and the little bags they strapped onto the back of her wheelchair. She hadn't been using any of it since she'd entered hospice in November, but his parents weren't making any moves toward packing, and Luke wasn't going to be the one to start. He wasn't going to break the silence to unfold a cardboard box and stuff all that was left of his sister inside.

So he lingered by his locker after school and tried not to think about why he hadn't told Marcos where he was going. Marcos had asked, especially when Luke hadn't followed them toward the auditorium after eighth period.

"Send my best to your mom," he'd said when Luke explained about the sorting and the packing. When he'd patted Luke on the arm and offered to help, Luke's stomach had flipped. He was a worm. No, he was worse than a worm. He was a grub.

He'd tell Marcos eventually, but he had to figure it out first.

Luke was circling the space in front of his locker when Eddie arrived from God knows where. He bounced on his toes as he led Luke into the empty theater classroom that doubled as the space for German and debate. Mrs. Danes led all three with a flair that came from a great deal of enthusiasm and very little preparation. And so, the room looked as though it had been dumped on its side and then righted again, without consideration for where anything was when it landed. Along one wall, lyrics from "99 Luftballoons" and film stills from old German movies overlapped with single phrases typed onto construction paper and stuck to the wall with bright red pushpins. Along another other wall, shelves wobbled under the weight of ancient textbooks and handbooks that spilled out onto the floor. Luke would never have known the room was used for anything other than German if it weren't for the tabletop podium perched on the desk at the front of the room and a tiny sign on one of the shelves that read "extra scripts" and pointed down.

Without the overhead fluorescents on and buzzing, the room sat dark. Windows lined the long wall opposite the door from just above Luke's head to the ceiling, but the light from the outside had to fight through frosted glass and years of grime to get inside. Every fall the principal made a show of getting the windows cleaned, if only to prove the job impossible. The official word was acid rain residue, but Mrs. Danes coughed under her breath about crappy glass.

In the middle of the room, several dozen ancient desks huddled together like survivors of a war. Their metal feet screeched across the floor as Eddie shoved them, one by one, toward the back of the room. When he had created a little clearing between the dry-erase board and the cluster of seats, he perched on top of the nearest desk and rooted through his backpack.

"My bad on the time," he said and shook his head. "My lacrosse coach wanted to talk about my chances of getting to play once the season gets going and, you know." He waved, as though Luke could obviously relate. *Those coaches, man. Right?*

"You play lacrosse?" Luke asked from the doorway and hoped his real question wasn't too obvious. Namely, *You play lacrosse, too?*

He assumed Eddie also chased tornados and cared for orphaned puppies whenever he wasn't running a drug cartel from under his bed.

Eddie laughed. "I play lacrosse really badly. Thankfully, the team here sucks, so that shouldn't be a problem." He pulled a manila folder from his bag and raised an eyebrow as Luke lingered in the doorway. "If your best friend is the team captain, and I just stepped in it again, I'm giving up."

Luke shook his head. *No. Not at all.* He only really knew Wes, and that was under duress. He just couldn't figure out whether to keep hovering near the door or to join Eddie on one of the desks. If he sat too far away, it seemed like he didn't want to be there. But, if he sat too close, it seemed like he *really* wanted to be there, and the last thing he wanted to do was make Eddie uncomfortable. It still wasn't clear if Eddie knew Luke had seen him in what amounted to his underwear.

Eddie made the decision for him. He waved Luke over to the desks and dropped the folder into his hands. "Okay," he said, "Here's what I've got." He snapped his fingers, and Luke flinched. "The official scene options were weak sauce, but I found a few that might have potential. I haven't given them serious time, but, you know, that'll come. By mid-March, I need six monologues with all the bells and whistles, right? But that's weeks away. Today, I say we grab a monologue from the top of the stack and go to town. I try a few things; you try a few things. We figure out a groove. Sound good?"

Luke nodded.

It didn't sound good at all, even if Eddie seemed fit to burst with excitement.

When Dee stepped in to direct for Mrs. Danes, she had an innate sense of how to pick one element out of a performance and grab onto it, like a producer who could fix a single guitar line in a sixteen-piece band. Luke assumed some of that skill was in the title. As long as he put on the director's hat and sat in the director's chair, Luke would be able to pretend he knew what he was doing.

Except, he didn't.

Eddie jumped into the first monologue, and it took all of thirty seconds for Luke to realize that he was in way over his head. If Eddie was floating on top of the Pacific Ocean, Luke was buried somewhere under the Marianas Trench. Eddie was doing Shakespeare and he was doing it really, really fast.

The speech was from *Romeo and Juliet*, but by the time Luke placed it, Eddie was already a dozen lines into Mercutio's monologue, and one word ran over the next as if he might run out of time. Luke tried to separate one idea from the next, but he couldn't when Eddie's hands and legs moved as quickly as his mouth. He moved left for the first lines and then pushed to the right before he charged up and planted himself in the center.

Luke swallowed hard. The speech was a riveting mess.

Eddie looked unhinged, but it wasn't the movement. It was his face. Mercutio was Romeo's best friend. He was also passionate and funny and effortlessly cool, the perfect antidote to Romeo's emo crap, but there was more to him than silliness and Eddie *got it*. His Mercutio bled pain. His eyes didn't just land on objects in the room, they cut stuff in half and branded them with rage. Luke knew the play. Theoretically. He'd seen *Romeo and Juliet* half a dozen times from backstage, but he'd never seen anything like this. He was good, really good. Luke didn't need more than a minute to tell that Eddie was disgustingly talented, but he was also trying to be everywhere at the same time.

When Eddie finished, he snapped back into his own skin like a rubber band. His shoulders relaxed, his hands unclenched and his eyes found their way back to Luke's face.

"Your turn," he said with a proud smile.

Luke blinked. "That was fast." *That was incredible. You're incredible. I don't know how to direct incredible.* "I—um," he stuttered. "It was—I couldn't really follow the story."

Eddie's smile faltered. "I rushed it that time," he said, quietly, as though he didn't entirely believe it. He frowned as Luke sank into his seat. "You know the play, right? I was Mercutio before the party. It's pretty intense."

"I know." Luke tried not to roll his eyes. Of course he knew *Romeo and Juliet.* He knew the play inside and out when other people did the parts. Eddie was just fast and talented and distracting. "Maybe if you tried it again, but a little slower this time," he said and frowned. *I sound like I'm directing a kindergarten Christmas pageant.* "Maybe don't move so much?"

Eddie's browed furrowed, as though Luke were speaking in code. "I can do that. I can slow down. For sure. I was just getting a feel for the room." Eddie backed up into the open space. "You just want me to stay in once place, yeah? Are there any particular parts where I should move or—?" Luke shook his head, and Eddie's face fell.

"Whenever you're ready," Luke said, quietly. *I told you I wasn't a director. I don't have anything to give you.*

"Always," Eddie said with a smile, but the light didn't reach his eyes.

For nearly an hour, Eddie tried going slower and holding still, but the energy didn't go away. His hands twitched when he paced, and the words didn't make any more sense. After Luke's third time telling him to ease up, Eddie suggested it might be time to let it lie. They could try again next time. Tuesdays and Thursdays were good for Luke, right? Once they got in the groove, Eddie knew they were going to be magic.

Who was Eddie trying to convince? Luke could have asked, but he couldn't bear to wait for the answer. As soon as Eddie turned to get his bag, Luke bolted and didn't look back.

At home, Luke went straight to his room and didn't check when his phone buzzed next to his bed. One rehearsal—if he could call it that—with Edward Sankawulo took away most of his ability to function around other human beings, and he needed anything left to decide whether to tackle another rehearsal. So, he made a list, two lists actually, one with the reasons he had to keep doing this project and one with the good, smart reasons that continuing was beyond stupid. When he should have been sleeping, he drew faceless bodies and wrote bullet points in the margins.

Pro: Class credit. He'd missed a lot of class, and even if his folks wouldn't care about another C, they'd notice if he failed English.

Con: *Not easy* class credit. Potentially *not possible* class credit. Eddie stared at him between tries, as if he was supposed to do something useful, and it would be a looong couple of months once he realized Luke didn't have anything to give.

Pro: More rehearsals equaled more chances to figure out who Eddie was.

Con: No time to do the musical.

Con: Lying to Dee and Marcos.

Con: Lying to his parents.

Con: Had he mentioned the lying?

Technically, he didn't have to lie. Marcos and Dee could know. But Luke couldn't tell them, not yet. Right now, the project with Eddie was a confusing, embarrassing mess, but it was *his mess*. He had to figure it out first, and part of that meant figuring out why he wasn't ready to share.

Eddie himself was on the con side too. Every time he got new information, something else stopped making sense. Was he a bad guy with a thing for theater or a good guy with a thing for guns? Was he *like Luke*, and did Luke even know what that meant?

Yesterday, Luke had spent the entire day trying to make time stop and today he was afraid to try. The last time he'd used the Hold, he'd walked into a mess so epic he couldn't even tell his best friends and had awoken with a headache that radiated down his shoulders and into his bones. He'd never been hung over, but he imagined that was what it would feel like if he drank everything on his dad's liquor shelf and then bashed his head into the bar. As a result, he knew next to nothing about what he could do, and there was no way he was going to try the Hold around Eddie.

Luke pressed his eyes until he saw stars.

For all he knew, Eddie was immune to his superpower. When he moved, that seemed obvious. Of course, Eddie would be the only person in the world with more energy than time itself. The fire behind his eyes probably made supernatural forces run the other way.

That fire was on the pro side too, along with Eddie's hands. Hell, his body had its own list. He saved number four for the way Eddie's back lined up with his hips when he changed direction, until he was one long, muscular line. Luke tried to draw it and got nothing but layers of motion lines as the body on the page tried to turn. He wasn't being a perv, mostly, although Eddie was the most beautiful boy Luke had ever seen in real life. This thing about Eddie's hands wasn't about beauty. He just had more energy in one finger than Luke had in his entire life. When he talked, Luke got it.

Some people are meant to be seen.

CHAPTER EIGHT

THEIR NEXT REHEARSAL WAS EVEN worse.

Luke arrived on Thursday already feeling foul. Yes, he was the worst asshat in the world. He was dirt, but there had to be some way to get Dee and Marcos to leave him alone. His parents mostly left him alone and that was a godsend just now. After nearly forty-eight hours of silence, Marcos and Dee apparently decided that two days were long enough to get over the emotional trauma of finding a secret superpower.

Cue the invasion.

"It's too early for a superhero name or a secret identity. We need time to figure out what you can do," Dee said when she appeared at his side between chemistry and English. Her eyes flashed when she was invested in a cause, as if the world better play along if it didn't want to get bitten. "When we have a full picture, we'll decide on a whole secret identity, and you can design your costume."

"Would you keep your voice down?" There was not going to be a costume.

She grinned and poked at the drawing pad in his hand, as Marcos appeared on his other side. They were uncanny. "You never know," he said. "Luke probably already has a secret identity."

"No, I don't." Luke said, as Dee shoved him toward his first hour class. "When would I have time? Right now, I don't even know if I have—"

A tall senior with a dark, wispy beard stepped into the gap at Dee's left, and Luke grabbed the first word that popped into his mind.

"—Chicken pox," Luke said. *Oh, good choice. I am a superspy.* "I don't know if I actually have chicken pox, and if I don't, that changes everything."

Dee snorted. "Not as much as if you actually do have *chicken pox*, Luke, and all signs point to yes. You're probably contagious." She threw up finger guns at her own joke and hooted all the way to her desk.

It continued after English, before lunch, after gym. By the end of the day, Dee was one step away from writing a backstory and selling it to DC Comics on the sly. "Come on, Luke!" she said, "Some part of your brain has to be excited about having chicken pox. I would literally kill to be able to make everyone stop moving any time I wanted to. How cool is that?" Her hands in the air, she spun to Marcos for backup.

Luke rolled his eyes. "It's what I've always dreamed of, really," he said and squatted along the wall near the theater. He wasn't going to lose them anyway. He'd been trying since nine that morning, and the traitorous part of his mind was starting to wish he hadn't told them anything. Hell, he was starting to wish he'd been adopted by a nice family in Canada. "Not to be ungrateful, but could we stop talking about it for five minutes? Everyone in the school is going to think I'm a walking plague vector."

"Not until we figure out a hook." And there she went with the *we* again, as though they'd all gone tromping into Eddie's house.

Dee squatted in front of him and grabbed his shoulders until he looked into her face. "Lucas Aday, you are amazing. Not that you weren't before, but now? You're a badass on the level of Doctor Fate or Luke Cage. Do you hear me? If any one of us deserved superpowers, it was clearly *moi,* but if I can't battle the forces of darkness myself, I am going to be the Mister Miyagi you obviously need. And not just because of the chicken pox thing." She poked him in the sternum, hard enough for him to feel it, but she had anxious eyes.

Marcos hovered at Luke's side, and gave Luke's shoulder a "me too" nudge.

Damn, damn, damn it.

He had to thank them for being there in his time of grief, but he just wanted to run until they stopped looking at him as though he were broken. Luke wasn't broken. He could do things no one else could, at least as far as he could imagine, so why did he feel like a car crash victim being inspected for new and exciting trauma? He might have been a crap director, but Eddie didn't look at him as if he were broken.

"Thank you, sensei," he said, more to the floor than Dee's face. "But before I get fitted for a cape—"

"You have to know why," Marcos said, as though that were where Luke's sentence was going. That wasn't where Luke's sentence was going. "Obviously, if Luke's going to be a superhero, he needs a reason why he got his powers. In the origin stories, it's all about the why."

Luke winced. "Is it?"

"Of course it is!" Dee said with a squeak and dropped back on her heels until she was sitting in the middle of the hallway. A band girl glared, and Dee stared back with placid amusement. "Keep it moving. I'm not that big, Courtney. Take one step to the left and you'll be on your way." Courtney scowled, but she did as she was told, and Dee turned back to the wall. "Marcos, you're brilliant, way smarter than Luke. We have to figure out the *why*. It's always a freak lab accident or genius technology—"

"Or a close encounter with aliens!" Marcos added. "Although I don't think you have any new superpowered accessories." He grinned until his eyes crinkled, and Luke couldn't smile back. They seemed so happy, as if they were born to be on a super-team, but he was just Luke. He'd never been chosen for anything in his life.

"You didn't get a grand genetic mission; no one destroyed *your city* and you haven't—" She stopped and her mouth shut with a snap.

"I haven't what?" Luke poked her in the shoulder, but she scooted away, her eyes anywhere but on him. "Dee, if I have to be anointed with oil or something to be mentored by a white lady Miyagi, just tell me."

Marcos coughed. "Death in the family," he said under his breath. "She was going to say that you haven't had a death in the family, but—" He dropped away and scooted to sit next to Luke against the wall.

Right. Of course. Someone always died: Spider-Man's uncle, Jessica Jones's entire family, Batman's parents, Superman's whole planet.

He squeezed Marcos's shoulder and pushed himself from the floor before Dee could apologize; she didn't have anything to apologize for. He gave her a tight smile and promised to call later, after the rehearsal they'd never know about. Dee didn't answer, and he wasn't going to call.

As he turned away, he laughed under his breath. Maybe he really was a superhero. Lizzy was dead, and he got the magical ability to turn a normal conversation into a funeral.

So, when he walked into his second meeting with Eddie, his brain wasn't anywhere near the theater/German/debate classroom. Half his mind was home in bed and the other half was still in the hallway hoping Marcos might drop his head onto his shoulder. None of him was left to play at powers he didn't have, and, if possible, Eddie looked even worse than he did.

Eddie had been twitchy the day before, just like in the hallway when they first met, but today something turned him up to eleven. He remained steady on his feet, but the rest of him was everywhere. As Luke arrived, he flipped scripts between his fingers and tapped out an uneven rhythm against his own thigh.

"Hey, stranger." Eddie said with a smile as Luke slouched into the room. "Come on. It's a brand new day!" He asked if Luke was ready to try again and didn't wait for an answer before launching into the same monologue.

Luke wasn't ready. He knew it, and by thirty minutes into the practice Eddie knew it too. Between the first and second run-throughs, Luke prepared a dozen canned suggestions, but he was still lost. When he tried to take notes, his ideas wouldn't clump together into words or sit in place on the page. Once or twice he thought he might have found a good direction to suggest. Sometimes he caught a moment that stood out as *more* amid the awesome, but when he wrote down the memory, it fell apart and he spent the rest of the monologue scrambling to pick up the pieces.

He drew disembodied hands and lips along the edge of his sketchpad and hoped that by the time Eddie finished the monologue, he'd figure out how to put them back together again, but they stayed separate and pointless.

After the run, Eddie waited and tapped. "Tell me the good news, Captain," he said, and Luke just stared at a page full of body parts without bone or muscle holding them together: eyes and lips in space.

"It's better," he said quietly and, when Eddie sighed, Luke heard a little part of Eddie give up.

Luke had been part of bad group projects before, but he'd never been the dead weight. This time, he was the anvil tied to the leg of Eddie's project, and the whole thing was sinking fast. The harder Eddie tried to motivate Luke to say something, the more Luke's words disappeared, until Eddie stopped expecting him to say anything at all. After each run-through, he just paused and then started over. Luke wasn't sure if that was to spare Luke the pressure or to spare himself the disappointment.

Once, Luke thought he was onto something. On Eddie's umpteenth time through the monologue, Luke stopped him and told him to play up the insanity. It made sense. The character was already ranting, and Eddie made sure he had the crazy-eyes, so it couldn't hurt to try one round with the crazy turned up to eleven.

"See if you like it," he said and waited for Eddie's relief. *Finally*, he would think, *finally my director started directing*, but Eddie wasn't relieved.

He stood in the middle of the dirty gap in the middle of the room and his hands went still. "That's not what I was doing," Eddie finally said through clenched teeth. He blinked hard and threw his backpack over his shoulder with a thud. "That can't be what I was doing."

He slipped out without disturbing the door.

I'm sorry. Come back.

Eddie couldn't leave. He had to come back to tell Luke what "that" was and why it was wrong. He had to let Luke explain that he didn't mean whatever he accidentally said. He didn't mean anything that would leave Eddie shell-shocked and quiet. Luke glared at the cracked door. *Come back.*

If he were a better person, he would have made Eddie stop. If he were in a movie, Luke would have said "stop" really quietly, and Eddie would have listened, because that's how movies worked. Luke scowled. *Real life needs better editing.* He scooted off the desk, stuffed his sketchpad into his backpack and walked into Eddie standing perfectly static outside the doorway.

He wasn't the only one. He'd dotted the hallway with statues in a picture so silent he could hear his shoes clip against the floor.

Luke hadn't just stopped Eddie. He'd stopped everything and he hadn't felt himself try. When Eddie had walked out the door, Luke had wanted him to stop and listen, but his demented mind had only managed one thing. He slid out into the hall with his back flat against the wall and his bag clenched against his stomach.

It had been less than a minute since Eddie picked up his bag. Luke couldn't have counted to one thousand in his head, and Eddie had already turned into someone new. The sad boy from their stage had disappeared. He had his back to the door and one hand in the air, as he turned toward a cluster of students in track pants and T-shirts. The whole group stood across the hallway with their mouths open and smiling, and, in the middle, a pretty girl stood on her tiptoes to wave back. Luke stepped closer to see her face. She glowed as if she made energy in her fingertips. Her skin was darker than Eddie's, and she had her hair piled into a ponytail that spilled from the back of her head in a high, elegant pouf. Three years at this school, and Luke couldn't have picked her out of a lineup, but she already knew Eddie. Luke had frozen the moment when her face lit up with joy. She was so happy to see him, and he—

Luke circled around to see Eddie's face, and he was beaming back at the girl. In the seconds it took him to step away from the classroom door, he'd been remade. Luke peered into Eddie's happy eyes and wanted to interrogate their shine.

How? He thought. *How did you learn to be everyone at the same time?*

He stumbled back to the wall and slid down to stare at the tableau. How was this his gift? On any other day the hall would have been empty and silent. No one would have been hurt if Luke sent out shock waves left and right, but then again—he thought of something Marcos had said. Luke couldn't remember where or when; he and Dee had been on him like limpets all day. At one time, though, he'd gotten stuck on the logistics of the Hold.

"What's your impact radius?" Marcos had asked, in all seriousness, and, for a second, Luke had thought he'd finally switched to a new topic. But Marcos had tried again. "If you go 'boom,'" he'd said, throwing out his fingers like a shocked octopus, "how far would you have to go to find someone who wasn't hit?"

Luke hadn't been able to answer. He'd assumed he could only hold on to the people and things in his immediate vicinity, but Marcos had made him wonder: What if there weren't boundaries? What if, when he held the world still in North Grove or Eddie's bedroom, what if that also meant that no one else, anywhere, could keep moving? Because of him, the little kid in Taiwan couldn't get up from bed, and the swimmer in Norway couldn't come up for air. He hugged his knees close to his chest.

None of them would know any better. After the Hold, they would go on with their swimming or their crying and never know the difference, but he would know. He would bring them all back to their waiting lives and know that, for just a bit, they'd been gone. The power turned his stomach. At the moment, he could do anything. He could rifle through Eddie's bag or smack the glowing girl's face, and neither of them would ever know. She'd walk around for the rest of the day with a phantom pain and never know where it came from.

The thought was horrifying and huge, a lot like the thought that, at this particular moment, he might be the only person in the world who could really be understood as alive. In this second, he hadn't just survived Lizzy; he'd survived them all.

Luke breathed. *Or no.* Luke tried to breathe past the tightness in his chest and didn't think about the needles at the corners of his eyes.

I can play with time like Hiro Nakamura. I'm infinite.

He laughed without smiling and pressed the back of his head against the wall. He was infinite, and he'd give it up in a second if Eddie could teach him how to be everyone at the same time.

LIZZY SPOKE TO HIM FOR the first time when she was fifteen, and it had felt like magic. One day Lizzy had laughed or made scrunchy faces when she was mad, and the next she'd had a whole library of mechanical words to use whenever she wanted. And she'd wanted to use them all the time.

The speech pathologists had set up the machine on a Saturday morning, and Lizzy had spent all weekend scrolling through the words on a big laptop screen. There'd been a paddle by her head, mounted on her wheelchair, and she'd tapped it with her head to make the machine move to the next word. She'd been able to pick words with her hands too, if she wanted, but she'd liked the one by her head. She'd been able do that one all on her own.

They plugged in words she'd want, like "silly" and "Kermit the Frog," and it had only taken a few hours to get used to hearing them pop out in a flat mechanical monotone.

"Silly."

"Happy."

"Hungry."

"Kermit the Frog."

"No." "Yes." "No." "No." "No."

Now, when people came to visit they'd talked about how the words didn't make sense. They'd smiled when she "spoke" to them, but Luke had understood. "Silly" was how she talked about herself. "Happy" meant music, and "Kermit" meant anything on the TV. "Hungry" meant go away. He hadn't known why; it just did.

They'd plugged all of the family names into the machine too: Mark, Janet, Elizabeth and Lucas. The others had been pictures, but he'd made his into a stick drawing, so she'd know it was him. After that, Lizzy had spent a whole hour just saying Luke's name over and over again, and each time it meant something new.

Sampson.
Regory: A my word wee'l not ...
Greg. No, for then we should ...

Greg. Do you quarrell fir?
... fir? no fir.
... fir, I am for you, I ferue as good
Nobetter? Samp. Well

CHAPTER NINE

[FROM DEE] OK. SONG TITLES with stop in the title, for the eventual soundtrack of Luke's superhero movie.

[From Marcos] Aren't you in chem?

[From Dee] Yes. Why? GOOO.

[From Marcos] Don't Stop Me Now. Don't Stop Believing.

[From Dee] Don't stop thinking about tomorrow.

[From Marcos] Stop in the Name of Love. But Luke calls it holding, not stopping. We need "hold" songs.

[From Marcos] Hold me closer tiny dancer.

[From Dee] YES. You're not gonna do any better than that, Luke.

[From Dee] Luke?

* * *

NEXT TUESDAY, LUKE WAS LATE for rehearsal. The clock ticked past 4:14 p.m. before he arrived, and he didn't have a reason.

He told himself that Eddie wouldn't be there. If he were Eddie, he wouldn't be there either. Then again, he would have given up on himself in the middle of their first rehearsal. Danes must have implied that he was the next messiah. Lucas Aday, Desi child of God. It was the only reason Luke could imagine why Eddie hadn't already kicked him to the curb.

Eddie was there.

He sat atop a desk in the middle of the first row, just as he had on their first day of rehearsals, and waved as Luke came in. "Captain, what's the holdup? You can tell me if you found a better actor in another room." He whipped out a piece of paper from the folder of scripts and held it out, just like before. Maybe someone hit the cosmic replay button and forgot to tell Eddie that he'd already done this scene.

"Take it, and let's get a move on," he said. "I'm ready to go if you are." His eyes focused on Luke's face as he waved the script, like an offer. *Take the paper,* his eyes said, *and we can forget yesterday ever happened.*

It was tempting, but Luke had spent too much time psyching himself up in the bathroom mirror to get comfortable.

"You're relaxed," he said slowly and leaned against the doorway. "I didn't know if you'd be here."

Eddie stared harder at the papers in his hand. "Almost wasn't. That's what happens when you show up thirty minutes late. Civilized people look down on that sort of thing." His voice was light as air and fake as hell.

"You can tell my mom all about how I'm uncivilized," Luke said. "I'm good, if you want me here."

"Why wouldn't I?"

Eddie seemed so genuinely confused Luke had to laugh. "Eddie," he said and wrapped his arms around his own body, "you walked out two days ago." *I almost made you cry.*

Eddie nodded, as if that was beside the point. "I was upset and so I left. Now, I'm not." He held out the paper again, and Luke didn't take it. "Look, something hit a little close to the bone for me. There's no way you could have known, and I didn't expect you to know."

Because you haven't told me anything. Luke nodded.

Eddie considered him for a second and turned away. "That reminds me of this time when I was five years old," he said, almost too casually. "I sprained my wrist. It was one of those stupid kid things." He smiled at the folder. "I was probably making life hell for my little brother and got what was coming to me. I don't even remember. I do remember a couple weeks later when I whacked my wrist against the stage in the community center—"

"The stage?" Luke asked, quietly. If he spoke too loud, Eddie might remember that he never talked about his own life.

"I used to do these kid's plays when we lived in Chicago, and that was play number one. I was one of, I don't know, thirty lost boys in *Peter Pan*. That day, I fell. I smacked my wrist into this hard wooden stage, and it felt as if my arm exploded. My father spent hours convincing me I didn't hurt it again. I was so sure because it ached like hell, but I didn't. I just hit the same spot and I didn't expect my body to still be mad at me." He rubbed his wrist while he spoke, as if he didn't know he was doing it. "That's what it was like, last time. I hit an old bruise and it hurt like a mother, but I'm not blaming you for it. You didn't know."

Eddie held the paper up again, and this time Luke took it.

"*Peter Pan?*"

Eddie's back relaxed as Luke sat. "Just imagine a little version of me in a giant white T-shirt and orange shorts all cut up like a Disney street kid. I've got a picture somewhere, and my hair's huge. I was rocking a baby fro."

"Were there other lost boys that, you know—" He pointed up to Eddie's hair.

Eddie laughed. "More than here. Have you been to Chicago? I'm not talking about Evanston. We were living downtown with my uncle, so—" His smile was fond. "I wasn't the only immigrant kid, but all those gaps feel like about a million miles when you're in middle school." He gave Luke a pointed look. "It would have been worse here."

Luke didn't deny it. If Eddie meant Minneapolis or St. Paul, then no. It probably would have been better, but North Grove was a different story. In elementary school he'd had to explain the difference between his kind of Indian and Squanto for three Thanksgivings straight. In third grade, a teacher asked him about "his culture" and got mad when he talked about *Spider-Man*. Eddie was probably right.

He turned to the monologue in his hand, while Eddie stretched in his chair. His shirt rode up when he reached for the ceiling, and there was nothing wrong with that, but Luke was too surprised by the monologue to really focus on Eddie's waist. "*Angels in America?*" he asked. There was no way in hell Mrs. Danes had included a speech from a former drag queen in a play about religion, AIDS, and gay sex in a stack for random students. Luke had first read that play under the covers with a flashlight, like porn. He'd been too young to understand the political parts or why some of it took place in Antarctica, but he figured out all of the male characters were into guys. That was kind of the point.

Luke didn't ask where the monologue came from or why it was in his hand, but a sly smile spread across Eddie's face. "Think about it," he said. "It's probably the only speech in that whole bookcase from a queer dude who looks anything like me." He hopped off the desk with studied ease.

"So, you're—" *Mind-boggling.*

"Bi. I'm the big B in the LGBTQA, or whatever the acronym is today. I can't say QUILTBAG with a straight face," Eddie said. He cocked his head, probably because Luke hadn't closed his mouth. "Is this something we have to talk about, too? Eventually I do have to go home."

"No! I just—um—me too. I mean, I'm the G," he said with a pained smile. *I'm the idiot.*

"All right." Eddie smiled and, that time, it went all the way up to his eyes. "I'm trying this from the top. You go ahead and do whatever it is you did last time. Just because I got all bruised up doesn't mean you weren't doing something right."

Luke nodded as Eddie rolled his shoulders and shook off the whole day like so many specks of dust. He wasn't sure he believed that he'd done anything right yet, but Eddie seemed certain enough for both of them.

CHAPTER TEN

[FROM MARCOS] WE'LL BE IN the theater after school today, if you want to come.

[From Marcos] I know you've got a lot going on, but if you can't do it, they might have to ask Vargassi to come back on board.

[From Marcos] Ok, not Vargassi, but someone.

[From Marcos] It's not the same without you.

[From Dee] Give it up, Boo Boo. He's not coming.

[From Marcos] Luke?

[From Luke] I'll be there.

* * *

"YOU ARE SUCH A LAZY sack of shit."

"I love you too, Dee." Luke tipped his head back until he saw her sitting on the catwalk above the North Grove High School stage. For the last hour she'd roamed the cats, fixing lights and marking the ones that needed maintenance before tech week.

Luke and Marcos perched on the edge of the stage, and their legs dangled from the edge. Luke had his drawing pad out and was sketching concept art for Audrey II, the giant man-eating monster plant at the center of the *Little Shop* set. Danes really should have stuck with *Spelling Bee*. If North Grove had any money, the process would have gone more smoothly. As it was, Luke's plans quickly outgrew anything they could possibly build on a budget of bake sale proceeds and donations from three enthusiastic moms. What began as a little Styrofoam pod head with painted teeth grew eighteen wire tentacles and a long, slavering tongue lolling out of Audrey's jaw. It was a beautiful sketch, with lips and spikes as real as life. He could almost see its fuzzy tentacles creep across the stage toward Maria Leitner and Jeremy Ng as they sang about skid row. Of course, even if his monster on the page magically came to life under Dee's command, the actors would probably care as much as they usually did about tech, which is to say, not at all until something broke.

Luke held the drawing at arm's length and squinted at its proportions. It was too much. He started to rip out the page, when Marcos poked him in the side. He didn't say anything, just poked and waited until Luke handed over the pad.

"It's her!" Marcos smiled, in awe. "Look what you did! You made Audrey II."

"Stop," Luke said. He could do better sketches in his sleep. Not that that was of any use. "We're never going to be able to build it. It's just a picture."

Marcos elbowed him in the side. "Does this look like a picture to you, punk? If I can move and I can talk, who's to say I can't do anything I want?" For a small guy, Marcos could do a passable Audrey II: sort of like Darth Vader, but as a plant.

"I'm not doing this." Because if he did the next line, Marcos would keep going, eventually they'd hit a song and then the jerk would try to make him to sing. Not a chance.

Marcos pouted at him, at least half serious. "Luuuke."

Luke said the next line.

Soon they lay on their backs with their heads together and their legs hanging off the edge of the stage. They'd quoted themselves through half of *Little Shop* and wandered on to mapping an imaginary staging across the ceiling. As Marcos spoke, Luke held his pencil over his head and drew a set in the air. The blues and grays of the buildings arced over the first and second levels of the flower shop, which was splashed in bright reds and greens. Marcos stole the pen to add invisible fire escapes that snaked up the side of the painted buildings.

By the time Dee yelled from the rafters that they had to "get their asses moving," they'd run out of pieces to add to the set and were just tossing the pen back and forth. It slapped into Luke's hand, and he didn't think about their shoulders pressed together against the stage, Marcos's left to his right. They fell that way, and Marcos never moved, so neither did Luke. He stared at the ceiling with the side of Marcos's cheek in his peripheral vision and let the moment seep into his bones. Marcos smelled like sweat, paint and the varnish they used on the flats. They hadn't been painting, but he always smelt a little as if he had.

I wonder if I smell like this place, too.

"You could, couldn't you?" Marcos jogged his shoulder, and Luke realized he'd missed a step, or six. "If you threw the pen and then froze everything, you could get up and get it yourself, right? And then you could play catch with yourself on a loop forever."

Luke's stomach tightened around the knot that was always there for Marcos Aldama. "Yeah, I could, I guess," he said and traced the splintered edge of the stage. He hated that stage. "I suppose anyone could play catch with themselves, though. We're doing it right now." He tossed the pen up into the air and let it land in his hands. "But I'm not doing that anymore, not until I know how it works." *Which will be never.*

"Okay," Marcos said, as if Luke had turned down a free trip to Hawaii, "but there's probably not a guidebook for this sort of thing. Unless there is, but it's undercover!" He punched the air with his right hand. "There could be a top secret guidebook to sudden superpowers buried under the hockey rink, and you have to uncover it to find your real mission."

"My real mission."

"Oh, yeah." And he lost Marcos. Marcos might as well have been on the moon. "When you read the book, you have all the tools to figure out why you have superpowers. Seriously, go back and read any comic with surprise superpowers. There's always some way of finding out the backstory so that you and your trusty sidekicks—that's us—have enough information to figure out why you have a superpower. Dude, we put the pieces together, and then it's all about fulfilling your destiny." He caught his breath and squinted up at the rafters. "I really hope it doesn't have anything to do with hockey."

"Does there have to be a reason? Couldn't it just be a thing I can do?"

"Not usually," Marcos said. If he noticed Luke's discomfort, it didn't show. "Sometimes you get superheroes with accidental powers, but even in those cases there's some logic behind the gift. Think about *The Flash*. No one roots for a superhero who doesn't deserve it."

"Right," Luke said, flat and dry. *Deserve it. What a cosmic, nauseating joke.*

Marcos smiled up at the ceiling. "You'll make a great superhero."

"And you'll both make completely useless theater techs," Dee called from backstage. The stairs from the cats dropped her far enough back to be invisible to an audience, but close enough that they could hear her speak. "Seriously, guys. From up there, you're actually less exciting than watching paint dry. And no offense, Boo Boo," she said, and squatted at Luke's side, "I'm not your sidekick, trusty or otherwise."

"No offense taken. You're my Mister Miyagi. If anything, I'd be the sidekick," Luke said. He tried to smile, but his face wouldn't behave, not when he wanted to puke off the side of the stage.

Dee's eyes narrowed over a frown, as though she wanted to ask a question. Instead, she poked Luke's side and pointed toward the rafters. "Okay, wonder twin number two, I need help with lamp replacements." She turned to Marcos. "You're on body mics. There are three boxes waiting in the control booth."

He saluted her from the floor.

Luke trailed behind Dee as she climbed the ladder to the cats and strapped them both into harnesses. He'd never tell her, but he couldn't go into the catwalks on his own. Five steps up the ladder would suddenly be way too far from the ground, and he'd have to make up some excuse about calling his mom so Mrs. Danes would let him back down. Oddly enough, the height was never a problem when Dee was there. She just made him feel closer to the ground.

Gloves in hand, they settled next to the cooling cyclorama strip lights; the stage was a distant checkerboard beneath the catwalk floor. She squatted on the metal slats, and he sat with his legs dangling. "Tough week," she said. It wasn't a question.

"Tough week," he said back, and she let him work.

Dee took out the old lamp and dropped it into his hands. It was warm, even through the gloves. Maybe it wasn't broken after all. Either that, or the problem was deeper than the part of the light they could see. He cleared his throat. It wasn't meant as a prologue, but the question came anyway.

"How do you keep up?"

Dee sat back on her heels, eyebrows raised.

"I mean—" He shook his head. In the darkness, the lamp's edges blurred into the grayish black shadows of the theater floor. "When you're directing, how do you keep up when everything happens so fast?" She was incredible on the job. Even with noise coming from the whole theater at the same time she always knew what was supposed to happen next. "I can't wrap my mind around how you do it. I can't even—" *No, wait, redirect.* "I mean, I can't imagine paying attention to one person and telling them what to do to make everything better the next time around." He especially couldn't imagine helping someone with antsy hands and feet that wouldn't stay still. Luke imagined an entire production full of Eddies playing every role, all of them smiling at the same time.

He coughed. *It would be a good show.* "I've just been thinking about it is all."

"Thinking about directing?"

"I think about things sometimes." Luke wanted to kick his feet against the scaffolding, but some things weren't advisable at fifty feet. "That looks harder than what we have to do." He gestured at Marcos, who was still picking his way through the box of mics, well out of earshot. "You don't have to answer if it's a stupid question."

"It's not," Dee said. She pulled off her gloves and slapped them against the metal slats of the catwalk as though that helped her think. It probably did. "I don't know how to explain it. You know when we did *Oklahoma* last year?" He nodded, even though the question was rhetorical. "I remember listening to 'The Farmer and the Cowman' and letting it flow right over me. We had the music basically right, and the choreography wasn't horrible anymore, so it was all about tweaking, and there's no way to pay attention to everything, so I let it flow until I noticed something was off."

Luke must have let the confusion show on his face, because Dee doubled back. "When I listened, it was as if I was walking and someone clipped me in the side. The wrong parts threw off the whole rhythm, so I could pick out offbeat moments and figure out what went wrong. Target and attack." She pointed her finger like a gun and shot out the light in Luke's hands. *Click. Boom.*

Luke's head spun. "What if you never, um, get clipped? What if you just kept walking and knew something was wrong, but—" The metaphor got away from him.

Dee shrugged. "By *Oklahoma,* I could usually pick out something, and that's why we have other directors. But," she said as she scrunched her nose at the ceiling, "if a director isn't picking up anything, they're probably coming at it the wrong way."

"Like, they should watch from the other side?"

"No!" She dropped her head until it smacked against the guardrail. "Sometimes you're so *literal*. Now put down the old lamp before I drop this and kill Marcos, and we have one less space cadet wandering through our lives." She yelled the last down at the booth, until Marcos tipped his head back and stuck his tongue out toward the ceiling.

"See?" Luke waved toward the Marcos-blur below. "We aren't twins. I would have flipped you off."

Dee rolled her eyes. "No, you really aren't twins, because that would make what you want to do to him illegal in almost all fifty states. Right now, it's only illegal in twelve."

Then he flipped her off.

CHAPTER ELEVEN

LUKE DIDN'T THINK OF IT as stalking. That would be creepy and screwed up, but after Dee's advice about directing, he started watching Eddie again.

It was better than thinking about his mom and how she didn't get out of bed. Luke didn't know if it was *couldn't* or *wouldn't*, or which would be worse. Either way, as he and his dad silently passed each other in the kitchen, her bedroom stayed silent, and her door stayed shut. Eddie was easier to watch and not nearly so still. Luke could probably piece together his entire schedule from glimpses in the hallway, and he couldn't shake the thought that Eddie could be different too. Maybe he had the ability to make everyone in the world like him. Maybe, if Eddie wanted to, he could snap his fingers like a genie and make the entire school fall at his feet. He definitely could do a funeral right. Eddie would perform grief like a soliloquy. His family and friends would leave feeling better about themselves because he cried in their arms.

The night before, it had been all he could think about: Eddie the secret superhero and Luke the—whatever he was. Maybe he could be the sidekick who held time while Eddie changed the world. They'd descend on a crime in progress. Maybe a little girl would be kidnapped or rival gangs would be in the middle of a showdown. Luke knew his idea of North Grove's seedy underworld sounded like a *Sesame Street* performance of *West Side Story*, but he didn't need realism. Realism wasn't working, so he thought about holding bad guys to a standstill while Eddie rained justice on moustache-twirling gangsters. By the time they were through, the kidnappers would send the little girl back to her parents and the gangs would hug it out like frat brothers, crying on each other's shoulders that "the world is full of love, man, so much love."

After watching Eddie for too long, Luke tweaked the fantasy. Eddie couldn't make everyone like him, but he could like everyone. Some people were utter dicks to him just as they were utter dicks to everyone else. Luke just hadn't realized it at first because Eddie turned asshole conversations around until it seemed as if everyone was on the same side.

Mostly, he was a wizard when it came to Dee's brother.

On Thursday, Luke was packing up after last period when Wes's voice rang down the hall like church bells: pissy, entitled church bells. Luke flinched, but Wes was bothering Eddie this time and, by the tone of his voice, he didn't think he was bothering anyone. "Dude, you gotta help me out here," he said. He pointed back to where Elliot and the others were trailing behind him. "What do they speak where you're from?"

Loud as anything, the question rolled down the hallway, and Eddie flinched, hard. Wes caught him in between classes, minutes after the bell. He couldn't have been expecting whatever bug Wes had up his butt, but he was still Eddie. He recovered. "Chicago?" He said, with a glaring smile. "Try English. They've got it all over these days."

Wes beamed. "Nah, man, don't be like that," he said, as Eddie turned to walk away. "You know what I'm talking about. In the motherland or whatever, what was the lingua franca?"

"The motherland is Russia, the lingua franca is French, and I spoke English, *really*. It's the official language in Liberia. If you don't believe me, I don't know, Google it." Eddie backed himself up against the closest wall, which happened to be across the hall from Luke's locker, where Luke was trying to make himself invisible. "I know a little Bassa too, but that was after we arrived in the States."

"Bassa. Cool." From Wes, the name of the language sounded flat, as though he were naming a new character in *The Lion King*. "Awesome," he said. "What can you say? You have to give us a sentence or something."

"Nah." Wes started to protest, but Eddie cut him off. Luke heard the smile. "It's not a party trick. Now, if you want to see me spin some plates on my hands, we could work something out. Give me time to put together a show."

Wes and the others didn't just laugh. They pressed their hands to their chests and roared. "Yeah, Sanka!" Wes said, happier than Luke had heard him in days. "You spin plates and we'll get Elijah to do a thing with dancing dogs."

"Cirque de Lacrosse!"

Eddie's low laugh carried them around the corner, until Luke couldn't hear them anymore. *Incredible.* Eddie wasn't the magical friendship guy. He was Darwin from *X-Men*. He adapted, even to a name like *Sanka*. Luke grimaced. That was new. It sounded like a brand-name energy drink, the kind that mixed Pixie Stix with alcohol and got banned in Europe.

Eew.

"Earth to Lucas. Earth to Lucas Aday. You with us?" Luke jerked and dropped his sketchpad on his foot. *Jesus Christ.* Eddie must have looped back for rehearsal and, once again, found Luke staring into the void.

He stooped to grab the sketchpad and slammed it shut before Eddie could see all the drawings of him. "Warn me or you're going to have to find another partner."

"Because I'm known for my stealth." Eddie gave a few stomps as he opened the door to the German room and waved Luke inside.

"Stealth, no, but timing," Luke said, with feeling. He had the worst timing. Eddie's eyebrows shot through the roof. His grin was equal parts surprised and delighted as Luke snapped, "I never know when you're going to show up, *Sanka*."

He tossed his bag into a corner and when he turned Eddie was perched on a desk; his smile was flat and tired.

Oh, no. When Luke apologized, Eddie waved him off. "No," he said. "It's—fine. I'm just—Sanka? Really?" He laughed up at the ceiling. "I sound like a character from *Cool Runnings*. You know, 'Sanka? You dead?'" His accent sounded like the kind of Jamaican who sold bananas to tourists. "My mom loves that movie. But if it catches on, I might as well break into 'Day-o' and pass out coconuts. They put me in the wrong country and, for all that, I hardly know any Bassa. You want to hear?"

Luke didn't have time to respond before Eddie kept going. Words rolled from his tongue like water, and Luke didn't even try to follow. "And that's what I've got," he said, as he finished. "Mostly, it's all proverbs and church songs. That one means 'to know nothing is to be foolish.'" He shook his head. "The irony kills me. My mom thought the mother tongue was too 'country,' so my uncles taught me stuff on the sly. I've hardly got enough to put on a show."

"What a tragedy."

"I know," Eddie said. "Poor Wes. I'll have to break it to him gently." He held up the *Romeo and Juliet* monologue and shifted back into his place on their imaginary stage, halfway between Mrs. Danes's desk and a wide crack in the tile Dee called *das Deutches asscrack*. When he found his imaginary mark, he smiled, a sly little thing that wasn't Eddie at all.

That was Mercutio's smile—filthy, witty and too smart by half.

When Eddie started, Luke let the words flow over him, just as Dee had told him to do. He stopped focusing on a critique, and he was still useless. When Eddie did something fantastic, Luke was too incompetent to do anything more than see it. He could ask Eddie to go back again and *again*. Sometimes he did, but that only highlighted the fact that he didn't know what to do and left them both too frustrated to look each other in the eye.

After the third run, Eddie suggested a break, and Luke's head dropped into his hands. "I vote we leave this room and never come back. Ever," he said through his fingers. He could probably recite the posters from left to right along the window-side wall. Hell, by the standards of the North Grove public school system, he probably knew German.

"And then I crash and burn alone?"

Luke glared up into Eddie's face. Poor, pathetic, trusting Eddie, who was getting screwed. "That's happening anyway," he said, and hoped Eddie would at least glare back. Luke couldn't help. He was too slow and he had an awesome superpower that made him even slower. "I'm tired and I'm crap at this."

"You're not crap," Eddie said. He crouched on his heels. His face was so gentle Luke wanted to hide under the desk. "You're just not *here*." He set his hand on Luke's foot, and it was awkwardly sweet. "I'm all over the place right now. You know it, I know it, and I need someone else's eyes to find the focus. Captain, I promise I'm not asking you to be the best director in the world. I'm only asking you to show the hell up."

Dee and Marcos wouldn't have said that.

It was a strange first thought, but there it was. Eddie pulled his hand away from Luke's shoe. His friends never would have gone there, and Luke wasn't sure how he felt about that.

Eddie slipped into the hallway to get a drink while Luke pulled himself together. Eddie's move was obvious—he always had a full water bottle in his bag—but Luke was grateful anyway. By the time Eddie got back, Luke had remembered how to smile. "Go. Act," he said, and tried to project presence from his hunched spot on the desk. "If something grabs me, I'll yell."

"And what a beautiful yell it will be."

Eddie slid into the speech they'd both seen ten billion times, and it was exactly the same, until it wasn't.

Between the first and second half of the speech, Eddie looked up with his hands pressed to his scalp, and Luke almost fell off his desk.

There was something *there*. Eddie was always spellbinding, but in that split-second movement he did something perfectly right.

"Stop." Luke swung his hand into the air over his head, and scrambled for his pad. "Stop. Stop. *Stop*." That was the moment, right there, with Eddie's hands in his hair. He had something, but he needed to gather his thoughts. He finally got ahold of the pad and looked up to where Eddie stood perfectly, unblinkingly still.

Oh, no.

"Can you hear me? Eddie?" Luke leaned forward with his eyes focused on Eddie's face. "If you can hear me, blink or something." Eddie didn't move.

Okay then.

Luke slid off the desk holding one hand in the air. "I don't know if you can't hear what I'm saying or if you just can't move, but I'm really, really sorry." He stopped a foot away from Eddie's face and peered into his wide eyes. Eddie didn't look like a man about to go for a walk. He looked like Mercutio. "For the record," Luke said, "I have no idea what you're doing that's so special right now." Eddie's feet were planted apart. His elbows were splayed wide as he held his head in his hands and stared into a vision above the audience's head.

Luke couldn't see what had made him fall off the desk, but he had time, so he drew.

He sketched Eddie's elbows as they angled away from his shoulders and the tension in his hands. Luke outlined the skin of Eddie's fingers against the darker brown of his hair, but he couldn't capture the pressure in his knuckles or the tight crease between wrist and hand. He couldn't come anywhere near the beauty of Eddie's face.

He was still staring at his drawing when the Hold dropped away. Luke didn't decide it was time. He got caught up in his drawings and let go.

"This is she!" Eddie finished, as though nothing had happened, and Luke slapped the sketchpad to his chest. It might have been his imagination, but Eddie already seemed sharper around the edges, as though he'd finally come into focus.

"Any notes, Captain?"

He was breathless, and Luke nodded. He'd found the something. Before today, he'd known Eddie's Mercutio was frantic, but he couldn't understand why. On the surface, the speech was nothing to make anyone frantic. Mercutio tells Romeo about a fairy who makes people have dreams about stuff that they like. Then, everybody gets upset. Luke assumed Romeo and the rest were worried because Mercutio was acting crazy. People weren't supposed to randomly yell about fairies. But, when Eddie held his hands to his head, the speech made sense for the first time, and Eddie's Mercutio wasn't crazy.

He was scared.

When Eddie looked up into the light from the frosted glass with his eyes wide and his mouth soft, he played Mercutio as one-hundred-percent afraid of imaginary dreams.

Mercutio was terrified and, just like that, the rest of the monologue snapped into place.

"There's something wrong with the dreams in the monologue," Luke said quietly. "There's a lawyer who dreams of money. There's a parson who dreams about a really great job. The soldier dreams about cutting throats. They all dream about great stuff they aren't supposed to have, right? They're hypocrites, and the fairy in the monologue makes them see it. They aren't the people they think they are. So then Romeo hears the story and realizes he's a hypocrite, too. They're all lying to themselves. That's why Mercutio gives the speech in the first place. He wants Romeo to think before he goes to the party, but it goes wrong, doesn't it?" Eddie listened, his attention focused on Luke's face.

Luke couldn't have stopped if he wanted to. "So, the problem is that Mercutio gets half-way through this speech to Romeo and realizes that he's full of it, too. All along, Mercutio's been the funny guy. He plays up the crazy, but then he gets smacked in the face with the fact that he's a huge liar, and that's terrifying."

Eddie opened his mouth as if to cut in, and Luke held up a hand.

"Shut up. I mean, wait. I got most of that from Wikipedia, but I think there's something here. I knew he was scared already, but I think your Mercutio figures it all out when he's talking about the soldier. When you talked about the soldier who dreams about cutting throats, you were looking up at the ceiling, like this." He turned toward the light, and Eddie's eyes followed. "That's the turning point for the whole monologue. Focus there, and everyone else will see it too."

Luke stopped and, for a moment, he thought Eddie might leave. He had that look in his eyes from the last practice, as if he Luke had turned into someone he couldn't recognize, but then his face split wide. "Wow, Captain," he said with a grin. "Speaking of liars. I only followed half of that, but now I know the truth. You've been holding out on me."

Luke sputtered. He had *not*, but Eddie laughed. "Welcome to rehearsals, Captain 2.0." He gave Luke a punch in the shoulder that was more of a pat, and Luke's shoulder stayed warm when Eddie pulled away.

"If you keep calling me Captain *anything*, I'm going throw things at you while you act."

"That wouldn't be very 2.0 of you," Eddie replied.

"Heavy things."

Eddie saluted, and the scene started over again.

THAT EVENING, LUKE HOVERED AROUND the kitchen table like a lost bird. He didn't notice he was doing it until his dad looked up from his laptop for the third time in five minutes, probably because Luke was staring intently at a full-page advertisement for vegan ice cream in *Bon Appétit*. Never mind the fact that Luke wasn't vegan.

After a complete inspection of a brand made with hemp and seaweed extract, he slunk back to his room, and his dad followed. He lingered in the hall longer than he would have in September or last summer, but he came.

"Want to talk?" he asked, as he sat at the foot of Luke's bed, and Luke almost laughed. Want had nothing to do with it. "If it's nothing, talk about nothing."

So he talked about classes and his friends, and it was all less than nothing until his dad got up to leave. That's when Luke cleared his throat, and his dad hovered by the door.

"Do you think we're good at stuff for a reason?" he asked, and his dad frowned in surprise. "I don't mean stuff we practice. Like, just imagine I woke up one day and could sing anything. Would there be a reason or would it just be this thing I knew how to do?" He didn't care what his dad said, not really, since he didn't have any idea what Luke was asking about, but when he answered, Luke leaned forward anyway.

"Well," he said with a sigh, "if I buy the assumption that you could wake up and sound like an opera singer, then my answer is yes and no. Do I think there's some power that decided you should be able to draw? No, I don't, but that's not to say it can't have meaning." He crossed his arms over his chest, and the words came out slowly, as if he were trying them on for size. "Think about it. I cook for you and your mom. She makes scrapbooks for your grandmother. You drew for Lizzy. We don't just do things. We do them for other people. Right?"

Luke nodded.

"Well then, there's your meaning."

He left with a sad smile, and Luke waited until a count of ten until he pulled the world to a standstill. There was no reason. He could hardly tell the difference alone in his room, but it was nice to pretend that the Hold was like cooking and that someone might notice if he got a little better.

CHAPTER TWELVE

LUKE DIDN'T MEAN TO CHEAT again. The next time he came to rehearsal with Eddie, he planned to focus like a normal person. It didn't matter what his dad said; he wasn't going to slow the world down to fit his own schedule. But then his brain wouldn't work on its own. The words kept flying past, like bullets, and Eddie asked, no, Eddie *told him* to get his ass in gear.

"I don't know if you got a visit from the ghost of Christmas past last time, but I vote you do it again. Ideally, now."

"Is that one with the Muppets?"

Eddie held his hand to his chest in mock horror, but he also checked his watch. Five minutes later, Luke gave in and stopped the scene. This time, the monologue was from Dostoevsky, and if Luke thought he was out of his depth with Shakespeare, well, this scene dumped him in the Atlantic without a lifejacket. He had never even heard of the novel it was from. He'd nodded when Eddie asked if he knew it, and now he felt like too much of an idiot to ask about the plot, the characters or why anyone would willingly read it.

After minutes, in which Luke stared into Eddie's frozen face and drew his outstretched hand, the plot finally fell into place. As best he could tell, it was all about this con man who pretended to be someone else and told the audience how he'd get away with it. This Dostoevsky guy sounded impressive, but he really just wrote a villain monologue in a Bond movie. The character had to play stupid, but in a friendly sort of way, and there was no nice way to tell Eddie that he was already pretty good at it.

"What if you try talking more slowly?" he said, as Eddie came out of the Hold. It was the best he could do and it was *pathetic*. "Unless you can think of other ways to seem more likable?"

"You don't think I'm likable?" Eddie said. "You know, Captain, that really hurts."

Luke's eyes shot back to his sketchpad. He didn't mean it like that. That was part of the problem. "There's always room for improvement," he muttered. "Think of a really likable person like Idris Elba. I'm sure there are people who can't stand him."

"I beg to differ."

Luke looked up at Eddie's pursed lips. "You're screwing with me."

"No. Of course not," Eddie said, with an innocent shrug. "Although that sounds like just the sort of thing an unlikable sort of person might do."

And so they went. For two rehearsals and then three. Luke and Eddie. Eddie and Luke. The rhythm settled under his skin. Eddie didn't need to know that for every minute they spent together, Luke spent at least two in the Hold, alone.

It's everything, said the voice in his head. *He thinks you're special.*
Luke knew better.

He wasn't anything like the "captain" Eddie wanted him to be, but that didn't stop the heat from crawling up Luke's neck when Eddie smiled. When Luke emerged from the Hold with ideas about where Eddie could move his hands or how he could use the space on the stage, Eddie lit up like a Christmas tree. He was so excited about Luke's ideas that Luke couldn't help grinning back like the smartest guy in the world.

That had to be why he added a new picture to the collage above his bed. One night, after a Thursday rehearsal, he stood up on his bed with a black sharpie and drew two little figures next to Wiccan from *Young Avengers* and just under Solstice from *Teen Titans*. The smaller one was just an outline in a too-big sweatshirt. The broader one, with his feet firmly planted on the ground, held a paper in his hand, and all around his head was an aura, as if he glowed. Both heads tilted up toward something in the distance. There wasn't a gun in sight.

Luke hadn't drawn that part yet, but in his head they looked out over a sea of superheroes and waited for someone to pick a fight.

* * *

"Hit me." Eddie burst into the classroom for rehearsal the following week with one hand pressed to the side of his forehead and the other tapping at his side. He didn't bother to check whether Luke was there before he spoke. Luke had been in the same spot, on top of a desk, every Tuesday and Thursday for a month. "I'm not joking," he said. "Do *something* painful enough to make me stop thinking about those idiots, or I swear to God, I will hit myself."

Luke couldn't begin to follow that logic. He raised his brows in confusion and Eddie started again.

"Thinking about morons takes up space in my brain," he explained slowly. "Intense pain should distract my brain long enough to refocus." It might have been a joke, but Luke couldn't tell. Eddie dropped to the floor with a pile of new scripts, but his knuckles kept tapping. "If you can't hit me, then don't ask. It's nothing. Wes was just being his charming self."

That was the most polite way to call someone a jackass Luke had ever heard. "And?"

"And nothing. Wes is in love with the idea that my mother tongue is a joke." Eddie sighed. "It isn't a party trick. It will never be a party trick." Eddie glared at his papers. "But it isn't important. I'm just being a little girl about it."

Luke crouched on the floor at Eddie's side and grabbed a stack of scripts. He didn't know what Eddie was trying to do with them, and he suspected Eddie didn't know either. "Sounds tough," he said. Luke shrugged as Eddie glanced up, eyebrow raised. "Being a little girl is hard core. I've got a herd of blonde five- and six-year-old cousins with names like Tiffany and Amber. They're all in ballet and, I don't know, I think they could take me."

Eddie looked even more confused. "Blonde?"

At first, Luke didn't understand the question. Then Eddie looked pointedly at Luke's hair. Luke's hair that wasn't blonde.

"Right," Luke said with a smile and imagined his mother's quiet frustration. It was by far the most tactful way he'd ever been asked the question. "Behold the power of adoption. My folks are like half Norwegian and half Finnish. Thus, the blonde."

"And your sister?" The question came out easily, as though Eddie was just asking about the weather. Luke never realized the kindness in pretending that Lizzy's death wasn't the end of the world. He loved Marcos and Dee, but Eddie never made him feel like a walking tragedy.

"She was their bio kid and blonde," he said, and smiled at his lap. "You'd never believe how many people thought a foreign kid was stealing their daughter."

Eddie's jaw dropped. "That's horrible."

"I know." Luke said as he bent close. "My mom's with you. She grounded me for saying that."

"You're such a rebel." Eddie rolled his eyes, but he didn't move away. "And your pants are buzzing."

They were, loudly too, but Luke hadn't noticed. He checked his phone and felt like a tool. Especially since Eddie still looked as though he wanted to either hug him or punch a wall.

[**To Luke**] We seeing you for the set build mi compadre?
[**To Luke**] By that, I mean, get your LAZY ASS to the set build or I will track you down and drag you in by your heels. *No disappearing act.*

Hi, Dee. She took spot number two on Luke's grand (and growing) list of guilt-inducing humans. He'd dropped off the planet before, but never for so long and never to spend his time in places and with people he hadn't explained. If he told Dee about the project with Eddie, he'd also have to talk about Eddie's house and the last month of absences from the tech crew and the mystery gun. It had been weeks since Eddie had stopped being a mystery for Luke to solve. He still didn't know why the money or the gun was under Eddie's bed, but for whole rehearsals, Luke forgot why he'd agreed to help in the first place. He'd just become *Eddie*, so it seemed easier to avoid explanations altogether.

Dee made him rethink that last part.

[**To Luke**] FYI: I don't miss you. I think you should stop being a reclusive dumbass, but other people might miss you. Other people might worry about you, but that's just because they haven't realized you're an undeserving sack of shit.

[**To Luke**] These people are idiots, but I like them. They're named Marcos. Come back.

Luke sighed. Dee was subtle like an anvil. This week, she had gotten it into her head that Marcos was flirting with him, or doing whatever passed for flirting in Marcos-world. To Luke's eyes, that looked exactly the same as usual-Marcos, but he wasn't the best judge. He'd spent so many years hoping Marcos might see the light and flirt with him, that he probably couldn't recognize the real deal if it landed in front of his face.

Either that, or Dee was full of it.

His phone buzzed again in his hand, but it wasn't Dee.

[**To Luke**] Are you tired? I would have asked you in person, but you know.

[**To Luke**] I've been tired this week. Mom says it's because Mercury is post-retrograde, and I'm dealing with lingering traces of chaos. Luke, it's harder to deal with her when you aren't here to play wingman.

That's not what a wingman does. He squinted at the phone. They'd talked about this.

[**To Luke**] What if we took her astrology seriously? That would be depressing. If the planets run the show and we have to act out some part the universe wrote for us? I'd hate that.

Luke blinked. There was absolutely nothing unusual about that message. That was pure Marcos. Other times he wanted to talk about how many flamingos could defeat a flying shark or what the world would look like if we switched off gravity. But thinking about it as flirting gave him a headache. To be fair, Marcos has sent more messages this week, and then there was the touching. Marcos had always been a casual cuddler, but this week he'd leaned against Luke's side when he walked and hugged him goodbye. Every time, Luke's stomach fluttered up into his chest, but he couldn't tell if Marcos actually touched him more, or if it just seemed like it because Dee caught his eye every time. Luke tried closing his eyes to avoid Dee's *significant looks*, but then he focused on Marcos's arms around his back.

[**To Luke**] Hope I get to see you.

Damn it, Marcos. Luke's stupid brain finally got used to the idea that his crush wasn't going to be useful in the real world. It was a blip, an adaptation with no practical application, like the appendix or nipples on men. Not that he wanted to think about anyone's chest—

Eddie coughed. His scripts sat in neat piles at his sides, and Luke had no idea how long he'd sat there, watching his director squint at his phone.

"Sorry. There was—I had a problem." It wasn't entirely a lie. His friends had a lot of feelings, and that was a problem. He never said the problem was new.

"It's all good." Eddie handed him a script and hopped to his feet. His eyes were sad, and Luke wanted to tug him back down to the floor, but once Eddie got going there was no pulling him back. "You need a minute?"

"No." Luke sighed as he settled onto the top of his desk. "I don't think there's anything I can do about it from here." Later, he could text his apologies for missing another build. Dee would send him angry emojis, and Marcos wouldn't say anything at all. "What about your problem? I know it's nothing, but if you want to talk—"

Eddie waved him off. "No, no," he said. "Remember, I'm a hard core, ass-kicking little girl, and nothing gets me down." He held up his script. "And today it also looks as if I get the chance to be Melville's Ishmael. From the top, Captain?" He wiggled his shoulders as he got into position, and Luke laughed out loud.

"From the top."

Luke's phone buzzed as Eddie began, and Luke turned it off.

CHAPTER THIRTEEN

LATER THAT WEEK, LUKE'S HEADACHE came back. Director superpowers were great and all, but they only went so far when he didn't know what the heck his actor was talking about. They were well into their Thursday rehearsal, and the newest monologue had all the realism and honesty of a used car commercial. He couldn't say that Eddie didn't try.

Oh, how he tried. "I do believe it was Love that first devised the torturer's profession here on earth," he began, and it was like watching a robot emote. "I'm tossed around, bandied about, goaded, whirled on the wheel of love, done to death, poor wretch that I am! I'm torn, torn asunder, disrupted, dismembered—"

"Stop. Oh God, please stop." Luke threw his hands up over his head, and Eddie did as he was told. "I'm sorry. This is going to sound rude—"

"Because it's going to be rude." Eddie pointed with his rolled script. "You're going to be rude and you're going to love it."

Luke ignored him.

"You don't believe anything you're saying right now, and if I can tell, then you're in trouble because I can't even pronounce your character's name."

"It's Alcesimarchus, like—" Eddie squinted at the posters. "I can't think of anything that it sounds like, but it isn't hard." He sounded it out—All-sess-ih-marcus—like the champion of the Scripps Spelling Bee. Luke caught him before he could go off on the etymology.

"Look at me," he said and waved his hands until Eddie looked. "You're talking about love. So why does it sound as if you could be talking about a roller coaster?" Luke was overselling his point, but it was also true. Eddie didn't seem caught in love so much as caught in a hurricane. Luke clutched his hand to his chest and moaned, "Save me. I'm on the Tilt-A-Whirl of love and I might die."

He went too far. That was definitely too far, but Eddie just grinned and waved toward the stage. "Why don't you show me how it's supposed to be done? Show me love if it's so easy to do." He sat back like a man who knew when he had checkmate.

Damn you for being right.

On the list of things that were not in Luke's wheelhouse, love monologues had to be entries one through fifteen. He was not going to show Eddie how to act, but he knew something was wrong. "I don't think love would be so—" He waved his hands like a chorus boy until the skin crinkled around Eddie's eyes. "I was expecting something quieter."

"Quieter," Eddie repeated, with deliberate care. "I hear you." He pressed his hands against the edge of the desk where he sat and looked into the distance, as though his ideas needed to be sorted before they could emerge. He was the loudest thinker Luke had ever known. "Let me start by saying I have never been, you know—"

"In love?" Luke wasn't sure why he was surprised or why his stomach curled up into his throat.

"Yeah. I don't think so," he said, more to the far wall than to Luke. "I mean, how do you know when a crush is more than a crush? But I used to like someone *a lot*, and there was nothing quiet about it. There was a girl in Chicago. I couldn't see her right away, but once I did, she was everywhere, you know? When she came into a room, I knew it. We never touched or anything, but my stupid body was still convinced it knew how her hair would feel." He smiled, crooked and faint. "A year ago, it's crazy, but I would have insisted hot and cold felt different with her around." He stared into the open space where the dirty light hit their makeshift stage and, for a moment, it seemed as though she might appear so Luke could see her too.

Eddie laughed under his breath. "I sound so soap opera right now, but that's how it seemed. You get it, right? My brain told me to snap out of it, but my brain didn't really have anything to do with it." He shook his head, as if he only just remembered to be embarrassed. "I don't think she ever knew."

"No?" Luke said, quietly.

"Nope. I never said anything, and she never said anything, and I left. Either she was the nicest girl in tenth grade at Jefferson High School, or there was a difference between what I felt and what she saw." He caught Luke's eye with a sheepish grimace. "Which is probably what you were trying to tell me in the first place. So, if you could have stopped me a few sentences ago, that would have been awesome."

Luke bit his lip and tried not to squirm. Eddie had a habit of giving him credit where he didn't deserve it. "I'm not that good," he said. "I don't know how to talk about all that hot and cold—"

Eddie leaned away as his jaw dropped. "You're laughing at me. I open myself up and my director laughs at me."

"I'm not laughing. I'm just—" He was definitely laughing. "When you get worked up, you open your mouth and poetry comes out. I don't know how you do that! When I get upset, I forget how to make words."

"But you think them."

He looked so certain, Luke almost believed him. "Really? How do you know I'm not sitting here thinking of white noise or the theme song from *Jaws*?"

"You're not," Eddie said. He looked away and beamed like a smug child. "Sometimes I can feel you thinking."

"You what?" Luke's smile dropped, but Eddie couldn't have seen the horror written across his face. He still smiled at the window, as if they were playing.

"Sometimes," he said with a grin, "your face goes all intense, like you're getting ready to jump off a cliff, and then, for a second, it's like I see the gears moving in your head." He looked back to Luke and held up his hands, as if to trace the gears as they moved in either direction. "I think it's part of the actor-director relationship, Captain. We're in sync. My last director was an ass. You, not so much."

He laughed, but Luke couldn't hear him over the panic. If Eddie could read his mind, even in fragments, he could find out about the bedroom and the gun and the Hold. He could find out about all kinds of things Luke didn't want anyone to know, least of all Eddie.

"Oh, no!" When Eddie finally turned around, he caught a glimpse of Luke's face and laughed even louder. "Don't panic," he said. "It's not like I can see your brain. It's more like—" He grabbed Luke's hand and held it to his own chest, just under the collar bone. "Feel right there. What do you get?"

"Your heartbeat," Luke murmured. *And mine.* He wasn't used to being manhandled by guys with Eddie's voice and his smile. Luke bit the inside of his cheek. He wasn't used to being manhandled at all. "You saw me thinking with your chest?"

"I felt you, and yes, sort of." Eddie looked at where their hands met on his chest. "It washed right over me. I thought I had vertigo, but it was you. You thought so hard, you just about knocked me off my feet."

"No way."

"I don't lie."

Luke wondered if he should laugh. That would be the normal thing to do if someone suggested he could make funny things happen with his mind, but he didn't want to laugh, not with his hand against Eddie's chest. For all Luke had worried about Eddie seeing him that night in his house, he hadn't considered what the Hold had seemed like for him. If he'd had to guess, Luke would have imagined coming out of it was like breaking out of a coma. He blinked hard. Maybe he hadn't thought about that night from Eddie's perspective because his version looked like torture.

He hadn't thought it could be nice, but Eddie's description was so beautiful Luke almost wished he could feel the Hold from the other side. He tried to imagine vibrations and a wash of sensation, but he only came back to silence. How could it be that on Eddie's side, the Hold didn't seem lonely? From Eddie's side, the Hold seemed like the kind of electricity that brought people back to life.

"You there?"

Eddie cocked his head, and Luke realized he'd been sitting with his hand on his project partner's chest for the better part of a minute.

"Yes!" He jerked away, and his hand whipped behind his back. "It sounds," *stunning, breathtaking,* "like a lot," he said as Eddie leaned away. "I can't explain it."

"I didn't ask you to," Eddie said, with a crooked smile. "I can live with uncertainty." He tapped Luke on the chest with one finger. "And you will just have to get used to power."

Luke almost asked him, then. Eddie turned to hop off the desk, and Luke almost asked him what he was doing on the night they met. It was almost the right time. The question bubbled up, but then Eddie had to go. He was late to help his brother, and Luke insisted the question could wait for another day.

Eddie held the door and ushered Luke into the hall as though they walked out of rehearsal together every day. They fell into step in the same direction, Eddie in the lead and Luke half a beat behind. The snap and squeak of their shoes echoed in the quiet hallway, but it wasn't the kind of silence that needed to be filled.

They were almost at the front door when Luke stuffed his sketchpad into his bag, and Eddie raised his eyebrows. "Someday," he said, "I am going to get you to show me that thing. Don't think I haven't seen it."

"It's nothing."

"Then, next Tuesday, I want to see the nothing. I'm not saying you're hiding Rembrandts, but I know you draw during rehearsal and I want to know if you're giving me horns."

He winked, and Luke's eyes went to the floor. "No horns," he said under his breath. There was only Eddie's face in every light. "I could draw you something if you wanted, but I'm not any good."

Eddie looked ready to argue, but he didn't get the chance.

"Hey, Sanka and—is that Punjab? Damn." Wes and Elliot turned the corner from the band hallway, directly in their path, and grinned like wolves on the hunt. "I wouldn't have expected to see you two together."

"Like Bambi and the Beast," Elliot replied and laughed as if it were an old joke they'd repeated a million times. Wes and Elliot probably had. Luke decided the universe could suck it and kept walking, but Eddie stopped cold.

"You know, Punjab," Wes said, "if I didn't know you better, I'd think you were trying to use your feminine wiles on a member of our defensive line."

Luke's jaw dropped. "My what?"

Wes shrugged, all innocence. "Hey, you're cozy in here after school hours, probably giggling about clothes or something. I'm just saying, our Sanka doesn't play like that, and I wouldn't want him to break your heart." He smirked, like the funniest asshole in the room. "Man, you know I'm kidding, right? You were probably just practicing Sanka's show. You don't want to disappoint the team moms, man."

"You just missed it, guys," Eddie said, with a tight smile, and Luke was reminded of negotiating tactics in a kidnapping. "I was just showing Luke how good I've gotten at spinning those plates. I should be able to do a little dance any day now."

Wes punched him on the shoulder. "You know, I have no idea if you're messing with me, but I'm cool with that." Eddie didn't punch back.

"Team moms?" Luke asked quietly.

"He's talking about the lacrosse awards ceremony. Players do stupid skits at the end, and everybody watches," Eddie said and his shoulders tensed. "I'm not doing it."

"You so are," Wes said with a grin. "I signed you up. New players go first, man, and extra points if you can get your folks into the skit. Last year, we got Elliot's dad to put on a skirt and pretend he was a mail-order bride from Taiwan that we got for coach, 'Me love you, Mister Murphy-san.'" He bowed with his palms together in front of his chest, giggling all the way. "Maybe your mom will do it this year."

As he spoke, Wes watched Eddie like a science experiment under glass. His face was perfectly, fiercely still, but as he looked away, his whole fist hit his leg, as if he wanted to make a bruise. "I don't have time for this," Eddie said through clenched teeth. "I said I'm not performing. I'm not even going to the ceremony. I won't be there and neither will my *mom*."

"Okay, okay, buzzkill." Wes rolled his eyes. "You don't have to do anything if you don't want to, but foreign stuff goes down big with the parents. If they flipped when Daniel performed in Spanish, just think about what they'd do for *Bassa*." He grinned back at Elliot. "Get ready to see them come in their pants."

Eddie sucked in a breath as Wes spoke. His lips were pursed tight, and his fist smacked the same spot on his thigh. He closed his eyes, and Luke was reminded of when he'd got shots as a kid. His mom had said if he closed his eyes he could pretend it wasn't happening, but that never worked. He'd always felt the needle go in.

When Eddie sucked in a hard breath, Luke told Wes to stop, and he stopped. So did the rest of the hall. Eddie was turned toward the door with his eyes closed, as Wes gestured toward his back with a predatory grin. Luke stepped away from Eddie's side and toward Wes's vacant eyes. Eddie had told him to get used to power, and that meant practice. Luke could definitely practice.

Maybe Wes didn't mean any of it. Maybe his life was such a game, he couldn't imagine a person could bruise, but that didn't matter. Eddie said no. He'd said no while laughing and smiling and maybe almost crying, and Wes didn't care. Luke looked back at Eddie in the middle of the hallway. He looked as if he'd tried to disappear into his own skin, and the thought of Edward Sankawulo wanting to be invisible made Luke want to gouge out Wes's eyes with his thumbs.

"Your sister taught you not to be an asshole, Wes," Luke said, quietly, into Wes's frozen grin. "You know better, but I think you need a reminder."

Wes didn't respond. He couldn't respond. He smiled at Eddie's back and, as he smiled, Luke created a reminder Wes couldn't ignore. When he finished, he let time snap back into place and pulled Eddie toward the main doors.

"You're okay," he said into Eddie's ear. "We're going." And Eddie nodded at the floor.

Wes didn't call after them, but as they pushed through the main doors, Elliot screamed. Luke didn't look back, but he imagined Wes's face as he discovered Sharpie up and down his arms. Luke's words were small, lopsided and upside down, but they said the same thing:

Leave him alone. Leave him alone. Leave him alone. Leave him alone. Fuck you. Leave him alone.

A minute later, Luke and Eddie walked through the main doors of the school in silence, but the quiet had changed. Eddie drew into himself; his quietness drew taut like the string on a violin. At his side, Luke replayed the previous five minutes on a loop.

The Hold worked. Wes finally shut up. *Eddie almost broke down, and I made it a little bit better. That was me. I'm the crappiest superhero in the world, but I also made that asshole leave Eddie alone.*

"Hey," he said as they reached the parking lot, "want me to go back and kick his ass?"

Eddie's eyes flicked up and then back to the ground. "No. He doesn't deserve it." He smiled softly. "Plus, I don't need my director in pieces."

"Fine, but I am taller than him. So are you," said Luke as he nudged Eddie with his shoulder. "Do you want me to go back and make fun of his mom? I've known her since I was eleven. You'll never believe what she reads when she thinks her kids aren't playing attention."

"Captain—"

"I could fill his shoes with mayonnaise. I am not constrained by traditional warfare."

"Luke." Eddie's smile made it all the way to his eyes, and Luke bounced on his toes. He'd made that happen too. "If I remember right, I'm supposed to say *Thank you and have a great day*." Luke snorted. "But really, thanks."

Luke dug his hands into the pockets of his coat and let the heat climb up his neck. "I didn't do anything. It was Wes being Wes, and we all have tough days."

Eddie shrugged with one shoulder and flicked the plastic loop on his backpack strap between his fingers. Luke wondered if his hands were warm. They looked warm and larger than Luke's by a mile. They were the same height, but somehow, if Eddie took his hand, Luke's would almost disappear. "I should get home." Eddie jerked his head toward the far end of the parking lot. "By the time I get there, my brother's going to have tried making his own mac and cheese and burned it all to hell."

"Yeah, no. Go." Luke waved him away and, as he did, he noticed his back pocket was too light. Where he usually kept his phone, he only had the imprint where it should have been. *Damn.* "I have to go back."

Luke had already turned away, but he heard Eddie's voice at his back. "See you next Tuesday, Captain."

"I'll practice thinking!"

Eddie's low laugh carried him up the hallway, even though he had his footsteps to keep him company. By the time he got to the classroom, Wes and his friends were long gone.

He found his phone easily. During rehearsals he sometimes set it aside and he usually remembered to pick it up again when he wasn't *distracted*. He grabbed it from the ledge of the whiteboard at the front of the room and turned to leave when he noticed a title in the mess of papers on Mrs. Danes's desk.

"Roster," it read. "Introduction to Theater Arts 126." He read the class name upside down and then went on to the names. The usual suspects were all there: Mia Robinson, Xi-Yi San, Margo Sawa, Vanessa Trent-Washington and so on. He grabbed the list and turned it around, so it was facing the right way. The roster listed the names in alphabetical order, but something was off. He read it again.

Eddie's name wasn't on the roster. It definitely wasn't where it belonged in the alphabetical order between Xi-Yi and Margo, but that wasn't strange. Sometimes teachers wrote new names along the bottoms of rosters. Printer paper costs came out of their pockets. But they never left someone off completely. North Grove was a small school; Intro 126 was the only theater class this semester, and Eddie couldn't have taken the class for months without having made his way onto a list.

Luke dropped onto the floor under the whiteboard and stared out at the empty room. They—he and Eddie—had spent more than a month practicing for a final Eddie was supposed to take for a class he was supposed to be in. But—he pressed his fingers to his temples—but Eddie wasn't on the roster. *Why would Eddie be the exception? No, worse than that. Why would Eddie pretend to have homework for someone else's class?*

It had to be a misunderstanding. Luke pulled his knees up to his chest and tried to breathe through memories of Mercutio and *All-sess-ih-marcus.* The project had to be real, and he had to be overreacting. Otherwise he had too many possibilities to handle.

It was all fake.

Or Eddie had played him.

Or Eddie still had money and guns and no reason to want Luke as a director.

Or Eddie had no reason to want Luke around at all.

"We were real."

The words died in the empty space, swallowed up by posters and the vacuum Eddie left behind.

CHAPTER FOURTEEN

FOR DAYS, LUKE LIVED IN a fog. Even as his mom fought her way out to the living room and the kitchen, Luke sank. He went to classes and went home, but most of him sat buried under thirteen layers of haze. He passed from English to math, and people slid past. If they said anything, he didn't notice. Dee was out sick, and Marcos was easy to avoid. Like Luke, he was a creature of habit and wouldn't read into the fact that he hadn't seen Luke for days. He might notice and he might even care, but it wouldn't occur to Marcos that his best friend in the world was avoiding him. Marcos never chose to hurt his friends, so why would they choose to hurt him?

Eddie, on the other hand, was a problem. After weeks of living on a separate plane of existence during the school day, he was around every corner. He appeared with the debate team, then with the lacrosse team—minus Wes—until Luke flattened himself against the nearest wall and buried his face in his phone. At least that was something to do. From somewhere in the building,

Marcos invited him to a movie, and Luke said yes before he'd fully read the text.

As he did, he shook off Dee's voice in his head. "Pretty fast for a rebound date," she said. "You only just got dumped by the boy who didn't know he was dating you." Luke scowled. Brain-Dee didn't know what she was talking about.

A kid with red, spiky hair narrowed his eyes at Luke as he passed, and Luke glared back. Sure, he might have mouthed out loud some of the conversation he was having in his mind, but it wasn't as though he were making a spectacle of himself.

He pushed off the wall and slouched toward fourth period before anyone could double back and magically end up in his hallway. Eddie's laugh could cut through the fog, and Luke didn't have the energy to stop being an emotional twit. Just because Danes hadn't written Eddie's name on the class roster didn't mean Eddie hadn't been there. But, Luke couldn't just walk up to her and ask. No matter what, Mrs. Danes would give him the same watery look every teacher had given him since he came back. He needed a sign strapped to his back: *Not everything inconvenient about me is a symptom*. Still, he didn't know; maybe that was a symptom, too.

Luke slumped against the wall near the front office and watched the secretaries flit back and forth on the other side of the glass doors. If he didn't put on the Hold, he was going to be late for pre-calc. The first bell had already rung, but he didn't care. The principal's head secretary, Mrs. Doe, tucked folders into other folders, and Luke dreamed of new superpowers. If he could control minds, this whole situation would be easier. Mind-control-Luke would probably be evil, but he could also walk into the main office and ask Mrs. Doe to hand over all the rosters for Danes's classes. He'd ask for Eddie's official transcript too, just to be sure that he'd spent the last month and a half working with a fraud. If she didn't remember handing him the folder, no one would ever know.

Mrs. Doe smiled and waved, absentmindedly, from the other side of the glass. She was wonderful, really, and more helpful than all the administrators put together. Luke waved back. Mrs. Doe wouldn't think anything of it if he went in to say hello. When Lizzy had gone into hospice, she'd brought a hotdish to the house. She was a sweetheart.

That must be why Luke felt like a monster. He didn't need her help. He didn't need her to hand him anything. Hell, he could walk away with her computer, her purse and the pencil in her hand without anyone batting an eye. The filing cabinets didn't have locks, and no one locked the office in the middle of the school day with everyone still inside. If he needed information, Luke 2.0 could get it himself, and Mrs. Doe would never have anything to forget.

Luke squeezed his eyes shut. He was sick, sick of monologues, and motion and boys with their own gravitational pull. He was sick of watching things happen in front of his face as if they weren't part of *his life*.

Somewhere in the building, Marcos was planning a movie night; Dee was home wondering why he'd become a cypher. His mom still mostly stayed in bed with memoirs about grief. And then there was Eddie. Eddie made up his own giant, swirling mass of questions Luke didn't know how to ask.

When Mrs. Doe took a seat at her desk, well away from the cabinets, Luke dropped his bag. He straightened his shoulders, stared into the glass and whispered, "Stop."

AFTER HE LEFT THE OFFICE, Luke wished he hadn't gone inside. He could have let the world spin on its wobbly axis and pretended everything was fine. In theory, he didn't have to know.

In reality, he'd walked through the doors and riffled through every student file while Mrs. Doe sat frozen at her desk. Luke had walked to her first, to make sure she didn't move, and he'd found himself grateful that her eyes were on the papers on her lap. The novelty of wide, staring eyes had worn off after day one and he'd appreciated the distance, as though he weren't actually breaking into the school's files in front of those eyes.

In the end, the evidence had been clean and precise, like the cut of a new knife. His name was Edward Sankawulo. He came from Chicago.

That was true.

He also wasn't in Mrs. Danes's theater class; he never had been. Eddie's name wasn't on the roster, Danes wasn't on his transcripts and there was nothing to suggest that Eddie's project wasn't a figment of his imagination.

He'd transferred to North Grove on January fifteenth as a junior, and among all of his classes from Chicago there wasn't anything about theater. For all he knew, Eddie was a pathological liar. Either that, or he wanted an excuse to keep an eye on the thief who stole things from his room.

Luke couldn't go down that path. It turned his stomach, but it was too easy. If Eddie would lie about a class for months, why wouldn't he lie about all the things that hadn't made sense from the beginning? Eddie could have kept an eye on him, or investigated him or found a way to become Luke's superhero arch-nemesis, and all of it would have made more sense than the idea that Eddie desperately needed to be his friend.

Outside the main office, Luke dropped the Hold and let traffic in the hallway go about its business. He was pretty good at keeping a grip when he wanted to, but he couldn't stop the world from moving and fight back tears. He scrubbed at his eyes with his sweatshirt sleeve. *Stop. I have to stop crying, and not just because people will see.* He didn't have the right to be betrayed. Since he'd agreed to help Eddie's imaginary project in order to find out more about him, he couldn't get all pissed off if Eddie had done the same thing.

"Luke!" He didn't hear Eddie coming and, once the voice was at his back, he didn't have an excuse to run. The day was foggy, but the last few minutes were perfectly clear.

I see you.

"Hey, Space Cadet," Eddie said, loud enough for the hallway to hear. "Found the door to Narnia?" He smiled, and Luke blinked back. He was still staring at the doorway to the main office.

"No," he said softly. *Why did you let me go?*

Eddie's smile faltered. "You headed that way?" He pointed down the hall. "I didn't know we had the same lunch period. I've never seen you." Luke was supposed to be in class and Eddie was supposed to be someone else.

"No." It came out louder, and this time Eddie stopped.

"Hey," Eddie said as he ducked his head. His hand hovered just above Luke's shoulder, and he pitched his voice low enough so only Luke could hear. "We don't usually meet on Mondays, I know, but if you need to—" His hand rubbed at the back of his neck, as if he were worried. Last week Luke might have swooned.

"I'm not in the mood right now, okay? I'm tired," Luke said in clipped syllables. "Let me be tired."

"Imagine how I feel after being all those people," Eddie said. Then he laughed.

"Exhausting." Luke looked up as Eddie leaned away, his eyes wide.

"You know it's a good tired." Eddie glanced behind Luke's back at their growing audience, with anxious energy shining in his eyes. Eight or nine students watched; Luke didn't know their names. Someone was probably already filming. "Do you want to see if there's a classroom free? We can talk—"

"Stop." The bite in his voice felt as good as Eddie's flinch. "Just stop."

"Hey—"

Luke rounded on him. Somewhere between the office and Eddie's stupid jokes his exhaustion had turned into a slow, empty, burn. "I don't want to go talk, *Edward*," he said. "I don't want to talk or practice or whatever else you had in mind, because today's my day off, and, believe it or not, I don't want to be stuck in a classroom that reeks of stale air when I could be anywhere else." He gave his bag a solid kick and didn't give a damn if it made him look like a child. Eddie backed away, and that was all he needed. "You're used to people falling at your feet to play whatever role you're working on at the moment—"

"Luke?" Eddie's voice fell to a whisper as Luke's rose. "What are you talking about?

"I'm not that person, if that's what you're looking for, okay?" Luke looked away as his calm fell to pieces. "I'm sure if you need a good critique partner, Mrs. Danes would be more than happy to give you all the help you could possibly need. I'm sure she'd love to help any student who's putting so much work into her *class*." He grabbed his bag from the floor. He needed to get out of the hallway, or he was going to sob. "Unfortunately, I can't work with you today because: one, I have a date, and two, fuck you."

Luke had no idea where that came from. Not the anger: the date. He seethed as the students in the crowd coughed and giggled into their hands. They were strangers, every last one.

"Oh," a voice said behind him, and Luke's heart sank. He knew that voice better than he knew his own. Marcos stood five feet behind Luke's back with one hand on his backpack and his face a perfect blank. "Okay then. A date. I—" He stopped. "That's good to know?"

It wasn't a question.

LIZZY WAS SEVENTEEN YEARS OLD when she'd had her first crush on a boy. She'd been in the hospital, in room 421 and he'd been down the hall in room 433. They'd been in school together, too, and his name had made her giggle for days. She'd curled into herself with her head against the hospital pillows, and Luke had said it again just for fun.

"*Anthony*. Anthony says hello, Lizzy," he'd said, and when she'd grinned her eyes had gone all squinty with joy.

He'd been ten, but he'd known the nurses and his parents weren't reacting right. They'd laughed about it, but not in a teasing way. She'd just been a teenager who liked a boy; it had been the most normal thing in the world. It had been funny because crushes were funny, but not because it was Lizzy. It hadn't been funny like that.

He hadn't been able to do anything about the adults, even if he'd known without a shadow of a doubt that he'd been right. So he hadn't laughed. He'd teased Lizzy and poked her in the side, and when the two of them went on "dates" in the hospital waiting room, he'd talked about it without the quotation marks. While his parents had talked about treatment options, he'd drawn Lizzy and Anthony. The picture hadn't really looked like them. It could have been anybody, but it had looked the way he'd imagined a date was supposed to be: two people who sat next to each other and smiled.

CHAPTER FIFTEEN

LUKE RAN HIS HAND UP the inside of the Westgate Cinema seat armrest, where the fabric met the metal. The red crushed velvet overlay stood in tiny spikes when he slid his hand against the grain. It should have been replaced years ago. There were more bald patches than velvet, but Luke was glad they hadn't replaced it. Without the fabric, the fogged lights above the bathrooms and the ancient curtain across the screen would seem out of place. According to every piece of signage in the building, that curtain had been here since the theater opened in 1951, and up close it was probably ugly as sin, but they'd hung it before the building opened and wouldn't tear it down until the walls around it were condemned.

Luke liked the theater, in a "wow, this smells funky" way, but Marcos was in love. He'd found this place before he should have gone to movies on his own. His folks wouldn't watch 70s movies every Friday night with their thirteen-year-old son, so Marcos had gone on his own. For a year he'd been the kid who knew all the words to *Harold and Maude*, until he'd known Luke and Dee well enough to drag them along. Luke couldn't count how many times he'd seen *Plan 9 from Outer Space* and *Back to the Future* in this freezer of a theater, usually with about four other audience members, all old enough to be his grandfather. The trio always sat in the same seats, three rows from the back, on the left, and he could use the faded patches as a map to five years of mimicking Christopher Lloyd and throwing popcorn at the screen.

Dee usually insisted she could see the outline of her own butt on her seat. "It's got a certain rounded definition there at the bottom—" she would say with pride.

Luke would reply that he'd never paid that much attention to her butt.

He'd never paid much attention to any of it. The Westgate was nothing. Of course, trips to the Westgate didn't usually seem like a matinee written, directed by and starring his bad decisions. As he sat down for the seven p.m. screening of *Star Wars: Episode VI—Return of the Jedi*, Luke looked at the back of a woman's head three rows away and willed himself to breathe quietly. Only two other people sat in the theater, both of them women who wouldn't have to fight for a senior citizen discount. They probably wouldn't turn around if he and Marcos started making out in the seats.

Not that Luke wanted to think about kissing. Thinking led to blood beating in his ears, because thinking about kissing led to thinking about kissing specific people and, worse yet, thinking about kissing Marcos, who sat one seat away. Luke-on-a-date wasn't allowed to think; he also wasn't allowed to sweat, fidget or ask questions. The candy advertisements rolled by as Luke squeezed the armrest, and the little spikes dug into his palms.

He'd thought that arguing with Eddie was rock bottom for the day, but apparently it had only been the beginning. Then Marcos had stood in the middle of the hallway with a pop in one hand and his backpack strap in the other. In his head, Luke had tried to explain, but everything came out inane. "Hey, Marcos," he'd imagined saying, "this is Eddie. You dared me to break into his house back in February, but since then I've been investigating him, because that's a normal reaction to finding out that someone has more secrets than I do. Also, I decided that our movie trip was a date. Surprise."

No matter what, he couldn't say *that*, so he'd ground a piece of dirt into the tile and willed the floor to open up under his feet.

After a long, quiet minute, Marcos had nudged him in the foot. "I'm still hungry. You?"

Luke hadn't been hungry, but he'd nodded anyway and followed Marcos down the hall. He hadn't looked back to check on Eddie. Eddie Sankawulo could go, stay or disappear in a puff of smoke for all he cared. He could be as chill as Marcos if he wanted to, and Marcos had been unbelievably chill. He'd been so unfazed; he might as well have walked in on Luke and Eddie talking about pizza.

After they'd gone through the lunch line and stopped at the vending machines, they'd settled against the wall inside the front door where they could stare into the wide-open hallway between the north entrance and the gym. Most of the students lingering in little herds along the walls had been seniors carrying clear plastic bags from Subway. It wasn't much better than the cafeteria, but it was close, off-campus and cheap as dirt.

Marcos had finally broken the silence. "Do you think you ever would have asked me?"

Luke thought about it, but there wasn't really a question. He shook his head.

Marcos's expression had been calm and blank as slate. "You could have, you know," he'd said. "I don't know how it's going to be different as a date, though. Flowers seem like too much for *Star Wars*, and I'm not going to bring, like, a bouquet of light sabers." He'd glanced at Luke's wide-eyed surprise. "Unless you changed your mind."

"No," Luke had stuttered. "No. I—Did you? I thought that you weren't into, you know—" He didn't think Marcos was into dating or guys or *dating guys.*

Marcos had nodded, as if he was considering several schools of philosophy: absurdism, utilitarianism and boys. "I might be into the whole—" He'd gestured at the space between their bodies with a smile. "You know I like you."

That was when Luke stopped breathing.

Marcos had shrugged down at his M&Ms. "You're pretty much my favorite person. I like talking to you and being around you basically twenty-four seven and I never seem to get tired of seeing you, so…" He'd nudged Luke's shoulder, and Luke had still felt it after he'd pulled away. "Seven-thirty?"

Luke had tried to say "yeah," as if it weren't a big deal, but he was already grinning. "Seven-thirty." He'd planned a date for seven-thirty.

Marcos had grinned back. "And you get to tell Dee all about it."

Luke had stopped smiling. Dee was going to kill him.

On the screen, the door to Jabba the Hut's palace slammed shut and jolted Luke back to the theater. Marcos smiled and mouthed along with the dialogue as usual, except this time Luke was on an actual date with the boy he'd had a crush on since he'd discovered hormones.

His phone buzzed in his pocket as a reminder that Dee hadn't actually killed him. In fact, when he'd told her, she hadn't stopped smiling until Luke had asked what was wrong with her face. He checked the message, and then wished he hadn't.

[From Dee] Are you sharing popcorn right now?

Luke considered Marcos's half-eaten bag and his own empty hands. *That would be a no.*

[From Dee] Are you being cute about sharing popcorn?

Definitely not. What does popcorn cuteness even look like? Butter hands aren't cute.

[From Dee] Oh God, did you even offer to buy him popcorn in the first place?

Luke closed his phone. *Damn it, woman.*

Marcos looked over as Luke shoved the phone back into his pocket. "You're going to miss your favorite scene," he said with a smile.

"It's not my favorite."

"That's not what you said last time or the time before…"

Luke rolled his eyes. It might have been his favorite. There was something *cool* about the first big escape when Luke catches the lightsaber in the air and everything goes to hell. When he was little, his dad had teased him that he wanted to see Princess Leia in the metal bikini. These days, Marcos and Dee had their own theories.

"I still don't have a thing for guys on springboards," Luke said under his breath as the other Luke sprang into the air. "It's just a cool jump. He's almost flying."

Marcos frowned, dubious. "There's also your thing for all the diving in the Summer Olympics. No one watches synchronized diving."

"And you're going to pin that on the springboards instead of the swimsuits?"

Marcos smiled. "It could be both." He held out his bag of popcorn, and Luke wondered when this had started to seem like a high-wire act between two burning buildings. He and Marcos had gone to movies for years. He knew how Marcos leaned forward in his chair and readied himself to whisper, "There is… another… Sky… Sky… walker" with Yoda's dying breath.

This time, when Marcos finished the line and grinned in triumph, Luke wondered if he maybe did it, just a little bit, for Luke, because *he* liked it. He always laughed.

Luke could do things to make Marcos laugh. If that was date-level flirting, he could probably do that. When the Luke on screen realized Leia was his sister, he gasped. "It couldn't be!" he whispered, "Not the only female character!"

The lady two rows ahead turned to shush them, and Marcos slapped both hands over his mouth. "That Skywalker." He giggled. "So quick."

"Nothing gets past him," Luke said with a grin. *Yes. This was absolutely (probably) flirting.* "You want more popcorn?" He pointed at the nearly empty bag and then toward the concession stand, but Marcos waved him off.

"Nah. If I keep going like this, you'll have to roll me out of here." He scooted down in his seat until his head pressed against the backrest and his knees pushed up against the next row of seats. Luke followed, and soon they were both low enough that they could only hear the movie playing as they stared at the back of the metal seats.

"Then we won't leave." Luke glanced over to check whether he'd taken the whole flirting thing a step too far, but Marcos just watched him. "We could set up a fort in the movie theater and live in it. You know the movie schedule."

"Everyone knows about Tarantino Tuesdays and Ed Woods Wednesdays."

"We could eat whatever we wanted from the concession stand. I get the hot dogs—" Luke said, with a smile.

"And I get everything else," Marcos finished.

"Exactly. No leaving and no rolling. Just *Star Wars* and popcorn."

"Sounds perfect," Marcos said. His eyes were still wide and unreadable, but he raised his hand from inside the armrest and inched it toward Luke's side, as if to take Luke's hand. This was when Luke was supposed to meet him in the middle. If he was a cool, date-having person, he could turn his hand over like an invitation.

"Ow. Oh, hey there, I'm sorry." A smack echoed from the entrance at the front of the theater, followed by a stream of apologies just close enough to a whisper to be audible in the entire theater. The voice sounded genuinely apologetic and familiar.

Luke dropped his hand from the armrest and peeked up over the top of the seats.

No.

Of course. Across the theater, Eddie walked into *Star Wars: Return of the Jedi* an hour late with the girl from track who'd waved at him from across the hall. *Renée Beauchene.* Luke might have looked her up. They wove their way toward the empty seats in the middle of the theater, and, as Renée tripped over her own feet, Luke realized with a start that they were drunk. Or, if not drunk, they had definitely taken something that would make running into an armrest *hilarious.*

Like a gentleman, Eddie offered her a hand into a seat several rows in front of Luke and Marcos. He waved her quiet with a shush louder than the laughter, and, when she bent to listen, she didn't move away. The movie kept going, and they sat there, with their heads together, as though it were the most natural thing in the world to watch movies glued to whoever happened to walk you into the theater.

On the screen, Han Solo handed the Millennium Falcon over to Lando Calrissian, and, in the theater, Luke banged his head against the back of his seat. *Why? Now?* Why did Eddie have to show up now, at this theater, on what looked an awful lot like a date? This was his moment. If Eddie had a superpower, it had to be the ability to hone in on exactly when Luke wouldn't want him around.

"You okay?"

Luke flinched. He hadn't realized he'd gripped his seat hard enough to leave marks.

He shook his head. "I'm fine," he said between clenched teeth. "I just don't like it when people come in late. They're going to ruin Endor."

"I think the Ewoks have that covered." Marcos shot him a look, but Luke didn't laugh.

"They're being obnoxious, and I like the Ewoks. They're funny."

It was weak, and they both knew it. No one liked the Ewoks, but Luke didn't have anything better to offer. Even if he explained how he knew the tipsy guy nuzzling his way into his date's neck, whom Luke just happened to yell at earlier that day, he couldn't explain how he'd gotten under Luke's skin. Eddie could have a date on the same night and in the same place as Luke. It was a free country.

He sat up in his seat with a huff and peered over Eddie's head as bikes raced through the woods of Endor. He couldn't remember why he liked this scene. The special effects were pathetic, and then there was the horde of creepy puppets. Out of his peripheral vision, Marcos reluctantly sat up in his seat, and his eyes were on Luke the entire way.

Luke stared at the middle of the screen and tried not to see Marcos's concern on the one hand and Eddie's googly eyes on the other. Technically, he couldn't see Eddie's eyes. He could only see the backs of Eddie's and Renée's heads, but he would have bet everything he owned that Eddie's eyes were sappy. As

Luke resolutely did not watch, Eddie reached around Renée's shoulders and let her lean against his chest. She tucked her head into his neck, as though the space had just been waiting for her to show up. When she got comfortable, she laughed. Luke couldn't have said what was happening on screen, but she must have loved it. She turned her head up to say something into Eddie's downturned face, and, as she did, his thumb drew soft circles where her shoulder met her upper arm. Eddie's fingers ghosted over her skin as though it was normal, but also like—Luke bit his lip.

He touched her as though she were precious.

"Do you think they have a reason for being obnoxious?" Marcos said, quietly. He'd leaned forward on the next row of seats, draped over the back of a seat with his chin resting on the top, and had his eyes fixed on Eddie's and Renée's backs. "I'm sure they have the usual reasons, but do you think they have any reason for being obnoxious right now?" he asked, genuinely curious. "Westgate and *Star Wars* aren't that romantic."

"Speak for yourself."

"Let me rephrase. *Star Wars* isn't romantic for people that aren't us."

Maybe it is for Eddie, Luke thought. It seemed fitting. "Maybe it's a dare," he said.

"She probably said there was no way that he could fit ten things from the 80s into one night," Marcos said, straight as anything.

"Obviously, that's what happened."

"They must have had a busy night, with all the Pac-Man and Michael Jackson."

"Naturally." Luke nodded. "They had to go somewhere else to watch *Dirty Dancing* and they had to drink—" Luke frowned at Eddie's and Renée's backs. "I have no idea what people drank in the 80s."

Marcos shrugged. "I'm sure they did their research. I mean, just look at all the 80s in one place." He pointed at the screen, where the bad guys were chasing an Ewok through an alien forest on their flying motorbikes. The little guy howled as he swung up into the trees, and Luke couldn't keep it together. He caught Marcos's eye, and they sank back in their chairs with their hands plastered over their mouths and their shoulders shaking.

Luke accidentally kicked the back of his chair and it shook along with them, until someone in front had to notice. Eddie might have looked up from where Renée was curled into his shoulder to check on all the noise, but it didn't matter. Luke and Marcos were both so low in their seats they couldn't see the screen, and no one in the theater could see them. Anyone who looked back would have seen a cluster of shaking seats, like an arrow that pointed to where people should have been.

Marcos clenched his teeth and gave a grin that said, "Oops?" or maybe, "Did I do that?" Luke grinned back. If they made themselves into the problem children in the theater, it was more Luke's fault than anyone else's, but he couldn't think clearly enough to take the blame, not when Marcos, grinning and out of breath with laughter, curled into the chair at his side. Marcos smiled all the time. It was what his face naturally did when it had no other plans. He had a resting happy face, but laughter transformed him. He shone. His eyes closed into happy little lines, and his hands curled into the middle of his chest, as though they had to be there to hold him together at the seams.

That laugh wasn't just Marcos, kind and vulnerable and so very young. That laugh with the crinkled eyes and the big grin was *them*. It was Luke and Marcos and Dee. Strangers didn't get to see that face. They'd all closed up as they got older, so Marcos only laughed like that with them. That laugh spoke of years walking on the greenway in the dark and sitting on someone's bed until it was too late to go to sleep: Dee and the idiot boys. When Marcos laughed, he was thirteen all over again, when he explained how Vargassi bit the dust in the middle of *West Side Story* rehearsal and didn't even get to the good part.

For years, his laugh had squeezed something in Luke's chest. He taught himself to think through all the parts of the color wheel until he could act like a proper human being, but this time, Luke didn't go anywhere. He leaned over the divide between their seats and stopped inches from Marcos's face.

"I—" *I'm sorry. I don't know what I'm doing.* "I—" Luke said, and Marcos closed the gap.

It was just closed lips to closed lips, and the pressure landed like a finger on his pulse. He turned his head, but their noses smashed together anyway, and he couldn't figure out when to breathe. If he took a breath, he had to pull away and he couldn't go yet. Luke had to stay, with the armrest pressed into his side and his lips on Marcos's lips. His hands landed on the seat of his own chair and wouldn't go any farther. He could reach over. It wasn't as though he'd never touched Marcos's arms, but he'd never gone anywhere near Marcos's arms or hands or legs while they kissed— *kissed*—and kissing made all the normal touch brand-new. No matter what he wanted, his hands wouldn't leave his seat, so he pushed against Marcos's lips.

And Marcos pushed back.

The rebels got themselves arrested on screen, and, as they raised their hands, Luke took in air. His chest burned, and his brain scrambled to go back to the kissing place. That was a great place; he didn't have to think. Marcos shifted back to his seat with his eyes wide and his lips pomegranate red. His mouth had never been that red, and when Luke realized he was the reason they'd changed color, speaking went right out the window.

They sat for the longest moment of Luke's life. Civilizations died while they sat. Marcos worried his lower lip between his teeth, and Luke squeezed the fabric of the chair between his thumb and forefinger, until Marcos finally leaned forward across the velvet divide. "Hey, Luke?" he said, just above a whisper. "It's a trap." The words came out of his mouth just as Admiral Akbar said them on screen. "It's a trap!" he repeated, already dissolving into giggles, and Luke almost slapped him.

"I—what did you—" he sputtered, but Marcos just grinned until Luke rolled his eyes and threw himself back into his seat. He couldn't hide the smile at the corners of his mouth, but he damn well wasn't giving Marcos the satisfaction. "I can't believe you," he said under his breath. "You're a five-year-old. I can't believe I just kissed a five-year-old in public. I'm going to get arrested."

Marcos didn't say anything, and Luke glanced back in alarm. He'd said the k-word out loud and he had no idea if that was against the kissing rules. But then Marcos's smile got softer around the edges and maybe, Luke thought, talking about the kissing had something to do with that. He kind of hoped it did.

He couldn't tell which of them turned back toward the screen first, but Marcos spoke first. "Would you rather fight ten Ewok-sized T. rex or one, giant T. rex-sized Ewok?"

"How angry is the Ewok?"

Luke answered as if nothing had changed, and maybe nothing had. Maybe, in the minutes between Eddie's appearance and Marcos's last smile, the whole world had been remade so well he couldn't tell the difference. Maybe a kissed Lucas was a totally different creature than one who only kissed Marcos in his mind, but as Marcos rattled off the conditions that might piss off an Ewok, Luke held onto the idea that the idiot boys didn't have to change.

CHAPTER SIXTEEN

THE NEXT DAY AT SCHOOL, Luke couldn't fight the feeling that he was supposed to be happy. No, he was supposed to be *ecstatic*.

He was maybe, sort-of-dating the boy he'd been in love with since middle school. There had been an actual date, and, when he'd come home, his mom had actually asked how it all went. For her, that was huge. He should have embarrassed himself with joy, but when Dee asked how he was doing, he only mustered a queasy grimace.

Then again, she grinned enough for the both of them. "Oh, I see." She beamed as she poked the sketchpad in his hands. "Do you not kiss and tell? I realize you've never had the opportunity before, but Luke, Boo Boo, telling is the *best part*."

"I think that means you're doing it wrong," Marcos said, as he materialized on Luke's other side, and Luke considered buying him a bell. "I might be wrong, but I think other bits are supposed to be the best part."

"Like the kissing?" Luke tried.

"Yup. That's a start."

Dee smothered a snort with her hand and kicked Luke in the shins as she backed away toward class. He was pretty sure that meant she was happy for them. So happy, in fact, that she didn't ask about the bags under Luke's eyes. It wasn't that Luke wasn't happy, per se. The joy was just tempered by a whole head-full of exhaustion.

Hours after coming back from *Star Wars* with Marcos, Luke still hadn't been able to close his eyes. The night had replayed in his head on an endless loop, sometimes with extra bits of rehearsal with Eddie or set-building with Dee cut in for bonus confusion.

Yoda. Leia. Hordes of Ewoks.

Eddie walked in with Renée. His hands played on her skin.

Luke turned into an Asshole. Capital A.

Marcos laughed. Marcos shined brighter than the movie.

They kissed, right on the lips, where anyone could have seen them, where Eddie could have seen them, and it all felt—

Luke had dropped his hands over his face and ground the heels of his hands into his eyes until he saw stars. When he'd replayed their date, his brain got to the part with the lips and threw out error messages like confetti. *Stop. Do not pass. Does not compute. Beep.* Kissing does not compute. So he'd traced the drawings on his ceiling with his eyes until he couldn't keep them open. The last time he remembered looking at his phone had been after three a.m.

"Do you have the time?"

Marcos bumped his shoulder and brought him back to the here and now. Luke held up his phone. It wasn't fair, not to Luke himself and definitely not to Marcos, but when Luke looked at him, he could only wonder why nothing stopped.

They'd kissed; it had been Luke's first kiss with his crush of a bajillion years, and he could literally stop time, but it hadn't occurred to him, not once. He hadn't even felt that metaphorical first-kiss stillness books always talked about. He absolutely remembered Marcos's breath and his lips and what his skin looked like up close, but he also remembered Han Solo getting arrested and the way the velvet chafed against his arm.

Maybe that was how all first kisses really were. Maybe they just had the world's best publicity department. But Luke couldn't help wondering if he'd missed a piece of the puzzle that would have made the whole date more *real*. Maybe if he'd asked Marcos out properly. Maybe if Eddie hadn't shown up, with Renée to keep him from tipping over. Maybe if Luke didn't have an easier time remembering what Eddie was wearing than reliving his first kiss, maybe then he'd know he'd done it right.

"Still busy after school, right?" Marcos squeezed his arm and was already backing away when Luke nodded. Luke had to go to Eddie's rehearsals, assuming Eddie would be there. He couldn't be the first one not to show up. He hadn't done anything wrong. "Cool. I'll text you."

Marcos caught his eye as he left, and Luke kept his smile tucked away for the rest of the day. His smile hadn't changed, even after the k-i-s-s-i-n-g. It was just the way Marcos smiled, with his eyes crinkled, but the sameness was deliciously *them*.

After school, Luke could have used a whole lifetime of smiles when he found himself, once again, watching Eddie march through a monologue that Luke didn't understand. They were back to the one about the con man, because, of course, Eddie didn't say anything about Luke's freak-out or his date and, of course, Luke had to watch Eddie celebrate tricking idiots who couldn't tell truth from fiction.

He hunched over and glared a hole into Eddie chest. *You are full of shit.*

He had no way of knowing where Eddie's fiction ended and his reality began. For all he knew, Eddie was a supervillain, with piles of money and guns, who'd monitored him for years. It was possible. It seemed as plausible as any other explanation for why he'd made up a fake school project just for the privilege of torturing someone who didn't want to be a director.

It figured. Luke *would* get a passive-aggressive villain.

"So?" Eddie finished his run-through and waited as sweat slipped under his collar. He cleared his throat, and Luke sighed, loudly. They were ten minutes into an hour-long rehearsal, and Luke couldn't find the give-a-shit to pretend.

"I don't know," he said. "It was fine. It was *acting*." Eddie was great at acting. Fantastic. If he wanted someone to play along, Luke could play, but he couldn't pretend to care about a project that *didn't exist*. He glared harder.

Eddie looked amused, but there was something else around the edges, something sharp. "Could you try that again with a little more apathy?" he said and turned away, his jaw tight. "I don't know what I did to you this time, but could we pretend I already apologized?"

Oh, no way.

Maybe it was the martyr routine, but Luke was over it. "For God's sake," he snapped. "You didn't do anything. You just did what you've been doing since the moment we met. You *lied.*" Eddie's jaw dropped, and Luke almost laughed. Eddie didn't get to be the victim here, not now. "Don't. Don't look at me like—"

Luke pushed off the desk and yanked his bag from the floor. Anger rose in his chest and gave him wings. "Danes isn't waiting for us to present, is she? She doesn't even know about any of these practices, because there isn't a project. You're not even in her class. Right now, I don't know what we're doing here, but I do want to know who in their right mind invents imaginary homework. Did I somehow piss you off before I knew your name?" Luke walked toward the door, but as it opened clapping echoed behind his back. Eddie clapped, slowly, like the Grand Marshal of the Sarcasm-day parade.

"We should switch places."

"Oh, fuck you," Luke said as he turned back, but Eddie kept going.

"No. I mean it," he said. "I'm especially impressed with how you managed to take all of that nonsense and make it about *you.*"

Luke sputtered. "I—what—I don't know how else to take it! There is no project."

"Of course there is."

Luke glared.

"There is." For the first time Eddie looked away, his lips pursed. His hands dropped to his waist and, if Luke didn't know better, he'd have thought Eddie was embarrassed. "It's not the same project that you thought we were working on, but the difference didn't seem that important when we started."

"How—"

"Because you're still getting class credit and so am I, just like I said on day one." He held up one hand for Luke to stay put and knelt to dig in his bag.

Luke stayed, but he moved his bag in front of his body like a shield. "Eddie," he said, "what are we doing?"

"This." Eddie pulled a shiny paper out of his backpack and dropped it into Luke's hand. It was a flyer, the kind with two folds that opened like a little door. Across the front, it read, "*En el Borde* Theater Company," and the text continued inside: "The company is committed to providing exceptional internship opportunities for the next generation of artists, educators and administrators. Through our program you will develop the tools you will need to move forward in your chosen field—observing, training and collaborating with professionals dedicated to diverse storytelling and performance." There was something else about college credit, but Luke couldn't keep reading.

Wait. Go back. Luke dropped his bag and leaned back against the wall. "What is this?"

"It's a theater internship program at the—"

"No, I can read. I'm asking what you're doing with it."

Eddie shrugged. "They're holding auditions."

"And you have to prepare six monologues?"

"Maybe," he said and cracked a smile. "I think it's overkill, but it's not my theater."

Luke didn't smile back. "And Danes, what, said I could get credit if I helped you get ready?"

"Yes?"

Luke glared down his nose at the tone, and Eddie had the good sense to look away. As he responded, he turned and walked away until he was talking to the windows along the far side of the room. "Okay," Eddie said, softly. "Full honesty, I asked Danes to direct, but she didn't have time, so she gave me a list of students who could get extra credit for taking her place. Your name happened to be first on the list." He wrapped his arms around his body and squeezed them close until his shoulders were almost at his ears. "I thought it was because you were new. Obviously, I was wrong. I tried to talk to you and then—boom." He turned back, and it was Luke's turn to avert his eyes.

Boom. Right. Enter Lucas Aday. Human wrecking ball. He slid down against the wall and said, "You have no idea how surprised I was when you asked again."

"Probably about as surprised as I was." Luke's eyebrows rose as Eddie laughed. "I wasn't planning on it. I crossed you off the list—twice—and I was going to go with Vargassi. He was the next one down." Luke's mouth twitched. "I don't know what changed, but the morning after you went—"

"Boom?"

"Right. I woke up absolutely certain that it had to be you. Nothing was different, but I knew this was your gig. You didn't know it yet, but you had to be my director, and that's all there was to it. It was like you crept in, and I just knew that it wasn't time for you to go yet."

Oh. Oh, no. As Eddie spoke, Luke's legs gave out, and he sat on the floor. Eddie crouched in front of him and ducked his head to catch Luke's eye. "I'm sorry if that sounded creepy, I wasn't going to be your actor stalker or anything. I just—" He stopped himself and started again, with care. "I woke up sure about you. I can't explain it, but one day I didn't know you and then, the next day, I did."

He shrugged, as if to apologize, and he had no idea how much it really wasn't his fault. The horror on Luke's face wasn't for Eddie. *God.* His stomach clenched in a sickly knot. Eddie woke up confident that Luke was his guy. *Apparently, staring at someone while semi-unconscious could have that effect.*

"Why didn't you just tell me about the audition?" Luke asked. He was a worm and a grade-A hypocrite, but still. "It's not even embarrassing, unless you don't want people to know you're in theater?" Or maybe that he was also into guys? The idea didn't fit anything he knew about Eddie, but it wasn't the biggest leap.

"No. Of course not." Eddie rocked back on his heels in disgust. "Have we met? If I'd gotten here a little earlier, I probably would have gone out for *Little Shop.*" His whole chest heaved when he let out a breath. "I understand if you call bullshit, but can I just say that the lie wasn't about school? I want to be honest with you, but—"

But I want some things to stay private.

Luke flashed back to that first day back at school after Lizzy's funeral, when everyone decided that an obituary meant that his life wasn't his own. Since when did Eddie's life stop being a private matter, not to mention anything in his room? Eddie didn't owe him half of what Luke had already taken.

When Luke didn't respond, Eddie pointed toward the door. "Hey," he said, "if you want me to go, I can just—I understand if the extra credit isn't really worth it anymore..." He trailed off and curled into himself as though Luke might yell at him and, worse, as though he might deserve it.

"No!" The response came out louder than Luke intended, but at least it came out. He pushed his way up from the floor before Eddie could bolt for the door. "You don't need to go anywhere. I'm good. Really," he said, quickly. "Actually—" Luke's voice slipped lower until he was mumbling at Eddie's ankles. "I should thank you for, you know, asking me and then asking again. It doesn't matter why. That was cool of you."

"You should what?" Luke started to repeat himself, but Eddie held up a hand. His face went so soft when he was off-balance, as if nothing stood between him and the whole world. Luke assumed that was just a character thing, but Mercutio didn't have Eddie's eyes. "I heard you," he said. "But it didn't make sense."

"I don't know," Luke said. He never seemed to run out of things that he didn't know. "You did that stuff, but you also asked. This whole audition meant a lot to you. You wanted to do a really good job and you thought that, I don't know, I was the right person to help you get there." It didn't matter that Eddie didn't understand where that confidence came from. Not really. It couldn't matter, because then Luke wouldn't be able to look at himself in the mirror. "You didn't know me, but you believed in me and you kept believing in me, even when I was being an ass."

Eddie opened his mouth, but Luke waved him off. "Don't say it. There's no version of events where I wasn't a monumental dick. Even you can't make it sound like I was nice."

"Want to bet?" Eddie asked, as he backed away. His face split into his first grin since Luke had come in and, once again, he became the only real light in the room.

Luke rolled his eyes. *This boy.* "What am I saying? You probably could." It was all too easy to imagine Eddie on stage in Luke's hoodie, as he acted out Luke's story, not that he wanted to think about Eddie in his clothing. "You'd turn me into some kind of misunderstood hero." He threw his hand up to his forehead in a sigh. "Oh, ye gods."

"Gods," Eddie echoed under his breath as he laughed.

Luke stepped into Eddie's space on their stage like a half-baked Romeo. He didn't recognize himself, but Eddie was sitting on top of his desk, giggling, and Luke couldn't bear it if he stopped. "I am undone," he moaned, "I have been called to the aid of a foreign cause without reason or explanation!"

"Those words mean the same thing," Eddie said, through his grin. "And, did you just call me foreign?"

Luke put his hand to his heart and soldiered on. "How shall I repay my foe for such treachery? Ah, I shall be a dickbag. My angst shall be so juvenile that the gods themselves couldn't mistake my meaning. Yes," he said. "I am pleased with this plan. There is no way this could lead to anything bad ever."

Luke lowered himself into a dramatic bow and, this time, when Eddie clapped, it was only mostly sarcastic. "That's your idea of a hero?"

Luke nodded, as seriously as he could. "This is why I should leave it to you. I can't even make myself sound nice as a parody."

"Maybe I wouldn't go for nice then." Eddie slowly leaned back, his smile coy. "Anyone can be *nice.* If I wanted to turn you into the hero of your own story, I'd probably go for frustrated, a little misguided and irritating—"

"Standing right here."

Eddie nodded. "—but you'd be fundamentally justified. I wouldn't make you *nice*. I'd make you like Hamlet. He's prickly and weird and he's so much more interesting."

"But without the thing where everyone dies at the end?" Luke smiled.

"Right," Eddie said. "Of course." He leaned back with his weight resting on his hands behind his back. His head tipped down until he had to look through his eyelashes to see Luke's face. The look had a weight, a purpose, and Luke was suddenly conscious of his own owl-eyes and too-big mouth.

He inched his way off the stage. "When's the actual audition?" he finally asked, but Eddie didn't stop looking. "It's got to be soon. You've been vibrating at a higher frequency than usual."

Eddie rolled his eyes, delighted. "Tomorrow, and screw you for being right. *En el Borde* shares the theater on Thirty-third. I've been over there on our off days to practice. They have a whole Greek-style theater set up on the roof and they don't use it until June, so I hang out up there until it gets dark." He laughed. "I think they notice me loitering, but they just don't bother making me leave."

"Don't you get cold?"

"Nah," Eddie said as he hopped off the desk. He headed for the windows and beckoned for Luke to follow. "It's been warmer for the last few weeks, and as long as I have a coat on I'm fine." He climbed on a desk next to the wall and pointed to where the windows faced the meeting point between North Grove and Minneapolis. "If you look just right, you can actually see the top of the building from here. Come on."

Eddie held out his hand, and Luke let himself get pulled up onto the desk beside him. He peered out toward the horizon, and there it was. If he followed Eddie's hand, he could just make out a taller building over the apartments on the edge of North Grove. It wasn't much, but he could almost imagine that roof as a quiet spot for rehearsal, even when sane people stayed inside. It was nice to think of Eddie up there on a real stage. To see, he had to be on top of a desk that wasn't meant for one person to stand on, let alone two. To keep his balance, he inched closer and held on to Eddie's arm. Lord, he was warm; even through his sweater Eddie exuded heat like a furnace. No wonder he could rehearse outside; he probably didn't get cold anywhere.

"You know," Eddie said, as he looked out at the theater, "you should check it out sometime. They show movies up there in the summers on a big blow-up screen. It's almost like going to an old-school drive-in movie, except you can buy sriracha popcorn."

"Eew." Luke ducked his head. The popcorn sounded disgusting, but the movies had promise. "Do they ever show *Star Wars?*" he asked, and Eddie's brow furrowed in confusion.

Oh, right.

Luke froze. They hadn't talked about that. Though he'd looked at the back of Eddie's head for an hour last night, Eddie and Renée had never seen him. For all Eddie knew, Luke must have had a date somewhere else, because normal people say hello in public. "Sorry," he said as he stepped back and only just remembered not to fall off the desk. "I meant like at the Westgate. I was at *Return of the Jedi* and I think I saw you there?" His voice rose several octaves at the end, and it didn't sound remotely like a real question.

Oh, well done, Secret Agent Aday.

"We were a couple rows behind you?" Luke pointed behind himself with his thumb as recognition lit across Eddie's face.

"You were the ghost seats."

"What?"

"That's what Renée called you. We heard someone talking, but when we looked back, we didn't see anybody, so she decided the theater was haunted. That makes you the ghost."

"I guess so; or at least I was one of them."

"Oh, right. Your date." He landed on the "t" in date and lingered there until it was sharp. "I forgot about that."

"Right," Luke said. "Marcos. You know, I should tell him about the ghost thing. He'll like that. It sounds like the kind of thing he'd say." He was babbling and he knew it, but talking about Marcos to Eddie seemed wrong, as though he might cross the streams of his life and make something explode. He inched farther and farther from the windows. "Did you have fun with Renée? She seems nice." She seemed like a lot more than nice. She seemed athletic, smart and probably funny too. Luke would have bet she wasn't an asshole to innocent people who didn't deserve it, and guys seem to appreciate that sort of thing.

"I did," Eddie said slowly. It sounded like a question. "She's…" He paused as he eased himself off of the desk. "I like her, but I don't think we're going to do that again."

Eddie walked to the front of the room, where he started gathering the piles of monologues into stacks, and Luke resisted the urge to follow after him like a puppy. *What does that even mean?*

"Why?" *Why aren't you going to see her? Why do I care?*

Eddie looked up from his spot on the floor and sat back on his heels. "Well, for one, I don't know how she feels."

Luke almost laughed. That was just stupid. Luke knew how she felt. It was written in the way she nuzzled into his neck and how she leaned into his hands, but more importantly, how could she not feel? Luke couldn't imagine anyone not giving something back if Eddie cared. *They'd have to ignore how he moved through space, as though the air just borrowed the room that, by rights, belonged to him. They'd have to miss how his whole face lit up when he was happy, because he had too much feeling to keep in his eyes or his chest. But mostly, they'd have to ignore the*—Luke grasped for the word. It was everywhere. Eddie existed to care about people who emphatically did not deserve it.

Oh.

Luke stopped following. He froze and watched.

When is a crush more than a crush?

"But how she feels doesn't really matter, I suppose," Eddie went on. Anyone else would think his voice was calm. Luke wasn't anyone else. "I care, of course, but I just can't see her again if I'm into someone else." Luke knew the moment Eddie's shoulders went tense, which was remarkable, because all of Luke's other brain functions had gone out the window.

Someone else. Into. Someone that is else. Lucas Aday has died. Please enjoy the friendly mannequin we've left in his place. Goodbye.

"Oh," he squeaked. "That makes sense. The not seeing if—" Luke made an abrupt turn toward the back of the room and started walking before he could finish that sentence. "Do you need anything from the script stacks before you go?"

"No," Eddie called back. "I'm good. What about you?" His voice was smiling. *The ass.* "Did you have fun with your fellow ghost friend? Marcos?"

"Yeah." Luke kept his eyes on the bookshelf and the stacks of undifferentiated papers. "You met him, actually, the other day? He showed up in the hallway."

"Ahhh. Nice. I mean he seemed nice."

"He is." The nicest, not at all like Hamlet. "But I'm probably not going to see him again either. You know."

Where did that come from? Luke stopped and held a random stack of papers close. It was true. He hadn't known he was going to say it, but it was true. He wasn't going to see Marcos again, not like that. He couldn't, but Marcos didn't know that yet.

"You're not. Okay." When Luke looked up, Eddie was watching him. "And that's good?"

Luke didn't have the first clue how to answer that question, which turned the clock above Eddie's head into a kind of blessing. It was so late. "Damn. I'm sorry for taking up your entire practice time, and now you've got the audition coming up," he said as he hurried back to the front of the room with the papers still in his hands. "I can stay if you still want to run through things a few times before you have to get home." Rehearsal he could handle. Rehearsal emotions belonged to someone else.

"No. Hey, Captain, calm down," Eddie said, his eyes still seeming concerned. "It's fine. I have to leave for lacrosse, anyway. We've got an exhibition game tonight." Luke's face must have gone blank, because the smile came back. "It's like a demonstration game, mostly for the parents. Our team plays against itself, and everyone wins. Before we got into the whole movie thing, I was going to see if you wanted to come along. It probably won't be boring." He raised an eyebrow, and Luke's heart fluttered in his chest.

"To the game? Tonight?"

"Yeah. It's just on our field, but this early in the season they turn on the floodlights for games, and it's all dramatic." Eddie ducked his head and fidgeted with his sweater. "I don't know why I told you that. You've probably been to a million games, and here I am talking about the lights."

Luke heard himself laugh. "Why would you think I've been to a million games of anything?" He pulled at his sleeve. "Was it the football tattoos? They always give me away."

Eddie replied with sheepish indignation. "You're friends with Dee and since Wes's on the team—"

Luke held up a hand. "Nooo. No. No," he said. "The first, vital mistake you made was in thinking that Dee would go to a game. Dee and Wes avoid breathing the same air, and I'm usually with Dee—"

"So no games."

"No games." *Yet.* He'd never gone before, but something in this room made him brave. "Still, those lights sound cool. I'm not saying that it's the only reason I'd go, but it helps to know you're not half-assing the effects."

"Never." Eddie watched him with a shy smile. "In lacrosse, we full-ass our tech."

"Good," Luke nodded. "Plus hot dogs?"

"Absolutely."

It occurred to Luke that this moment didn't have to end. If he wanted to, he could drag time to a halt and stay here, with his butterflies and Eddie's little smile, for as long as he cared to do so, but for the first time in a long while, he didn't want to stop time.

CHAPTER SEVENTEEN

WHEN LUKE SAID HE HADN'T been to a game, he might have lied.

He hadn't actually seen the team live and in person at the North Grove field, but he'd come close. Once, when Dee's folks had dragged her to one of Wes's games, she'd bugged out as soon as she could and called the boys to keep her company. They'd sat together on the hill that looked over the field and watched as the tiny bodies moved in the pool of light. From that far away, they hadn't been able to make out plays or teams, and Luke had been fine with that. He'd never learned enough to know what he was watching.

Dee had been fine with it too. She'd said she didn't mind watching once they were up the hill because "at that point, the crowd could have been cheering for anything. They could all suddenly start cheering for the hot dogs, and it would sound exactly the same."

That was when Marcos had decided that they were all cheering for the weather. "Go wind!" he'd yelled down at the field, and the crowd had cheered back.

That had been more than a year ago and none of them had mentioned Wes's games since, so both Dee and Marcos could have been excused for their confusion when Luke texted that he wanted to go to the exhibition game that night and he needed company.

"I still don't understand why you have to see a fake lacrosse game," Dee said as she juggled her hot dog, pop and bag. They made their way down the middle of the bleachers before the game started, and Luke tried to gauge how close he could get to the field without drawing attention. "Who even gets a need to watch a game they don't like? That's like getting a craving for pickles and ice cream when you aren't pregnant." She looked him up and down. "Luke, are you pregnant?"

He glared over her head. Eye contact wasn't a good idea right now. Dee was his own personal bad psychic; she could reach into his soul and assume everything. "No," he hissed. "I am not pregnant."

"That would require sex and a uterus," Marcos added.

"Right. And I don't understand what's so bizarre about wanting to get involved with something on campus that doesn't begin and end on stage. I don't actually want to live there." He was so full of it. He'd hardly been to anything tech-related in weeks.

"I think it's nice that you want to expand your horizons," Marcos said. He meant it too, and Luke was absolutely no better than the stain on the bottom of someone's shoe. *Good old shoe-stain Luke.*

He muttered his thanks and turned to lead them to an empty row. Even for a pretend game, the crowd was small. A cluster of parents took up the far right side, but the rest was just a smattering of friends and probably girlfriends. Based on what he'd heard from Eddie, the team wasn't football-level quality, so having any audience was reason to celebrate. They landed two or three rows up from the field, and, if that seemed almost too close, there wasn't much that Luke could do about it. He certainly couldn't turn to his friends and say, "Sorry. We have to move, because the boy I like and whom I've been kind of hanging out with for the last few months will be on the field, and I want him to know that I came to the game, but I'm not sure what to do if he actually sees me."

Instead, he sat, dug a bag of chips out of his bag and stared at the open field until Dee leaned behind his back and started talking to Marcos on Luke's other side. Luke didn't mean to look at anything. The wide-open space was a convenient excuse to look busy, but the field itself was beautiful. In the daylight, from the school grounds, it was just a giant patch of green with painted lines and dirty silver bleachers, but under the floodlights, the space was enchanted. The white of the lines popped out against the green, and, past the field, a line of houses stood silhouetted against the vestiges of the setting sun. Even the neon scoreboard gained an iconic dignity in the darkness.

Luke gripped the edge of the bench. He hadn't meant to be so close. The team wasn't out yet, and he didn't know when they'd emerge from wherever the school had them socked away. Not that it mattered. It was just a stupid game. Luke squeezed tighter.

"Hey, Luke? Do you want one?" Marcos reached over with an open bag of jelly beans in his hand. "You're looking a little—" He pointed up to his face and, by his expression, he could have meant tired, hungry or terrified. Luke took the bag with a nod. "Didn't see you after school," he said.

Luke shrugged. "You know, I had that project again. It's gotten kind of intense." A couple days ago he would have felt bad saying that he was working on a project, but now it seemed right again. He wasn't exactly lying. He was working on a project. It just wasn't entirely for school. He passed the bag back as he said, "it should be done pretty soon, and then you won't be able to get rid of me again."

"Really?" Marcos cocked his head and he might have gone on if the team hadn't come running onto the field.

Part of Luke, a big polite part, felt bad for cutting off the conversation, but the rest of his brain was too occupied to care. He hadn't put thought into the actual act of watching lacrosse, beyond the fact that he didn't know the rules. Other than that, he hadn't considered the drama of the lighting or the rush of sitting with excited parents and he absolutely hadn't considered the uniform. Luke swallowed as the team ran across the field. Usually, Eddie wore pants and shirts that were just tight enough to show movement. They weren't too tight or too baggy; they were just normal-sized, preppy clothing with a little give, except maybe across the shoulders and, there, Luke just pretended not to notice. But lacrosse-Eddie wore a whole lot less, pretty much everywhere, and Luke had no choice but to pay attention.

Eddie wasn't exactly big. He and Luke were almost the same height, but it turned out Eddie had arms. Eddie had legs with thick thighs and calves. Eddie had all kinds of muscles that Luke had never seen, and they moved together across the grass with a grace that Luke knew all too well. On the field, he had the same ease as he did in their classroom. It was twitchy and just a little awkward, but also beautifully stable. The whole rest of the team could tumble to the ground, but he knew Eddie wouldn't fall. Even if he tried, the ground wouldn't let him.

"I'll take that for a yes." Marcos said, his head still cocked. He took the candy bag back and followed Luke's gaze onto the field.

Luke blinked as he muttered, "We should probably talk." He glanced to his left and thanked everything that Dee had gotten herself into a conversation with a line of girls in the row behind them. He couldn't bring himself to look to his right, but if he trained his eyes on the horizon he wouldn't have to see Eddie or whatever happened on Marcos's face. "Yesterday was amazing, but I don't know if we should do it again," he said. His voice faded away to nothing, and he tucked his hands between his knees. He wasn't sure about the appropriate posture for hurting someone he'd loved since he was thirteen. "I'm sorry."

"You mean date?" Marcos hummed under his breath and popped a jellybean in his mouth. "Yeah. I figured."

"It's not that I don't like you, because of course I like you, but—wait, what?" Luke looked up, startled, and Marcos kept watching the field as though he'd said something about *Battlestar Galactica*. "What do you mean you *figured?*" Marcos smiled, and Luke poked him in the side. "No. No! You do not get to go all Yoda on me. What does that mean?"

"It means you're not as subtle as you think you are," Marcos said with a grin.

"You know I hate you right now."

"Seriously?" Dee's voice sounded in Luke's ear, and he turned to find a glare directed at the back of Marcos's head. "Was this supposed to be a date? This whole idea was weird, but I assumed it was, like, a group weirdness," she said, and her eyes got even wider. "Why didn't you just tell me?"

"We're not on a date," Luke sputtered, but his smile didn't help. Neither did Marcos, who'd gone back to his candy. "Feel free to jump in and help any time you like."

"I don't know, Luke. I'm not sure I can bear to hear you disparage our love."

"Oh, my God."

Dee groaned. "I'm just going to sit somewhere else so that you two can *hate* each other in peace." She pointed to the bench on Marcos's far side and almost made it out of her seat before Luke dragged her back down.

"No, Dee. Don't get up," Luke insisted and tugged her back into her seat. "I promise we're good, but can you just tell me what's going on?" He pointed out to the field as a referee in red blew a whistle. The players snapped into motion, and Luke didn't have a clue what was going on.

Dee sat without another word. The last time Luke had seen anyone as excited as she was, the person had been a three-year-old and had just been given a bag of sugar. A twinge of guilt yanked at his gut. He had to explain to her everything that was going on with Marcos and Eddie and he needed to do it soon, but she was distracted. Dee might not have wanted to be at her brother's games, but information was in her blood. She would have called it "teaching" and she would have been wrong.

"Okay, the basic concept is simple, but it gets tricky because there are so many rules." She turned her body his way, and Luke felt the full force of Dee in her element. "Any player worth their salt has to have good stick skills. Plus, they have to communicate as a team so the defenders can slide and the offense can set picks, and that's not even getting into stalling or penalties."

Luke scooted back, his hands in the air. "Whoa, *Sports Night*. How about we try that again on the beginner setting. For example," he said as he turned toward the field, "what's that guy doing with the ball?" A player with long red hair had a little ball in a net at the end of a stick and seemed to be running somewhere with it, dodging other people as he went. Luke was aware that the redhead probably wanted to get it to the other end of the field. He had seen football once or twice, but if playing dumb made Dee turn red, it was worth it.

"You know," she said, "I don't even know if you're messing with me right now and I think that says more about you than it does about me." She echoed his turn and faced the field. "That's Ricky Otto. He's on Wes's team for the scrimmage. You can tell because they're all wearing green. Now Ricky here would like to get the ball past the silver team's goalie to score what is known as a goal, but that would make the silver team super sad."

Marcos snorted. "Wow. She's not talking to me, and even I feel like a toddler."

Dee shoved him behind Luke's back, and the process started all over again. She couldn't quite find the balance between too much information and too little, but ten minutes later, when she started into defensemen, midfielders and attackmen, Luke convinced her to write it down. For five minutes, she drew a stickman version of the field, complete with where all the positions had to stay, and then handed it over with pride. He stared at the sheet, overwhelmed. "I'm just going to—"

"Yeah. Yeah," she said and waved him off; her eyes were back on the field. "Give our regards to the void."

Luke elbowed her in the side, and put the game on hold. It might have been self-indulgent, but Dee's drawing was easier to understand when everyone stopped moving. In stillness, he could actually see how green players charged down the field and silver players moved in to cut off the attack. Offense and defense. Check.

The Hold also gave him the chance to inspect Eddie's game stance, but that was a bonus. The game stance wasn't as intense as Eddie's "I'm doing Shakespeare" stance, but it was still intimidating as hell. He was on the silver team, and Luke caught him in a full run, legs extended, as he barreled down the field. If he were on the other team, Luke would have dropped to the ground and handed over the ball, but as himself he just stared. It was beautiful. He was beautiful, and Luke would have drawn the moment on the back of Dee's directions if it weren't for the twitch.

Eddie twitched. In the middle of the Hold, when the whole game and maybe the whole world stood still, Luke could have sworn that Eddie moved his head toward the bleachers and toward him.

Luke dropped the drawing and the Hold. The diagram almost slipped between the slats on the bleachers, but he caught it in time to see Eddie slam full-bodied into Wes's side. They landed in a pile of sticks and shoulder pads and shoved each other away almost before they hit the ground. Wes hadn't been the player with the ball. Eddie had no reason to hit him, unless—

"Watch where you're going! It's a practice!" Dee yelled at the field and glared over at Luke and Marcos's surprised coughs. "What? He's still my brother, and that was dangerous."

"Yeah, idiot," Luke echoed back, but his eyes stayed on Eddie as he wobbled to his feet. The hit wasn't hard enough to worry about concussions, but Eddie looked as if he couldn't figure out how he'd ended up on the field, let alone on the ground. He blinked as Wes cussed him out, and the other half of the silver team pulled him away. When play started again, Eddie ran at half pace, three steps behind the rest of his team. Luke quietly thanked Dee for the diagram, and made a show of borrowing Marcos's candy, but he didn't look away from the field.

Based on Dee's picture, Eddie was supposed to be one of the defensive guys on his end of the field, but after the hit he lost track of his team. The other defensemen had their areas on the field to control, but Eddie never landed in the right place at the right time. Luke wanted someone to yell for a timeout and shake Eddie back into the game, but he didn't have that power and he had to at least pretend to watch Wes. After all, from Dee's perspective, Wes was the only person he actually knew on the team. Weirdly enough, watching Wes easily turned into watching Eddie, because wherever Eddie was on the field, Wes appeared too.

At first, Luke thought he'd mixed up the players. They all could have been the same person in the masks, but then it became impossible to ignore. No matter how far Eddie wandered from his zone, Wes showed up and got in his space. He lingered, and when the ref focused on other parts of the field, he threw an elbow or shoved Eddie in the side. The first couple of times, Eddie moved away, but Wes followed until Eddie stopped fighting his new shadow. Once, when Eddie's stick came out of his hands, Wes had his mouth by Eddie's ear, and Eddie's shoulders pulled tight.

"He really takes his game seriously, doesn't he?" Luke said. "Wes, I mean?" He pulled himself away from the game and willed the anxiety out of his voice.

If he sounded anything like he felt, Dee couldn't tell. She laughed and said, "Right. I forget you haven't seen him in the zone before. He goes all game-face when he's on the field. Grr." She pursed her lips and narrowed her eyes, but the result looked more like angry puppy. "It's hilarious, but it also means that he's exhausted after practice, so I'm glad he gets his stupid little yayas out."

When she smiled, he tried to smile back, but it wouldn't come. He wanted to ask why Wes had to "get his yayas out" all over a guy who should have been pulled off the field ten minutes ago, but he couldn't do that, so he dug into his bag for his sketchpad.

"Not your game?" Marcus cocked his head and tapped the sketchpad. Luke kept drawing, but he sensed Marcos's nod. "I get it," he said quietly. "It's not easy watching people you care about get pushed around."

Luke stopped drawing with his pen frozen on the skyline. *People* could mean anyone, but Marcos didn't sound as if he were talking about just anyone. "How are you so cool with this?" he whispered. "And I don't mean the game. How are you so cool with this?" He gestured to himself, to his everything. How could Marcos be okay when Luke couldn't watch a stupid exhibition game because a team member pushed his *friend*?

Marcos peered at Luke's paper so, for a second, they looked at his fake skyline together. "I don't know," Marcos said. "It's not hard. I know that you're one of my people and you always will be, but I don't mind if he's your person too." He looked out at the field, but Luke had to keep his eyes the page. If he looked up now, he might cry, and Dee would wonder what they'd been drinking.

"You know I'm crazy lucky to have you, right?" Luke said quietly. "Even if we're not, you know, just the fact that you could say that—"

"Luke." Marcos's hand landed on Luke's knee.

Luke shook his head as the crowd noise grew on either side. "Please let me finish. Otherwise I might never say it out loud."

"No." Marcos's voice caught and he pulled Luke to his feet. "Look." He pointed at the field, just past the sideline closest to the crowd, where Eddie had Wes by the front of his jersey, and his feet were all but off the ground.

The little crowd grew louder. It bellowed because the game had stopped and a player was coughing and sputtering in the air. Eddie and Wes's helmets lay in the grass and, beyond them, a scattered semi-circle of players watched, their faces caught between confusion and delight. Wes yelled something inaudible over the crush of people. He screamed, and Eddie didn't flinch. He wasn't large enough to dwarf anyone, but in his stillness, Eddie might have been twice Wes's size. He might have taken up the whole field, and Luke didn't recognize any part of his face. He'd seen Eddie with narrow pursed lips, but that was just anger. None of his characters had wanted to kill.

Parents ran toward the sideline, but as they came, Eddie pushed Wes backward, off the side of the field. Luke could have sworn the push happened in slow motion as Wes's back arced through the air like a dive. But if time slowed down, it wasn't Luke's fault. None of it was his fault; he only watched as Wes's head cracked against the corner of a bench, loud enough to echo against the bleachers, and his body landed with a solid, sickening thud.

Wes didn't move. Even when the coach, his face stunned, crouched to touch the bench and then Wes's head, Wes lay with his face planted in the grass and his arms splayed wide.

A high wail rose like a siren, and for the longest time Luke didn't realize it was Dee. By the time he looked away from Wes's body, she was already halfway down to the field; she was no match for the coaches and assistant coaches who tried to hold back the crowd and call 911. She ducked under arms and shoved through huddles of frightened students to reach the field, but once she got there, she froze. Wes lay on the ground, surrounded by a wall of bodies. Even if she knew what to do or what to say, she couldn't get to him. So she stared at Eddie: Eddie, who needed to be private; Eddie, whose face was blank; Eddie, who might have just killed her brother.

He backed away into the field, until he stood alone in a circle of light.

They took Eddie away, eventually. Long after the screams turned to sirens, three white men with guns on their belts walked him toward the school. He went quietly, and Luke let him go.

CHAPTER EIGHTEEN

Three hours later, it was eleven o'clock, and Luke had déjà vu.

He hadn't been to the hospital for two months, and it had been a lot longer since he'd spent any time in the emergency room. Nothing about the last months of Lizzy's life had been an emergency, but the ER hadn't changed. The hospital hadn't changed. He hadn't expected it to. He still knew the nurses. He knew its hollow smell of disinfectant and age, but he also knew the numb flutter in his chest that said, "You're here, and someone isn't going to be okay."

He and Marcos sat in the plastic and metal chairs in the second ER waiting room, and Luke kept breathing. He had all of his old tricks. If he tipped the chairs right, he could get the front legs off the ground. Then he had to try to tap the tiled floor with the legs of the chair without making a sound. If someone noticed, he lost the game. He'd invented it months ago, and sometimes it worked. Like today. They'd been sitting in these chairs—as opposed to the chairs in the first waiting room—for almost an hour, and no one had noticed Luke tapping in the corner. Marcos sat two seats away. He'd slid down in his chair until he could stare straight at the ceiling with his feet wide apart on the floor and his arms wrapped tight around his body.

Dee paced. When Luke wasn't counting taps, he counted her trips past the chairs, around the nurse's station and past the vending machines. He lost track at seventy-two. Seventy-two rotations, leaving an imaginary groove in the plastic tiles. Marcos had tried catching her hand at round five, but she'd shaken him off and walked harder. Luke didn't think she'd stop until someone told her something useful about Wes or her mom finally showed up.

Three hours ago, when they'd trailed the ambulance to the ER, Dee had texted, then called, and her mother had screamed expletives into the phone. For the first couple of hours, if Dee didn't check in every five minutes, her mom had called, convinced that the worst had happened and they were too busy grieving to give her the bad news. It had been almost a relief when she had boarded a plane in Salt Lake City and lost contact. Dee had passed her phone to Marcos; he could deal with anyone who called now. She paced.

Luke had never been a pacer. It wasn't his way, but he had the path from the room to the elevator and down to the cafeteria recorded in his bones. He'd gone when his folks needed real food and when they hadn't, because it was a place to go and a thing to do when it wasn't nice to throw things at the wall.

"What are they doing to him back there?" Dee asked, quietly. She paused as she passed Luke's chair and stared toward Wes's room. She wasn't really talking to him or Marcos, but there wasn't anyone else to ask. "I mean it. What can they possibly be doing to him that could take *hours*? They would tell us if he was going to have surgery. They have to tell before they can cut him open. That's the law." Her voice rose, but nothing lay behind it. Dee didn't have the first clue what they could legally do to Wes without asking. Neither did Luke. "They have to get our consent." She said, her teeth clenched and, finally, she let Marcos take her hand.

"Of course they do." He squeezed her hand, and she let him. "I'm sure they'll be out to tell us that he's okay any minute now."

Luke shifted toward them. "It can't be that serious, Dee. Otherwise they would have taken him back right away."

"Really?" Her voice wobbled.

"Of course," Luke said. "It's against HIPAA, or something." He didn't think about the number of times they'd sat with Lizzy in waiting rooms for a lot longer than that. Those times had been less serious, usually.

Dee let out a long, shuddery breath and let Marcos tug her back into a chair. "I wish they'd just tell me. He shouldn't even be here. He never gets hurt."

Luke nodded. As long as Luke had known the Corellis, Dee had been the one who broke. It hadn't made sense at first. Wes had played lacrosse and run before he walked. In middle school, he'd gone everywhere on a skateboard, but injuries had seemed to rush to get out of his way. He'd been the kid who could get in a four-person collision on the field and come out without a scratch. Dee, on the other hand, had attracted damage. For every show she'd stage managed, she'd found a way to break a bone or tear a ligament. Sometimes she'd just tripped over her own feet, but if she were in a cast for opening night that would give her another way to threaten her team into submission. Her injuries had been her war wounds and they'd said, "If a broken tibia can't keep me from doing my job, what chance do you think you have?"

Dee was a different sort of threat now, as she perched on her chair and stared at Wes's closed door. By Luke's count, she lasted two minutes before she got back on her feet.

"I can't believe he almost got—" She switched direction. "I can't believe it was someone on his own team. If it had been a fight with another team, that would have been one thing, but his teammate put him here. He shoved Wes like it was nothing." She trailed off with her eyes fixed on a point in the distance. "How could they let him play?"

"Who?" Luke's breath was caught somewhere between his throat and his lungs. "Let who play?"

"That monster." Dee started pacing again, but this time she stayed closer and tracked a tight circle around their chairs. "He'd have to be some kind of psycho to go crazy on his own team. I know Wes's a little shit, but he's not—he doesn't deserve—" She blinked up at the lights.

"Of course he doesn't," Marcos said softly. He looked to Luke for an echo, and Luke didn't look back. He wasn't so sure of that. He wasn't so sure of anything. If Wes didn't deserve to be unconscious, then that made Eddie the monster who had put him there, and that image wouldn't hold. The Eddie who shoved Wes's limp body melted away into the Eddie who smiled when it seemed as if Luke could break him in two. He was fragile and sweet and a complete stranger. Dee's broken face said it all. Luke had forgotten; Eddie might have become *something*, but he wasn't family.

"It's nuts. I've been going to team fundraisers and to their stupid parties for years, and I don't even know who he is."

"Yes, you do. Sort of." Luke heard himself say the words before he knew why he was saying them. He sounded numb to his own ears, maybe because he needed to be. Marcos watched, his face unreadable.

"What?" Dee stopped mid-circle. "How?"

Luke blinked. He could have laughed. "It was his house, back when you two wanted me to go be a badass and 'bring something back from inside.' That was his house, and he was there," he said and turned to stare at the blank white wall. He had enough images in his head: a bedroom filled with plays and money and Eddie's wide-eyed, frozen face. "I guess you don't really know him, but maybe you should. We broke into his house."

Dee's jaw dropped and her eyes froze. "You—we—didn't take anything, did we? You said you didn't take anything." Luke sensed Marcos staring at his back, eyes narrow. He knew that look, and it burned. "He didn't even know you were there," Dee said.

"I don't know. I don't know what he saw or if we did anything. You know, it could have been a lot worse," he said, and the words just kept coming, like an avalanche. "He had a gun, too." He coughed out a low laugh and turned to see Dee sit down, hard.

"Yep." Luke laughed again. "E—the guy had a gun under his bed and a whole pile of money. For all we know, he could be selling meth out of his garage." He could also be the next Patrick Stewart or Meryl Streep. Maybe he was that good. Seven hours ago, Luke would have sworn that Eddie was exactly that good, but he didn't know anything anymore. "I'm sorry I didn't say anything. I—I was confused. I never thought anything like this could happen." He pulled his knees up to his chest and hugged them for dear life.

"Of course you didn't." In the silence, Dee's voice was the softest he'd ever heard it, as if someone could blow on her and she'd float away. "No one expects this."

Marcos still didn't speak. He'd settled back into his chair; his back was slouched in a curve against the plastic, and his eyes were fixed on Luke's shaking hands.

"Excuse me, are you Deana Corelli?" A nurse emerged and peered at them from behind Dee's back. Luke hadn't seen her coming, but then again, he wasn't paying attention. She was shorter than Dee, with dark hair in a bob that dipped below her chin. It was a style Luke associated with young moms and aunts who didn't care about being cool. She frowned, as if she were worried that Dee wasn't actually Deana and that she'd have to go somewhere else.

Dee nodded, and the nurse beckoned her into Wes's room. For a second, it seemed as though Dee might ask if they could come too, but the moment passed and she let the nurse lead her inside.

"We can be here for her when she comes out," Marcos said quietly. "She'll be okay."

Luke nodded. He knew that. In any other situation, he'd be asking her what to do next. She would have laughed at him for keeping it all inside and for being a drama queen. She'd have loved the irony, but she also would have told him what to do. But now, it was too late. Wes was in a hospital bed, and Luke might as well have put Wes there with his own two hands.

I'm sorry. I'm sorry. I'm sorry. It was never going to be enough.

The guy had a gun under his bed. The guy. Luke closed his eyes and let Marcos pull away. It was true. Luke should have been happy. So why couldn't he stop shaking? He'd finally chosen his family over some guy who wouldn't even tell him the truth, but if there was any relief, he couldn't find it. The crush in his chest wasn't relief. It wasn't even fear for Wes. Most of all, Luke couldn't breathe through the terror for a boy with wide eyes and twitchy hands.

Eddie, where are you? I shouldn't want to know and I don't care if you lie. Please tell me you're okay.

CHAPTER NINETEEN

THE NEXT MORNING, NO ONE was surprised when Eddie arrived late for school. They were shocked he showed up at all.

Luke wasn't in any of Eddie's early classes and he wasn't at the doors when Eddie arrived, but Becca Germain-Frost in AP English got a message from Emma Cassid who was in Eddie's first hour. As she said, she wasn't watching for him, but she couldn't pretend she didn't notice when he walked in.

By the end of first period, Luke would have bet his life savings that everyone but the teachers knew four things:

1. Eddie Sankawulo kicked Wes's ass in the middle of a lacrosse game.
2. Eddie got interviewed as a "person of interest" after the game.
3. The police let Eddie go without charges.

They didn't know why or how long he'd been held. They didn't even know if the cops had any reason to question Eddie in the first place, but they all knew one more thing:

4. Eddie had a gun.

Becca told him about it in a hushed whisper, as though she were revealing the location of the Lindbergh baby and leaned back in her desk, flush with pride. Luke just gaped, his mouth open and his stomach in his throat. There was no point in trying to hide his horror. She just took his slack-jawed silence for fear of Eddie, what Eddie was, what he could do with his teammate-punching insanity and the arsenal under his bed. She took it as fear of the boy who hadn't come to school yet, not of her or of whoever gave her the chance to spread the word.

By the end of first period, Luke couldn't hear anything else. In the hallway, where there should have been a wall of chatter about games and homework and who was having probably-not-actual-sex with whom, he heard the echo of bullet fire and every permutation of *gun*. Hallways full of students and a few teachers whispered behind their hands, and he kept waiting for them to look at him.

They didn't. Ever.

He was as invisible as he had ever been, just another frightened face in the crowd. No one had any reason to connect him with Eddie or Eddie's gun except Marcos or Dee, and she, at least, was missing in action. He saw Marcos from a distance, but Dee might as well have fallen off the face of his earth.

Luke shouldered his way through the students on their way to second period classes until he found an open spot of wall and stared at his silent phone. He'd tried texting Dee when she hadn't met him at the doors on his way in, and then again after Becca made her mark. She hadn't texted back. Luke opened the one-sided wall of messages and his stomach clenched. There were only so many reasons Dee would have gone AWOL, and every one of them left Wes's condition worse than when they'd left him last night. At three a.m. the nurse had insisted that he was out of the woods. He was awake and as coherent as he'd ever been, but anything could have happened in the hours between then and now. Dee might not have had the time to let them know where she was going, and that might have been the scariest part.

"He's here."

Luke couldn't tell where the whispers began, but they rippled up the hall. One of the mock trial girls told someone near the world history classroom, who flagged down the head of debate. By the time he'd texted Dee for the millionth time, the freshmen in the D-wing had to be whispering to each other around the drinking fountain between the vending machines and the gym. Odds were they didn't know who "he" was or why they were supposed to care, but they nodded toward the main entrance on the other side of the courtyard anyway and said, in hushed whispers, "I can't believe he's actually here."

Along the wall of lockers, where the rest of the crowd determinedly wasn't staring, Luke saw flashes of Eddie inside the front doors. Eddie was little more than an outline in the distance, but even from a full hallway away, he wasn't okay.

Luke didn't realize that he'd grabbed onto the Hold until he was winding his way toward the front doors and everyone else stayed in place. He ducked around huddles of bodies frozen mid-whisper with their eyes wide with scandal and their hands close to their chests. He could almost hear group after group reenacting their versions of last night's fight. He wondered what sound they used for the moment when Wes's head hit the corner of the bench. In his head, it still sounded like a cross between a bullet crack and a hard, sickening thud.

In front of the tile mural and a body's length in front of Eddie's face, Luke stopped. He couldn't go any farther. Eddie was smaller, somehow, as though the last day had cut him off at the knees. He hunched into himself as he watched the North Grove crowd not watching him. The students who'd stood near the door when he entered naturally formed a wide circle around his body, as if a force field had turned him into the center of a moving target.

Luke walked the perimeter of Eddie's human circle, and Eddie's eyes seemed to follow. He was overdressed, even by Eddie standards. A black dress shirt under a black blazer gave him the air of young preacher on his way to a high-class funeral. But under all of that, he was the same. Even now, he was Eddie Sankawulo: the boy who beamed when he invited Luke to the game and who sent Wes flying as if it were nothing. *There you are. Why am I disappointed?*

It was stupid, but part of him thought he'd be able to see a difference. Surely, after the thud and the sirens and the hours in the hospital, Eddie would have to have changed. Luke wanted to see a monster, but Eddie looked like adrenaline and a tug in the chest and the metallic taste of being alive.

Luke wasn't sure how long he stood before weaving his way back to where he'd begun. He'd given up keeping his own time during the Hold. He just let it stay until he'd pressed his forehead and palms against the cool tile wall. The air filled his lungs for a count of *one, two, three,* and then he let the world spin back to life. When he turned toward class, he didn't look down the hall, but he sensed Eddie's eyes on his back the entire way to class.

[FROM LUKE] I'M WORRIED ABOUT you.

    [**From Luke**] Pls say that ur ok.

    [**From Luke**] I'm gonna have my phone turned off for a while, but I'll be back again later. Let me know.

    [**From Luke**] DeeDeeDeeDeeDeeee. Don't make me start quoting Trek at you.

    [**From Luke**] If you go seriously AWOL I'll start quoting it wrong.

    [**From Dee**] Anything but that. Jerk.

    [**From Luke**] Hi.

    [**From Luke**] You ok? Or not ok, but the not ok kind of ok?

    [**From Dee**] … yeah. I'm that one.

    [**From Luke**] I'm sorry.

LUKE HAD BEEN THIRTEEN WHEN he'd pushed Lizzy into the street. He hadn't meant to do it, but that hadn't been important when cars had swerved into other lanes, and his mom had run in front of a truck.

He hadn't been paying attention, is all. They'd been walking to the park as a family. He'd pushed her chair while his parents walked behind him, and they hadn't stopped talking at him for blocks and blocks. He needed to join things, they'd said. He needed to find clubs and groups, so he could do something after school other than sit in his room and draw. They hadn't said he needed friends, but it had been there in the fine print.

She'd said, "You'll be happier, honey," and he hadn't shot back that she'd been talking about herself. His mom was the one who'd have been happier if he'd gotten out of the house. Luke had already been happy. He'd liked drawing more than he'd liked people anyway. He'd been fine. Then his dad had joined in, and he'd been so upset he hadn't said anything at all.

So, he hadn't noticed the car that blew into the crosswalk until it slammed on its brakes. The wheels squealed, and, in his shock, he'd let go. Lizzy hadn't gone far, but he'd been pushing her hard, with all the rage he hadn't sent back to his folks, and he'd frozen as she'd drifted out into all the traffic that hadn't stopped.

She had been fine. His mom had gotten to her before anything could happen, and five minutes later they'd been listening to music at the park, but Luke's parents hadn't settled down. Hours later, his dad still hovered, and his mom had fluttered around the house fixing things that weren't broken.

The next day, Luke had joined his first tech crew. It was like a club, and they'd both been right. He'd met an odd girl who'd insisted on being his friend, and his mom had been unbearably, unspeakably happy.

CHAPTER TWENTY

AFTER SCHOOL, LUKE STOOD OUTSIDE their classroom, his and Eddie's, and composed an opus on why he should leave.

There was nothing waiting for him. Eddie wouldn't show up, and, if he did, Luke didn't have to be here too. He had to go home. He had to talk to his parents about where he'd been all night. They'd noticed this time and were worried. They wanted to have "a talk," and Luke had almost forgotten what that was like. If he didn't go home, he had to go to the hospital and sit with Dee. She needed him, but the selfish parts of his brain wouldn't let him go. He'd almost given up his people for this boy, and Eddie owed him more than words.

Luke shoved open the door hard enough for it to crack against the wall on the other side—and found no one. The room sat empty in the half-dark of the late afternoon as a flecked glow seeped through the frosted windows. The light wasn't strong enough to illuminate the graffiti on the desks or the permanent residue on the whiteboard, but the room was prettier in the dark.

"Afternoon, Captain. How was your day?"

Eddie perched on a stool in the far back corner of the room, in the nook between the bookshelves and the farthest window. His voice was numb and brittle and numb again, like blown glass wrapped in layers of cotton.

"Afternoon." Luke straightened his spine. In his mind, the word landed like a challenge. *I saw you. I know you*, it said, but if Eddie noticed, that didn't show.

"My day sucked," Eddie said, and, as he stared up at the ceiling, his eyes sparked like flint. "My gym teacher about died when I showed up for class, but I guess that was better than the students. They just got scared." He spat out the last word, and Luke inched back with his hand on the doorframe. *Do I look scared, too?* Eddie laughed under his breath. "What are we waiting for? I have three hours until my audition. Plenty of time to pack in a few go-rounds." He pointed toward *En el Borde*. "What do you want to do with me?"

"What?" Luke balked. He couldn't answer that question. The day before, he'd wanted to tear Eddie's bullshit apart like a surgeon, but now? He'd settle for the chance to drag Eddie into the hospital, point at Wes's body and ask him *why*.

"I'm thinking we start with the Dostoevsky bit. It's never been up to snuff, not like the others. It's just not there yet. You know?" Eddie moved with studied focus toward their fake stage. "Maybe if we give it another try we can give it a boost. I don't think it's going to make the difference, but I don't know. What do I know?" His smile spread, joyless and wide. "That might be all it takes."

"You really want to practice." He really thought Luke could practice.

"I don't have a choice, *El Capitan*, and I don't think you get that. This audition is happening and, funny thing, I didn't get any sleep last night. I might have had too much caffeine, or it could have to do with some guy's head slamming into the ground—"

"Eddie!" Luke snapped. *Don't you dare.* And Eddie faltered, as if he'd forgotten where he was. His hands dropped and he breathed in long shaky drags. When he finally spoke again, his voice came out small.

"Is Wes okay? Is he okay or is he still in the hospital? I—" His jaw clenched. "It's fine if you don't want to tell me. I understand if I don't get to know, but the police wouldn't tell me if he was okay. I'm still here, and no one's said anything so I assumed he didn't…" He swallowed hard over the word that wouldn't come. "But there's a lot of space between, you know, *that* and okay."

"Yeah." Luke said. There was infinite space between that and okay. "I don't know. I mean I don't know how he's doing right now. Dee's not talking that much, and I don't blame her. Last night though, he was—" Wes's limp body flashed behind his eyes. "He wasn't okay, but he was on his way to okay. Does that make sense?" Eddie nodded, slowly. Luke took a breath. He couldn't explain why Eddie got to hear any of this. He didn't deserve to know, but he'd asked, and it was true. He said, quietly, "He was out for a while, but there doesn't seem to be any permanent damage. He's still Wes. I don't think the knockout improved his personality. He *is* still Wes. When he first woke up, he wanted to know if he'd made anybody cry. Really. He specifically asked if 'any hotties got emotional.'"

Eddie held the back of a hand over his mouth, as if he wasn't allowed to laugh. "You're kidding."

"I swear to God," Luke said, his hand over his heart. "Dee almost gave him a second concussion." And he didn't blame her. Umpteen hours waiting in the hospital, and the little shit just wanted to get laid.

"I can't figure out how it happened," Eddie said, and he could have been talking to Luke or to himself. He sat on top of a desk and stared at the wall as if he could still see the field. "One minute Wes was up in my face, and the next he was on the ground like—" He stopped before he could say *a body*. Or worse. "The next thing I knew, security had me in the principal's office and they wouldn't tell me what happened after I left. God damn." He rubbed at the back of his neck where the skin went raw.

"I thought I killed him and that I'd find out on Facebook or something before they came back to get me for real." Eddie squeezed his eyes shut, as if the thought stood in front of him, and it was too bright to see. "But Wes is fine?"

Luke nodded and didn't think about how long it had been since he had heard from Dee. Wes was fine. He had to be. Luke wanted to feel bad for talking about Wes in here with *him*, but he couldn't. Eddie was too much himself for Luke to do anything else. Dee wouldn't understand. He couldn't understand, but Luke-and-Eddie space had different rules. Their rules were all confusing and upside-down, but they were still true.

"Thanks." Eddie sounded so thankful Luke almost couldn't look. "For telling me about Wes and, I mean—" He broke into a weak smile with the shine again in his eyes. "You came to the game. It was a crappy game, but you were there."

Luke inched in the door and sat on top of the desk closest to the door. The two desks between them might as well have been two miles. "Of course I came." He didn't say, "I came because you asked," or "I had to go because you wanted me there," because that didn't make any sense at all. "I didn't really know what I was watching, but I tried. Dee gave me a crash course in lacrosse."

"Next time, I'll come over and give you a tutorial," Eddie said with a shaky grin. "You see, there's this ball, and the whole team is trying to make sure it goes into the other team's net."

"Shut up." Luke rolled his eyes, but he couldn't help smiling back. *Next time.* He said, *next time. What happened to Wes?* "I'm sorry, but I can't take lacrosse lessons from a man who looks like he's going to the opera."

Eddie eyed his black-on-black. "I look like I'm going to an audition," he finally said. "I don't know. Today, I wanted to look good."

You do, Luke thought. *You are.*

He opened his mouth, but the words stuck in his throat. He felt the influence of *their room*, just like all the rehearsals before this one. Even when he couldn't find a good direction to save his life, he eventually sank into their place, their stage and Eddie's smile, as if he could stay here forever. As long as Eddie kept looking at him as if he were the smartest, funniest, most talented boy he'd ever known, part of him was sure the outside world would hold its breath and wait. Outside, there were secrets and questions and too many hospital beds, but in here—Luke's stomach clenched. It would be glowing and perfect for a while, but then he had to go.

"Captain?" Eddie asked, because he'd gone silent, for how long, Luke couldn't tell. "You know I'm not actually pissed about the suit—"

"Tell me what Wes said." Luke replied. His back straightened as Eddie's collapsed. "I think I deserve at least that. What did he say that was so bad?"

Eddie's gaze fell. "It was nothing." The twitch in his hands came back. "No, not nothing, but nothing *new*. He said worse stuff about my mom every day, like it was supposed to be funny." He pursed his lips in a scowl. "I don't know why I let it get under my skin."

"Your mom?" Luke had almost forgotten Eddie had parents. If Luke tried to imagine them, he only conjured a blurry picture of Eddie's face on older bodies. He never talked about them, and Luke had never even noticed. "What does Wes know about your mom?"

"Nothing," Eddie spat, but then he seemed to register Luke's confusion and his eyes went wide. "Oh. You're serious. I can't—" He pushed off the desk and paced into the open space with his hands at his neck. "You have to understand. On my way here today, I heard three different groups of freshmen go on about how I had a loaded gun under my jacket and how I was secretly a drug dealer. I didn't know any of them, but they were dead certain I was selling crack from under my bed. That's the stupidity going around, and the team didn't say anything." He almost smiled. "That's nice, I guess."

"You mean you don't really have a gun?" *Because I know better,* Luke didn't say. He held his breath.

"No." Eddie rolled his eyes, and Luke's stomach sank. "I mean, I do, but it's not on me and it's not loaded. It's never been loaded." Eddie threw open his jacket and shook his pockets, as though a semi-automatic might fall out onto the floor. "My father has a permit and he never bought bullets because it was never supposed to shoot anyone. You wouldn't believe how much guns scare him. He wouldn't even let it stay in their bedroom, but she needed to have it in the house. *Where* in the house didn't matter."

"Why?" He was pretty sure he already knew who "she" had to be.

Eddie rubbed his hands across his face and his eyes and suddenly looked so tired. "It was supposed to make her feel safe. She hasn't felt like that for a long time."

Luke thought of walking through a house without being invited. He started to get up. "Eddie, you don't have to tell me about—"

"No, clearly I do," Eddie said, his hand out. He spoke as if he was reading from a list, but his hand didn't stop tapping the entire time. "I was really young when we came to America. All of my memories start in Chicago, but my parents spent years in a refugee camp in Ghana—it was called Buduburam—and, before that, too many years watching their lives in Liberia disappear. They were from professional families before the Wars and then—" He blinked at the ceiling until his eyes stopped shining. "When they finally got out, they spent most of my life living in a room in my uncle's basement in Chicago before they saved enough to get their own place. It probably doesn't make sense to you or to Wes or anyone else, but for my mom, in a new city and new home, having some money outside of a bank and a useless gun felt like—"

"Like safety."

Eddie pointed at him, as if he'd won a prize, but his voice was tired and so sad. "We were fine. We were *coping*. My parents never talk about the Wars, let alone PTSD, but we were okay, and then the whole lacrosse team got involved." He waved toward the field with a tight, sarcastic smile. "She picked me up after practice. She never came to school, especially on the hard days, but my little brother had to go to a doctor's appointment, and she didn't have a choice, you know?" He gathered himself, and Luke didn't say a word. "She was in a bad place from a thunderstorm the day before, and I guess a car backfired the in the parking lot, so by the time I got out there she couldn't stop crying. It would have passed, I think, but the other parents didn't react well. They got scared because she couldn't say what was wrong. Then I freaked out, and Wes filled in the rest."

Eddie swallowed, and Luke saw his mom, in bed and motionless. "Wes isn't good at being a human being, but he really isn't stupid," Eddie said. "The mom stuff started because it worked. I guess he was looking for something that would throw me off, and I let him find it. It started with little stuff like, 'Hey, is your mom coming today?' I didn't know if it was all in my head, but then he was all, 'There's crazy, and then there's crazy, you know? Of course you know.' If I'd brushed it off, he would have let it go, but I didn't. I couldn't." He blinked at the ceiling, and his eyes were red and shining. "After we saw him in the hallway, when he was going on about the talent show, it got worse. I don't know. It got more personal. He started making jokes about how I had a special asylum reservation waiting for me when I turned eighteen."

Luke clapped a hand over his mouth. He thought about permanent markers and black lines on pale skin. After that day, Wes had gotten worse, and Luke had made that happen, just as he'd confused Eddie on the field. He'd talked about the gun. He'd seen the gun in the first place. It all came spiraling back to Luke. And he'd been so proud.

Eddie kept going, quietly, as if Luke wasn't even in the room. "When I ran into him during the game, he sang 'happy birthday' under his breath, except it was 'happy birthday, dear schizo.' That's when—" he gestured back at the field. "You saw the rest." He leaned back against the board. "I put him in the hospital, but he still won and he never even touched me."

No. Luke couldn't move. He could say whatever he wanted about superpowers and confusion, but it all came down to one simple fact: He'd seen Eddie with a gun and turned him into a monster. One look and he'd thought *this man is a bank robber, gang member, drug dealer.* Luke swallowed bile. If he'd been in anyone else's room, would he have jumped to that conclusion? What if it had been Wes's room or Dee's? He didn't have to answer that question. "Is that really what you took away from all this?" Luke asked. That couldn't be the moral of the story. "He spent, what, months giving you shit, and it's all on you?"

"No," Eddie said, without conviction. "I'm just—I shouldn't have let it get to me."

"You can't control that." When Luke was little, he hadn't told people that Lizzy was in the hospital. He hadn't wanted to deal with how they'd look at him, as though he should have been more upset. "We get embarrassed about weird stuff."

"Embarrassed?" Eddie dropped his hands, stunned. "Is—is that what you think it was? Do you think I was embarrassed or, what, *ashamed* of my mother? Screw you." He said it the way he'd tell Luke that he'd misspelled a word, like a fact. "I'm not ashamed of her because she's never done anything wrong. She's coping. I am ashamed of how people react to her. Even my good, enlightened teammates wouldn't look me in the eye for a week after she showed up, kind of like you're doing right now. I'm ashamed for how I *know* people will react before I say anything and, yeah, I get to save a little bit of shame for myself. I should have just trusted her."

"What?" Luke asked. Eddie wouldn't meet his eyes.

"I didn't tell my mom about the audition, okay? I didn't tell anyone I didn't have to tell because I didn't want it getting back to my parents," he said in a rush with his hands tight against the whiteboard. "It sounds stupid when I say it out loud. Don't get me wrong. They went to see everything I did in Chicago, but there's a big difference between a kid who acts and a son who wants to be an actor. Acting kids do other things with their lives. Actors starve. There's nothing *safe* about that."

His voice dropped so low, Luke wasn't sure he was supposed to be listening. The shine in his eyes turned into tears, and Eddie didn't wipe them away. "I didn't want them to have to deal with it until I knew it was for sure. If I got the internship, I could say that I was going to be okay. I could promise to be okay. And now? I haven't even seen them yet. By the time I got home, they were already in bed, but she must have seen the news. She watches Channel 5 when she wakes up, but she doesn't have a cell phone. Neither of them does, so I haven't had to—I don't even know—" his voice cracked. "How do I say, 'this is what I did for you?'"

Eddie stopped too close. He planted his hands on the desk, one on either side of Luke's folded legs, but Luke couldn't look away. This wasn't a challenge. This was an actual question begging for an actual answer from a boy in tears, and Luke only had a pile of things he couldn't say.

I'm sorry. I'm sorry. I'm sorry. Please stop shaking. I'm sorry I'm an idiot.

If the directors at your audition can't see you, then they're idiots. You're the only beautiful person in a school full of idiots.

"You're wrong."

Luke didn't realize he actually said anything until Eddie flinched and, by then, it was too late. "I know that's not what you want to hear, but you're dead wrong. Sure, actors aren't safe. They pretend to be other people for a living, but you aren't just *actors*. You're, you're Edward Sankawulo, and what's safer than doing the only thing you were ever supposed to do? When you get on stage, that's the only place you were ever supposed to be. I don't know your mom, but if she knows you and loves you as much as you say she does, then she has to know that's who you are. You are Mercutio and that conman with the weird name, and you *make* that safe because, for you, it's like breathing. So yeah, you're wrong. You're trying to make her feel safe by taking yourself out of the equation, but it's the rest of the world that's scary. Eddie, your success is the only safe bet she's ever made."

Luke was crying. He started in a whisper and ended on a sob and half of his words were lost between gasps for breath. Eddie never moved back. "You don't know that," he said. "You don't—"

"Yes, I do. You—why do you think I'm still here?"

Luke wasn't sure who moved forward first, but they landed in the middle, off-center and off-balance. Luke was half past Eddie's mouth, and Eddie was practically on Luke's cheek, but they were kissing. Luke kissed Eddie Sankawulo and for a universe of seconds he couldn't have found his own hands. They existed somewhere; it didn't matter, because Edward Sankawulo breathed him in; his mouth was open as if Luke were air. His hand held Luke's jaw, as he stood over the desk, their desk in their room, and the touch pulled up from Luke's gut a curling, delicate heat that squeezed his heart and tingled under his skin. Under his hands, Luke became real and made of light. He made Luke precious.

Luke caught his breath in a gasp, a quiet "oh."

This is who Lucas Aday is. He kisses Eddie Sankawulo. He blinked, and found Eddie's head down and his eyes closed tight. He was breathing so quietly Luke couldn't hear him over the blood that rang in his ears, but he felt it. Little gusts of breath burst against his skin, filled with *want,* and it took everything Luke had not to kiss him again.

"Yeah, *oh*," Eddie echoed, his eyes still closed. "Okay. Okay. I—" He bit his lip in a smile. "I'm going to say something, and I need you not to freak out." He opened his eyes, and Luke had never seen eyes so brown or so close. "I have to go."

Luke eased back and nodded slowly. "Yeah. Okay." Cool. They kissed, and Eddie had to go. He couldn't imagine why that might be upsetting. At least Eddie wasn't still crying. He wiped under his eyes with his palms and leaned back into Luke's space. "I'm getting mixed messages."

Eddie blinked, and his hands landed on Luke's shoulders. "Captain," he said, slowly. "I'm going to go because I got all dressed up for my audition and if I stick around I'm either going to start crying or I'm going to kiss you again." His pursed lips bloomed into a grin. "With us, you never know. But, either way,

I'm missing my audition." He pressed a kiss to Luke's forehead. The kiss smelled of sweetness and leather and him. "I promise I'm not going for mixed anything." He watched until Luke went hot behind the neck and smiled back. *Point made.*

"I suppose," Luke said. "If you promise."

"Cross my heart and hope to die, Captain." He pushed off the desk and leaned down to grab his bag, just far enough away to avoid Luke's kick at his leg. "I am going to go, but later I am going to call and prove that my intentions are entirely honorable." He laughed as Luke's eyebrows shot toward the ceiling. "For now. We can revisit that later."

Eddie held up a hand and backed into the hallway with a grin that looked as if it might pull him apart at the seams. He glowed, and, if he hadn't turned to go, Luke might have come apart with him. Eddie's eyes lingered on Luke's face; his happiness was as intimate as a kiss. Finally, Eddie tapped his hand against the doorframe and then he was gone.

Luke hopped off the desk and followed Eddie to the door. He grabbed the doorframe just below where Eddie had tapped and hung there, holding on to the metal and letting his body tingle with joy. He watched Eddie run through the empty hall until he turned the corner, and then there were only steps that echoed against the tiles. He didn't turn around once, and Luke almost couldn't handle the joy.

Luke knew Eddie didn't turn because he couldn't. If he looked back, he would want to come back and keep kissing. He knew Eddie wanted to keep kissing so much he would have missed his audition and, most importantly, he knew Eddie wanted to keep kissing *him*. Luke swung from the doorway like a five-year-old on a jungle gym and let the joy slip through his veins. He'd never been drunk, but he could hope real drunkenness felt something like this. He could be drunk and dizzy on Eddie's voice and Eddie's eyes and Eddie's arms under his hands.

He giggled when he realized the best part: He had no idea if he'd stopped anything during the kiss. He could have stopped time or space. Hell, he could have knocked down a building next door with the power of his mind and he wouldn't have noticed. "I'm sorry, officer," he would have explained. "I have no idea what happened after school last night. I understand that the gymnasium exploded, but you see, I kissed my—" He didn't know what Eddie was in relation to him. But there was a relation. Eddie was his *something* and the lack of a real name didn't make it any less real.

"He's my something," Luke whispered, and he grinned down the hall until he could swear the hall was grinning back.

"Is he?" A voice came from the hallway, from where the wide expanse turned the corner into the junior commons.

"Dee?"

She couldn't have been there a moment ago. No one had been in the hallway when Eddie ran toward the doors. Luke would have seen her if she'd watched him go. But when they had been in the classroom, she could have been anywhere. The door had been open. Luke wouldn't have noticed if she'd stood outside and screamed at the top of her lungs.

She had her arms and ankles crossed, almost casually, as she leaned against the wall, but there was nothing casual about her voice. "As long as he's a *something*, a super-special something, I guess it's all just fine." She laughed under her breath, and it was brittle enough to break against his skin. "Hi, Bestie," she said.

He'd never heard that word sound like a slap. "I missed you today. Not all day, because I wasn't here all day. You wouldn't know, but I spent the morning going back and forth from class to the hospital, because at first Wes was perfectly fine and then he wasn't."

Luke's knuckles went pale against the doorframe. She couldn't have been saying what it sounded like she was saying, because it wasn't possible.

Dee bit the inside of her lip. "Don't look at me like that; he's not dead. I do assume you care even if other people don't." She walked toward him, and Luke shrank into the doorway.

"How long have you been out here?" He really wanted to ask how long she'd been watching. She wrapped her arms around herself, and her glare hardened as Luke spoke. "Never mind. I don't care. You just have to listen." He pointed down the silent hallway. "Eddie didn't mean to hurt him."

Her eyes went wide over a flinty smile. "Oh, it's Eddie now," she said, "Not Edward or 'that one sociopath,' but Eddie. Is he *your Eddie*, Luke? Is he your little secret?"

Luke couldn't look her in the eye. *How could she be so wrong and so right at the same time?* "Wes isn't some innocent victim here. You know that," he said, quietly.

"Oh, my God." She spun away until she was yelling into open space, and it wasn't for the sake of drama or flair. She just couldn't bear to look at him. "Does it matter? I don't care why you landed on *Eddie's* face, but you clearly didn't just meet him. You've been hooking up with a secret drug dealer for God knows how long, and you didn't think for one second that it might be a good idea to tell us? We have been keeping your big, world-changing secret like saints for months, and you couldn't bring yourself to tell us that you'd started dating a guy who keeps an Uzi under his bed."

"It's not an Uzi—"

"Who cares?" She cut him off, and he stopped as her shoulders shook. "Marcos likes you, Luke. I mean he really likes you. I thought that you felt the same way, or that at least if you didn't feel the same way you'd have the decency not to start some secret thing behind his back. That's wrong, and you know it."

"What? No. Marcos is fine." As soon as the words came out of his mouth, Luke knew he should have stopped.

In a breath, she turned, and the anger drained from her cheeks. "He knew," she said.

"Dee."

"No. I'm right. Marcos knew about this *thing* you had going on with the gun nut. He knew."

"But I didn't tell him! He just knew." Luke stepped toward her, half afraid that she'd run away. It wasn't his fault that Marcos knew him better than he knew himself. "I wasn't even trying to keep it from you." *Except when I was.*

Dee held her sides as if they might split apart. "Good. That makes it all better then," she said. "You two had this brilliant, dangerous, idiotic little secret, and no one thought that maybe—" Her eyes dropped as her voice grew too waterlogged for words. Even in the hospital, Dee hadn't cried. "I looked for you. When I came back, after the hospital, everyone was gone, and I looked for you, because I thought maybe you could share." Luke stared in confusion. He didn't have anything to share. "I know that's probably not how your whatever—Hold—works, but I thought maybe if you could stop time, you could maybe wrap me up in it and let it stop for me too, because right now he doesn't even look like Wes. He's, like this little body that's lucky to be alive, like he could just shut off." She found his eyes, and the shields snapped back into place. "I wanted it all to stop for a few a few minutes, and you weren't there because you were off in your special little room having a special little moment with the monster that put him there."

"I—"

"Shut up. *Shut up.* I know Wes is a little shit. Wes. I, I know he's not some angel, but he's my little shit, okay? He's *mine* and no one, not you and definitely not that asshole, gets to take him away from me."

"I'm sorry." He wasn't sure what he was sorry for. He was sorry for not telling her and sorry for not realizing that there was something to tell. He was sorry for not being there when she needed him, that most of all. He didn't know if he could share the Hold, but for her he would have tried. "It's only that—" Luke looked down the hall as if Eddie might have been waiting at the other end. "I know it doesn't make sense to you, but I care about him too. I care about him a lot, and I know he's not family. It's not the same at all, but I wouldn't be okay if I lost him either."

Dee's mouth fell into a thin, pale line. "You should get used to it."

"I should what?" Luke backed up against the wall.

A second ago, Dee had been screaming and shaking, but this was worse. This was stillness and control. "The police should have arrested him yesterday," she said, quietly. "They held him for questioning, but then they let him go. Like they think Wes just fell over and smashed himself into a bench. That's not how it works, Luke. And no, it doesn't matter if he didn't mean it." She walked forward until she was in his space. "Your Eddie has to explain himself. He has to tell me why some innocent guy just happened to attack his own teammate and why he just happened to have a pile of money under his bed that he probably stole with his shiny, innocent gun."

Luke swallowed a gasp. She wasn't listening. She wasn't even making sense. Her two points didn't have anything to do with each other, unless—Dee stared him down, and Luke couldn't look away. "The police don't know about the gun," he said, his voice flat. "The police wouldn't know about the gun because no one would tell them, right?" Just as no one would tell Becca and she wouldn't tell half the school. He couldn't breathe. "Right, Dee?"

"I looked for you," she said, and the shudder came back in her lower lip. "I couldn't find you when she called and I couldn't stop thinking about him." She jerked her head down the hall to where Eddie had long since ceased to be. Her eyes had gone glassy. "Your special friend could come into school any day he wanted and blow us all away. Becca was right. You were the one who said that he had a gun, and I wasn't doing anything to stop him."

"Who called, Dee?" He stepped forward. His hand hovered near her shoulder. "Who did you talk to?"

"My mom," she said. "I called my mom. I didn't know she'd call the police, but I ..." Luke didn't need her to complete the thought. When Dee knew, she didn't care. Of course her mom called the police. That's what monsters deserved. "She knew he'd be leaving school soon because I saw him *with you* and she knew he had a gun, but that's all. Everyone already knew about the game. I didn't tell her anything that wasn't true."

"Dee." Luke stared, and Dee glared back, her jaw set. She didn't understand. She couldn't understand. Dee didn't say that he had access to a gun or that there was a gun stashed away in his home, probably under three layers of dust. She said "had," and Dee and her mother were nothing if not absolutely, perfectly precise.

Eddie might very well not make it to the audition or to the theater. He wasn't going to get to practice on the roof because, according to the North Grove police department, Edward Sankawulo was walking the streets at dusk, dangerously unstable, and carrying a gun. If he made a wrong move, or if he didn't move fast enough, or just because he was black and armed—

Luke ran.

CHAPTER TWENTY-ONE

LUKE WASN'T A RUNNER, BUT he ran.

The tiled school floor gave way to the parking lot and then the sidewalk as he sprinted toward the only place Eddie could have gone.

Up.

He had two hours until his audition and he'd be on the roof of the theater, staring out over the edge and ranting about soldiers to the setting sun.

God. He loved that stupid, stupid, pain-in-the-ass Mercutio monologue. Luke never had to make him practice that one; Eddie sank into Shakespeare like coming home. They'd never talked about the fact that Mercutio died.

He closed his eyes as he ran up Dakota Avenue and into the wind from the lake. If he cut through Carpenter Park and the thirtieth block of Colorado Avenue he'd practically be on *En el Borde*'s doorstep. He could make the fifteen-minute walk in a ten-minute sprint if he stayed on his feet. By the time he passed the park playground, his chest burned, and his eyes watered until the buildings blurred into a stream of grays, yellows and blues. If there were people, they blurred too, and if they saw him running, he didn't care. His hands went numb, and his feet chilled through from puddles he didn't avoid.

As he turned the corner of Brunswick Avenue, the theater emerged across the street. The old building rose from behind a line of apartment buildings, six stories of white brick against the gray sky. The front door popped out from the rest of the street in stop-sign red, and the theater name, on the side of the building, disappeared behind a pair of police cars each parked with two wheels up on the curb.

Two empty police cars.

Luke stopped running. Blood screamed in his ears, louder than the cars on Twenty-ninth Street, but voices echoed from the rooftop above the theater. He didn't know them. They were just strange voices yelling, and none of them was Eddie.

He squinted up at the edge of roof. If he blocked the rest with his hands, there was only the white and the long line where blue spots moved back and forth across the edge of the rooftop. Then they disappeared, and he was left with the line where the concrete met the sky.

Luke had to move. He couldn't move. The space where the blue shirt had been stood empty, and the drivers on the street kept on driving, as if nothing had changed. Couldn't they see that there was something very, very wrong over their heads? He had to go into the theater or, better yet, find someone who could help. On his own, he was useless. No matter what was happening above his head, he couldn't do anything about it. Even if he made the world stop for a minute or ten minutes or a million minutes, he'd eventually let go, and it would all be hell again. It would be a disaster. Someone would disappear again, and if he had to take that one more time—

"—I don't know what you're talking about!"

That voice. *I know that voice.*

He'd missed everything before and he missed what was said after, but Eddie was on that roof. Luke stared straight up the building, as if he could will Eddie to the edge to tell him he was okay. He couldn't do it, and not just because he didn't have the power. Eddie wasn't okay. His voice sounded too small to be his own. For a second, Luke wondered if that's how Eddie sounded to his mother. Maybe, for her, he never stopped being a little boy.

Eddie's voice echoed again, and Luke was halfway up the second flight of stairs before he realized that he'd moved. He made it halfway up the third flight before he noticed that the echoes had gone silent. He passed a woman in a green blouse who was frozen in the doorway to the fourth floor with her face caught in a placid smile, and kept climbing. So there it was. He didn't choose to use the Hold or tell the world to stop, it just did, somewhere between the receptionist and the stairs.

At the top, Luke fell through the doorway and headlong into a man frozen on the other side. The officer's shirt was the same color as the blue flashes he'd seen from the street. He stood taller than Luke; his features were sharp and small like the cherub figurines on his mother's shelves. Along the edge of the roof, a second white officer stood frozen in profile; her dark ponytail was thrown behind her head in arrested motion. She stood nearly ten feet from the door, but the man could have whispered in Luke's face. His mouth stood open mid-scream, and his hands held a gun pointed toward the skyline. Together, they formed an almost perfect right angle between the woman, the man and the boy with his hands in the air.

Luke knew that back.

No.

The sob caught as he sucked in a mouthful of cold air. *No.* That boy should have had a jacket on and a suit coat. It was cold. He must have left them on another part of the roof, before people showed up to scream and wave guns at his back. He stood in his black shirtsleeves and his best shoes with his back to the door as he stared into the gray sky. Luke didn't know what Eddie saw over the edge of the roof, but he couldn't have turned without looking down the barrel of a gun.

Without breathing, Luke inched toward Eddie's back and around his body. No one else moved, but the Hold already tugged on the back of his mind like an anchor. If he tripped or lost focus, he might let go, and that couldn't happen. Not now. He focused so hard on control that he didn't prepare to see Eddie's face. Eddie had his eyes screwed shut so tight wrinkles pulled at his temples. His open palms had stopped near his ears and his mouth was open just far enough that he could have been whispering—or praying. *Hands up. Don't shoot.*

"Eddie?" he said. He had no plan. He had a heartbeat in his throat and sweat freezing on his neck. "I know you can hear me. I saw you on the field during the game and that day in your room. You looked and you saw me even when nobody else could." Luke wasn't sure if he was talking about the Hold. He braced himself on Eddie's side, just above his waist, and did not cry. "You saw me and I, I made everything awful. I didn't know I was doing it, but that doesn't make it any better. I'm sorry. I know you don't want to, but I need you to open your eyes."

Eddie didn't move. He stood with his tight face and his frightened hands. "Damn it, Eddie." He couldn't leave this boy or drag him away. "I know you're in there. Just move. You don't have to do it for me. I don't deserve that." He squeezed Eddie's arm so hard it had to hurt. Fabric crumpled under his hand. "If you've ever listened to me, listen to me now. I will work harder than I've ever worked to make everything all right, but I can't do that unless you open your eyes, you stubborn sonofabitch."

Wake up. Wake up. Wake up.

"I'm not—" Eddie's eyes cracked, and Luke's chest cracked wide. "Don't do that." His eyes twitched from Luke to the sky to the ground in a bleary haze. "Ow."

"Are you okay?" Luke ducked as he lost his balance. "Did I hurt your arm?"

"No." Eddie squinted, as if the muscles in his face weren't his own. "You called me a sonofabitch." He sounded out the word one syllable at a time, like a foreign word. Son-of-a-bitch. "That's—I don't think I deserve that. You're way more—*Oh.*"

Eddie looked over his shoulder and stopped at the officer aiming a gun at his back. "They're here." He pointed at Luke's feet. He was shaking. "You're here. You're here now, too, but why aren't they—" He turned back and blinked with groggy focus into the sunset, like a child shaking off a bad dream. "Luke, I don't understand."

"I know," Luke said, quietly. If he knew anything, he knew that was true. "I know you're confused, but I need you to listen to me. We have to go."

Eddie didn't show any sign that he'd heard him. "It was you?" And his eyes went wide. "It was you during the game and during rehearsals and—" He found Luke's gaze, and the clarity there landed like a blow. "You were in my home. I thought it was in my head. You came into my room." He stumbled backward, and Luke let him go. He nodded, and a light disappeared from Eddie's eyes. "And you never said anything."

No, I never said a thing, until I told my friends about your gun.

Luke had had a dream like this once, not long ago, when his chest was tight and the sweat seeped through his shirt. In the dream, he was eleven and he was supposed to watch his sister. It was dream logic, upended, but his parents left him to watch his sister as they did a million times, but this time she disappeared. Luke was supposed to hold on to her wheelchair while they were gone; that was the only rule of the dream. He couldn't stop holding on. He couldn't let go, but he forgot.

He blinked, and his hands were empty, pawing the air where her chair was supposed to be. He ran out into the front yard and screamed down the street as though she might come back, as if she might be waiting for him and laughing, but she wasn't there. He let go and he knew deeper than he knew his name that she wouldn't come back. He'd wakened screaming gibberish at his bedroom ceiling, with tears caked on his cheeks. For three years, that dream had come back, always exactly the same.

This was worse. In the dream, he was alone.

"How?" Eddie pointed back at the officers on his right and at his back. He didn't have to explain. They were there and they weren't moving.

"This isn't the time —" Luke said, quietly. The cops still had guns.

"Tell me how," Eddie said again, and his eyes weren't confused anymore.

"I don't know." Luke didn't know anything. "I don't know how it works or why and I don't know why you can—" His voice cracked, and he bit his lip. "I just know that I can stop everything and I mean everything—people, time, all of it—but I can't stop you. I didn't mean to mess with your head, not during the game and absolutely not—" He swallowed. "Not in your home with your family, but I did. That was me." Eddie looked away, as if Luke were too much to see, and Luke didn't blame him. If Eddie never talked to him again they wouldn't be even, but Luke would miss those eyes. "It's my fault you were confused during the game and this is all my fault too, but it doesn't have to stay this way." He held out his hand, palm up, and let it hang in the air. "Come with me."

"No."

"Eddie. I'm not leaving you here." And he couldn't stay. He could only imagine how little it would help if he dropped the Hold and they suddenly had to explain why some other punk had appeared out of nowhere. The headlines practically wrote themselves: "Gunmen Menace North Grove in Coordinated Attack," or better yet, "Thugs Threaten Area Theater." And there was no need to mention that they would both be gone by the time the newspapers hit the pavement.

"Then that's your choice, but I can't go." Eddie turned from Luke's edge of the roof and walked toward the policeman near the stairs. He wobbled, but he kept moving. When he was level with the gun, he peered into the officer's face. Luke forced himself to watch. "Why does this man think I need to be arrested?"

"He thinks you have a gun. I didn't tell them that, but someone did and—" He made himself return Eddie's stare. "And they think you have a gun."

His face a blank, Eddie turned back to the officer. "Guns are legal. I could have a gun."

"I know."

"So they think I'm going to do something with it? They think I'm going to hurt someone?" Eddie flinched as he asked the question, as if it hurt to form the words.

"I guess they do," Luke muttered. Or they thought he was a Black Man with a Gun, but he didn't need to say that out loud.

Eddie nodded anyway and slowly backed away from the barrel of the gun. "That's why I can't go."

"That doesn't make any sense!" Luke felt himself losing control, not of the Hold, but of himself.

"Of course it does." He adjusted the name badge on the officer's chest and, for the first time, wonder flashed across his face. He was moving and the officer couldn't do a thing to stop him. "According to you, Mr. Hagerty and whatshername over there think I'm carrying a gun. Fine." He turned back, his mouth as straight as a line. "I have never owned a gun, I have never carried a gun and I absolutely don't have a gun on my person, so no. I'm not going anywhere."

Luke gaped. Eddie meant it. He literally looked down the barrel of a frozen gun pointed at his head and refused to move. "You're staying here because, theoretically, you could have a gun you don't even want?"

"No," Eddie said, his hands on his hips. Where Luke expected anger he only heard exhaustion. "I'm staying because I didn't do anything wrong. Yesterday was different. Regardless of what part you played in that mess, I made that mistake. That was mine, but today, I'm just a guy getting ready for an audition and if I run they'll think I'm guilty." His voice was certain, and scared. "If I disappear, they're going to find me again, and then I'll be the guy that ran."

"Then don't run." Luke's pulse raced in his ears, and his voice was desperate even to his own ears, but he couldn't keep this going forever. Already, the Hold's pull at the back of his mind had turned into a piercing ache. Arguing with Eddie wasn't easy in the best of circumstances, but the Hold made it feel like juggling knives. In one minute or five, either the argument or the Hold had to drop, and Luke didn't know which would go first. "I made this happen, so let me fix it," he said. "If you don't want to come with me, I can just take the guns away, so that they can't hurt you, but that might not be enough. You need to not be here when these cops wake up. Please." Luke held out his hand. "Eddie, I know I have no right to say this, but there are other people who need you to be okay tomorrow. Do this for your mom."

Eddie's jaw clenched, and for a brief, horrible, second Luke was sure he would say no. He'd refuse to leave, and Luke would have no choice but to let go. The thought alone was enough to steal his breath, until Eddie looked back.

"You're right," he said, quietly. "You have no right to say that," but he reached for Luke's hand. His jaw was tense, and he wouldn't look Luke in the eye, but also he didn't let go.

Luke gave an experimental tug, and Eddie followed him toward the stairs, one step behind. They ducked around the officer near the door, and Luke was afraid that he'd knock him over by mistake. All they needed was for a cop to get magically hurt by Edward Sankawulo, disappearing felon. Eddie was unsteady on his feet as they stepped over the threshold, but Luke didn't look back. He just squeezed his hand when the door closed behind their backs.

Thank you. Thank you. Thank you for not making me leave you.

When they pushed open the door on the first floor and stepped back out into Twenty-ninth Street, Eddie squeezed back.

THEY RAN FOR FIVE BREATHLESS blocks before Luke stopped waiting for the cops to follow and six blocks before a car nearly ran Eddie into a curb.

He'd stepped off the sidewalk onto Idaho Avenue and jumped back when a Subaru took the turn at full speed. He spun to where Luke had fallen behind and pointed at the car. "How long have they been back?" Eddie yelled. The cars were moving again. They weren't the only people in the world. Not anymore.

"Two blocks!" Luke called back. As soon as they got off the busy streets and into the neighborhood, Luke had had to let it go. The farther they got from the theater, the more apparent it had been that the Hold had reached *everywhere*. They could have run for miles in their frozen city, and he'd felt it all. Even after he'd let time snap back into place, the back of his mind ached like an open wound. For two blocks, they'd been running next to moving cars, and Eddie hadn't noticed. "Be careful," he'd said, too late, and felt ridiculous. What did careful even look like on the run from the cops?

Luckily, there weren't many people on the street. The darkness and the bad weather were enough to cut the lazy street traffic down to a trickle, and even the people who were out and about had their own places to be. They almost ran into a middle-aged woman in a full-length parka at the corner of Jersey Street, but she was moving just as quickly toward the bus stop and didn't bat an eye. Two rude teenagers didn't warrant attention.

"Excuse me," Luke muttered and directed Eddie down a side street and back toward the school. His single, half-baked plan, invented between the second and third block on the run, might have been beyond horrible, but it was all he had, and it meant more running. When they had ducked down two more streets and past a line of familiar houses, he grabbed the back of Eddie's shirt and tugged him to a stop behind a short line of naked elms. There was no one on the street as far as Luke could see, but the cover was still a relief. "Wait here," he said. "I have to make a call."

"Right now?" Eddie said, in disbelief. He had a hand to his chest as he hunched over to catch his breath. "Who could you possibly have to call right now?"

Luke swallowed and pulled out his phone. "You're not going to like the answer, but I have to call Deanna Corelli because this is her house, and I have to convince her to let us in."

CHAPTER TWENTY-TWO

LUKE MIGHT HAVE UNDERESTIMATED HOW much Eddie didn't like that idea. They stood outside of Dee's house for fifteen minutes, and Luke spent the first five leaving Dee messages while he waited for Eddie to talk to him.

Finally, she texted that the key was under the mat. *I know*, he said to his phone. That key had been there since middle school, but getting in was beside the point.

The point, every point, was Eddie, and Eddie needed more time. "Tell me again what happened," he said, with his head down and his shoulders tense. "Tell me what she did." The *tell me what you did*, was implied and also the question he couldn't ask and Luke couldn't answer: Why should I trust her with my life?

In the end, Luke entered in front, with Eddie at his back and with a clear set of directions at the ready. He would be the mouthpiece in Dee's house, but this wasn't his mission.

They found Dee waiting in the kitchen with her phone clutched in her hand. She was hunkered down behind the table with the corner at her back, as far as she could stand from the door while technically existing in the same room. From the doorway, the line of cereal boxes looked like a cardboard bunker, but that was an accident of fate. Dee's family always had empty boxes on the kitchen table, just as she had clean laundry piled on the sofa. It wasn't messiness so much as a consistent ethos. Like its people, things in Corelli-house tended to get halfway from one place to another before getting distracted. Except Dee. If she stopped in the middle, it was because she meant it.

And if she placed every inch of the kitchen between herself and Lucas Aday, she definitely meant it.

Luke made it three steps into the kitchen before he balked. Most of his plan, such as it was, focused on getting Dee to let him in, but he hadn't been prepared to see her.

"Thanks for, you know." He pointed at the door and shoved his hands into his pockets. "I don't think the police figured out where we went because, um, they didn't actually see us go anywhere. I did the thing—the Hold—and we were pretty far away from the theater when it dropped." She had her arms crossed and was looking at him and, at the same time, she wasn't. Her gaze went through him and came out the other side. "I don't know where they'd go next. They might try Eddie's house or maybe go back to the school. Do you think they might call your mom back?" Luke was aware that he was babbling. He was filling air, but he hadn't seen enough *Law and Order* for this.

"Sit down," Dee said and pushed a chair out with one foot. The treads squeaked across the floor. "Before your thank-yous, before questions, and way the hell before you tell me about the great escape, you need to sit down and start from the beginning.

Talk. Luke, you sit right here." She pointed to the chair she'd kicked. "Your friend can sit wherever he likes."

Eddie sucked in a breath, and Luke had to grab the chair to stop himself from kicking it back. "My friend's name is Eddie," he said, "and you can't speak to him like that. If you do, we're leaving. I deserve it. I didn't tell you the truth, but he didn't do anything." *And we almost killed him.*

Eddie stood in the doorway and his hand tapped at his side. With anyone else, this would have been the time when he'd have stepped in to smooth the way with all of his warmth trained on his new best friend. Now, as Luke spoke, all of Eddie's attention landed on Dee, but it was cold steel. She watched, and he didn't look away.

She frowned, her mouth tense and thin, but she got up and pulled out the chair closest to the door. "I'm serious," she said. "Less than an hour ago, I basically said I wanted you dead, and now my best friend thinks that my home is the best place for you to be safe. Sound accurate?" She turned back to Luke, and he nodded. It wasn't entirely true, but she was close. There were other ways to make this better, but Luke and Dee had to be the ones to do it. She had to look Eddie in the eye. Dee sighed and crossed her arms tighter over her chest. "Perfect. Given that blazingly clear logic, I would like an explanation. Luke, start talking. Everything. Now."

So he spoke. He started on the day that he first came back to school and barreled forward though months of missed practices and silence. He hesitated at the room where he threw his backpack at the board, but she'd asked for everything, and they both deserved that and more. Once he'd gotten through the first Hold, with the crying and the first sea of frozen faces, it got easier. He just stared down at the long crack where the leaves of the kitchen table fit together and let the stories come.

When he got to Eddie's bedroom, when he walked through the Hold, Dee went pale. When he got to Wes in the hallway, with taunts about parents and words crawling up his arms, she sat on the windowsill, hard. Eddie could have been doing anything, for all that Luke knew. He couldn't bear to look. It wasn't shame, not exactly. He just couldn't talk about rehearsals or the game without sounding like a love-soaked mess. Even when he kept the story short and to the point, feelings seeped in around the edges. There had to be a reason that he wrote, "leave him alone" on Wes's arms or drew Eddie's hands in his sketchbook. It was just a fact. He couldn't go anywhere near their classroom without making it perfectly clear that Eddie took his breath away.

As he approached today's mess of a rehearsal, he forced himself to bring Eddie in. "I don't know if I should keep going," he said. There was so much that wasn't his in their last meeting—the harassment, the audition jitters, Eddie's mom—but Eddie nodded him on. His gaze stayed, intense, on Luke's face, but it wasn't filled with anger. It was just *full*.

Luke got as far as the game before he had to stop. He whispered, "happy birthday, dear schizo," and anything else felt irrelevant. "You know the rest," he said, even though Dee wasn't watching. When he'd got to Wes's jokes about Eddie's mom and the "special asylum," she'd covered her eyes and hadn't looked back. He wondered if she was thinking about how Wes used to love playing jail with her Barbies. He'd lock them up over and over, until he ran out of ways to set them free. Or until he forgot.

Luke blinked, and Dee was on her feet. She said, "I'll be right back. I'm sorry," and reached into her pocket while scrubbing at her cheeks with her other hand. By the time she got to the kitchen door, her phone was already at her ear. "Please, don't move."

He didn't. For all he knew, she was in the living room calling the police, but they didn't have anywhere else to go. At Eddie's house the police might show up any second, and at Luke's, he'd have to explain everything all over again. That thought alone made him want to curl up and hide. *No.* He'd dumped all his cards on the table, and there was nothing to do but let the wall clock tick seconds into the silence. That, and avoid thinking about why Eddie wasn't talking.

Finally, it came. "Do you have it with you?" Eddie asked, and Luke must have looked bewildered. "The notebook, from rehearsals. Do you have it on you, or—" He nodded toward the floor, where Luke usually dumped his backpack. "I'd like to see it." There wasn't any urgency in the question, just curiosity, as though he'd given up finding answers and wanted to see how far the rabbit hole would go.

Luke reached into his jacket pocket, the big one on the inside, and handed it over without a word. He only had the little notebook with him. He'd left the large rehearsal notebook in the classroom by his bag, but if Eddie wanted what Luke thought he wanted, then the little one would do well enough. Eddie flipped through the whole thing, from cover to cover, page by page. He leaned over the kitchen table and spread out the little sketchpad like a butterfly on a pin. He flipped past quick sketches of Luke's life BE—before Eddie—or maybe WL—with Lizzy: a misshapen mug from his mom's pottery class, Dee's profile, an early sketch of Ms. Marvel (alias Kamala Kahn) he'd done before he drew her on his bedroom ceiling, little flashes of nothing. But then he slowed. Luke didn't need to look. First there were pages of sketchy hands, then arms, and finally Eddie's face mid-monologue. By the last drawing, his drawn chin was turned up toward the corner of the page; the shading of light appeared on his cheeks and the bridge of his nose. His lips were parted, and his eyes were wide with Mercutio's fear.

Stunned and stunning.

He'd stared at that picture for what could have been hours, trying to map the alchemy between Eddie's bare throat and the line of his jaw. Then he'd drawn it again, and now he watched Eddie looking at himself. He had to register his reaction to the drawing. His disgust had to show somehow, but his face remained fixed, so focused he may have been reading a play.

"Is that what I look like?" he asked, finally, with his eyes on the page.

Luke faltered. "I guess so, in parts. You saw how rough my drawing was in the beginning, but I got better." He didn't say that he hadn't come close to doing Eddie justice. Sure, by the end his nose had started to look right, but Luke hadn't come close to the light behind his eyes or the energy in his veins. The drawings were all too *still*.

Eddie looked up, his eyes narrow. "No," he said and shook his head. "I mean, do I look like that?" He flipped back to a drawing of just his hand and lower arm. It was an early attempt, before Luke had learned to trust the Hold, all rushed lines and motion. Eddie pointed to his wrist mid-turn. Even with the clear anatomy of bones and muscles, the drawing was more than just a human wrist. There was poetry in the flair of his fingers and the curve of his palm. "Do I look like that *to you?*" he asked, slowly, and Luke understood.

"Yeah." Luke said, quietly. "I mean, yes." Eddie didn't look away. "You really do."

Eddie's eyes flickered—to the table, to the drawing and back to Luke's face—as though he couldn't find words. "Luke," he began, but Dee had already rushed back in.

"Okay," she announced. "Luke, I have an idea. I think you might hate it and I wouldn't blame you, but you have to believe that it's the best one I've got." She turned to Eddie, and her eyes went soft around the edges. "It's your call. If you think my idea's crap, then I'll come up with another one, but give me a chance to explain?" Eddie leaned back, and Dee mirrored him against the window frame. "I think we should go to the police station."

"No. Hell no," Luke said before she could finish. "We can't send him back, especially not if *you're* going to walk him in!" Dee watched Eddie with clasped hands and nervous eyes, but nerves weren't enough. Nerves didn't take the idea back. "He's going to be arrested on sight," said Luke. *Or worse.*

Dee sighed. "No, he's not. Not if he walks in with his apologetic, visibly contrite, wrongful accuser." She brought her hands back to tap on her own chest and said, "That would be me." She paused, but Eddie didn't respond. "I know it sounds like I'm telling you to hand your life away, but the only way we're going to get you out of this is if we put on a show. I play the emotionally compromised idiot who got scared; you play the victim who would like the police to leave him alone for something he didn't do; and we both get out of there before the end of the day." She shrugged. "Maybe faster if I cry. What do you think?"

"He thinks it's a stupid idea," Luke said between clenched teeth.

Dee glanced up to where Luke was leaning over the table and then went back to Eddie's face. "Maybe so," she said, "but I'm asking him." Dee might have sounded confident—Marcos liked to say that she could sell salt water in San Francisco—but even the best poker players had their tells. As she waited for Eddie to respond, Dee bit her bottom lip raw. "It's a good story," he finally said, with a nod, and the air rushed out of her chest in a puff of relief.

"It helps when they're true," she said, and her eyes shone, but it could have been the light. "You game?"

Eddie glanced at the sketchpad before he answered. "Only if Luke's in charge."

They both responded so quickly, Luke couldn't hear himself speak.

"Not a chance in hell," Dee said, and it was the first time Luke agreed with her all night. "He hasn't done enough?"

"I shouldn't—" Luke sputtered, as he backed away from the table. "You should be in charge. You're the actor. I'm just—"

"A director?" Eddie asked, as if it was the most obvious thing in the world, as if directing a monologue was remotely the same as orchestrating a con to save Eddie's life. "You asked to help, and this is what I need." He turned back to Dee with his elbows on the table and his hands clasped under his chin. "You're with me, and Luke plans the big picture, or I'm out."

"Done, but he's not coming in with us."

"Dee!" Luke rounded on her, but her eyes stayed on Eddie and his aggravating calm. Her tight lips said she wasn't happy about the decision, but she'd make it anyway, which was all well and good, except for the fact that it put Luke in charge. "Thanks for the vote of confidence, but I can't direct away Wes or anything that happened at the theater. Your brother's in the hospital for something I basically made Eddie do—"

"You didn't *make me* do anything," Eddie said and had the gall to roll his eyes. "At worst, you get an assist."

Luke kept pushing. "Fine, but Wes doesn't know that, and the police officers who tried to arrest you won't care."

"Wes isn't going to be a problem," Dee said. "He's had a change of heart and won't be pressing charges. What do you think I was doing before you got here?"

Probably planning how to kill me.

"I called Wes as soon as you left school. I figured there was more to the story." She pushed away from the wall and walked toward the fridge, with a look that said she knew exactly what he'd been thinking. "I could believe you were hooking up with a, well—" she glanced at Eddie, and he looked back. "I'm sorry. You know what I said. If I wasn't seeing straight, I could make myself believe you were being stupid and casual, but, really, you didn't sound like you were talking about something casual." She held out a Britta filter like an apology. "Either of you want something to drink?"

Heat crawled up Luke's neck, and the boys shook their heads in unison.

"Anyway, I knew if you cared about him that much, I was missing part of the picture." Dee leaned against the counter and sipped water from a mug that said *Stage Managers Do It with Authority*. "Obviously, I care about my asshole little brother. He's my family, and nothing tops that. I *love* him," she said with such fierce affection that Luke worried for the mug. "But, if I have to choose between your version of reality and his, there's no competition. Dude, you win." This time, Luke knew he wasn't imagining the shine in her eyes.

"There's no way he told you what happened," Eddie said, quietly.

Dee shook her head. "He said enough." She scowled into her glass. "We had a talk, and let's just say you don't have to worry about him anymore, at least not in a legal sense." She snorted, and her smile came back around the edges. "If I tell our mom even half of what you said today, she'll have him sent to a boarding school in Saskatchewan."

Good. But Canada isn't far enough away. "And the roof?" Luke asked. "What do we do about that?"

Dee shrugged, but Eddie was already half out of his seat with his hand in the air as if he had to be called on to speak. "Nothing," he said, and looked far too happy about it for Luke's taste. "We do nothing, because it never happened." Luke stared at him. Eddie wasn't making sense, but Dee nodded as though she should have gotten there first. "We do nothing," Eddie went on, "because the only people who know it happened either can't or won't talk about it. I won't incriminate myself, you weren't officially there and what are the police officers going to say? 'We had him on the roof of a five-story building, sir, but then he disappeared into thin air? No sir, we aren't high. Why do you ask?'" Eddie grinned, and Luke felt it down to his toes.

Dee snorted. "Exactly. If they really wanted to, they could probably prove you were there, but how hard are they going to try?" *Not hard at all if we get this right.*

So they planned. Dee and Eddie tossed out ideas, and Luke pulled them together into something like a show. If he thought about it like just another monologue, it wasn't so difficult. It was just another page of pictures in the notebook, and this time Eddie got to see him put the pieces together. Dee was new, too, but the least surprising thing that happened all day might have been how easily Dee and Eddie fell into step. They made sense together, like two halves of a brittle, brilliant whole, but he wasn't sure they would notice.

Something tight and warm curled in his chest, and he cut them off before he could get sappy. "Are we ready?" It wasn't really a question, but Dee waited for Eddie's nod before heading for the door.

As she passed his chair, Eddie laid a hand on her arm. "I'm glad your brother's okay," he said, quietly, more to the table than to Dee.

She squeezed his hand. "Thanks. I don't know if I feel the same way." When she caught Luke's eye, her smile was strained. "Let's ride. We have to get you home so that you can have a long, hard think about the value of communication."

Eddie pursed his lips over a laugh and shrugged as if to say, *she's not wrong.*

They took Dee's SUV to the station. Walking would have meant more time on the streets and more time for the police to find Eddie on their own. Dee's silver Nissan—alias "Bruno"—had always seemed like a tank, gross and pointlessly huge. He'd never liked the thing before, but it was growing on him. The city passed by in a haze, and Luke breathed foggy circles onto the glass. In the front seat, Eddie's knuckles tapped a nervous off-beat against the door. That's the sort of thing that usually would have gotten him dumped onto the sidewalk, but Dee just turned up the radio and glanced at Luke in the rearview mirror. He shouldn't have been surprised at how fast they got to his house; he lived just five minutes away from Dee, but he still jumped when she called his name.

"This is you," she said, and he focused on looking calm. His stomach might have been somewhere around his ribcage, but neither his parents nor Eddie needed to know that.

When he was fairly sure his lunch wasn't going to land on his shoes, he pushed open the car door, and it took him a second to realize that Eddie's was open, too.

He climbed halfway out of the front seat and asked, "Is it okay if I borrow you for a second?" Luke wasn't sure if Eddie was really asking, but he shrugged and let himself be led toward his own front door. Eddie stopped at the steps and turned with one hand on Luke's arm. "We could change the plan so you can come too," he said, with an edge of hope and, after the day he'd had, Luke didn't know where Eddie found optimism; he had to have a pipeline right to the source.

"I know we have a plan and I know it was my idea to let you make the plan," Eddie said and held his hand to his chest, just below his collarbone. "But I'm an idiot. You belong in there with us. So you screwed up—"

"So much."

"Yeah," Eddie smiled, "so, so much, but you also saved my life." He cocked his head with his eyebrows raised, and Luke couldn't help but smile back. Eddie couldn't look at him like that; it wasn't fair. "That's right. You saved me. You were like a crazy-brave, stupid superhero, and no one gets to know that you were even there." He finally let go of Luke's arm. "I know why you can't come, but I wish you could be there to finish the job." He rocked back on the balls of his feet, and it was so darling Luke could have cried.

"Remember when I first said I was calling Dee?" Luke asked.

Eddie almost laughed. "Of course. I kind of stopped breathing." Luke followed his gaze back to the car where Dee was patiently *not watching*.

"I didn't want to tell you," Luke said, "but at that moment, that was the whole plan." He smiled, and Eddie stopped rocking. "We got out of the theater, and she was the only strategy I had. I wanted her to see what she did and to fix it, but I also figured she could actually help. Together, you two are the smartest people I've ever met. When she isn't scared and pissed off and wrong as hell about something, she knows how to get the job done."

Eddie's eyes softened. "But then I made it your job."

"Yeah, you did," Luke said, quietly. "Still can't believe you did that."

"Still glad I did, *Captain*."

"Then you should get back in the car and let my plan work. It's going to be okay," he said and found that he believed it.

Eddie's eyes narrowed, as if he were trying to memorize Luke's face on the sly. "It's weird," he said, "but I know." He held out his hands and tugged Luke to plant a kiss on his forehead. His breath whispered against Luke's skin. "I just have to get used to the idea that you're a superpowered secret agent. No big deal."

"I think you just made yourself a Bond girl," Luke said into his collarbone, and his head spun. By all rights, Eddie should have left him crying on the curb. *I don't deserve you.*

"That may have been intentional," Eddie said with a grin. "They get the best outfits."

And Luke was going to save that thought for another time. "Go. I'll see you." Then he pushed, and Eddie laughed his way back to the street.

He had to go inside and explain to his parents where he had been since school ended and all of the previous night. If he explained about Wes, they'd want to know why he was at the game, and it would all spiral out from there. For all he knew, that night could turn into one of the marathon conversations he remembered from the beginning of high school when they all had sat on his bed and hashed out Luke's silences until dawn. He couldn't say they didn't care. It had just been a while since they'd remembered to ask.

The first conversation after he came out had been *intense.* His dad had told stories about his own "coming of age" at the beginning of the Reagan era, stories that Luke never wanted to know, and his mom had gotten all excited when she'd thought he'd started dating. Boys or girls, she'd wanted to have his "little friends" over for dinner. It had been exhausting, but also endearing. They would ask questions that would make Luke want to crawl into the floor, but if it meant that they could talk to him again, he'd answer any questions in the world.

He had to go inside, but first he could watch Eddie go.

CHAPTER TWENTY-THREE

IN THE MADE-FOR-TV VERSION OF Luke's life story, the plan, which Eddie eventually named "The Cop Drama," would have gone perfectly to plan. Dee would have been contrite; Eddie would have forgiven her—so selflessly—and the police would have fallen over themselves to apologize for their *grievous* error. At least, that's how it worked in the better, happier half of Luke's directorial imagination.

The reality was less dramatic.

No one seemed shocked when Dee and Eddie walked into the station, probably because no one knew who they were or what they were doing there. Eddie didn't get arrested on sight, and, if the officer on duty was shocked when he explained why he wanted to make a statement, she did a good job of keeping it under wraps. Granted, she spent the next thirty minutes readjusting her glasses, but that could have been a coincidence. Her name was Officer Mallory Craik and, mostly, she listened. She took notes on a yellow legal pad while Dee explained her mistake. "It was a personal misunderstanding, ma'am," Dee said, or rather sobbed, and kept her hand on Eddie's arm. "I didn't have the right context and I was so upset I couldn't think straight."

Then Eddie cried.

That wasn't part of Luke's plan. Eddie was supposed to be more stoic, almost saintly in the face of Dee's emotion, but he said the tears seemed right in the moment. He was playing off Dee's energy, so they rolled with it and bawled all over the bewildered officer's table until she left, muttering something about pop. She came back with a Coke for each of them and three more officers in tow, none of whom knew what to make of the soggy teenagers in interrogation room two. Suddenly, they had no accuser, no weapon, no apparent crime and no one involved seemed to understand the concept of getting a lawyer.

Plus, the blond girl kept *crying*.

Luke also hadn't counted on that fact that the police would call everyone's parents. By the time they were released, three hours later, Luke was waiting in the lobby, but so was Eddie's dad. Luke had called Marcos after an hour of waiting, so he was there, too, and when Eddie emerged, he waved as though they were all trying to get their licenses renewed at the DMV.

Outside the station, Eddie's dad watched with trepidation as his son spoke with the "nice boy" who had apparently gotten him in trouble and then gotten him out of it again. Eddie had promised to tell the entire—well-edited—story at home, in exchange for five minutes in the parking lot. Luke wanted to make good use of the time, but he couldn't stop thanking all the gods that Dee's parents had shown up first. Now they were long gone, but Luke's blood still surged in his ears.

And Eddie? Eddie looked fantastic. He wiped his eyes on his sleeve and smiled like a conquering hero, tired but alive. The station wouldn't apologize any time soon because, apparently, "it wasn't their mistake," and the fact that that sentence wasn't the most disgusting thing Luke had heard all day said more about the day than the department. Eddie seemed ready to agree, but, then again, he didn't have to worry any more about anyone showing up at his house to interrogate his parents. He could have been ten pounds lighter, and that was just in the shoulders. He'd walked away from the station, and the officers weren't even upset that they couldn't make him stay. He was *safe*.

Dee, on the other hand, had sworn the entire squad was ready to arrest her out of sheer irritation. "They hated me," she'd chirped before her mother dragged her home. "I insisted that we wanted to drop the charges, just like we practiced, even though there weren't any charges to drop. I think I actually saw smoke coming out of the oldest guy's ears." She'd squeezed Eddie's arm, and Luke had seen something pass between them that he couldn't read. He only hoped it had been an acknowledgement that Dee was the only one of them who could afford to piss off the cops.

It took nearly five minutes curled into the backseat of Luke's car before Eddie stopped shaking. He took even longer to remember that he'd missed his audition. His time slot had long since passed, and he couldn't explain to the theater folks that he'd missed his shot because he was being arrested on their roof. From Luke's perspective in the driver's seat, Eddie took the realization in stride.

He was fine, Eddie insisted. It was just one play. Compared to Wes and everything else—he was fine, he said again and, for the moment, Luke let it lie.

Greg. Do you quarrel sir?

Regory: A my   No, for then we should be Colliars.   Greg. No, for then we should be Colliars.   Mora. No better?   Samp. W

CHAPTER TWENTY-FOUR

It took two weeks and two days for Luke and Marcos to talk about Eddie or Wes or any of it, because—as Dee would say—it was *them*.

Luke couldn't argue with that. Every time he wanted to say something, he ended up asking about class or whatever comic Marcos had in his lap. Once he talked about pie. Marcos didn't even like pie.

It was just that everything was so good. Eddie and Marcos talked—a lot—and from what he could tell, Marcos liked having Eddie around. He wasn't sure how it had happened, but they'd bonded early over old—some would say obscure—musicals and recording artists that Luke couldn't have picked out of a lineup. The mind-meld wasn't instantaneous. Luke spent a lot of time providing real-time Marcos translations for Eddie, especially when Marcos forgot that everyone didn't necessarily know the backstory for inside jokes that required knowing all the voice actors for the *Legend of Korra* or all the ways that Luke had traumatized himself in eighth grade. Eddie was happy to learn.

It wasn't a perfect fit. Eddie's comics knowledge ended with the movies, and Marcos got lost just thinking about lacrosse, but they could both sing through *Bat Boy: The Musical* from start to finish. Eddie was fine. Marcos was fine. Luke was mostly fine, and none of that had to change, until—all at once—it did.

It was eleven o'clock and Luke was on his back in bed. He tossed his phone toward the ceiling and caught it again before it could land on his chest. He couldn't have said he was actually trying to sleep. To do that, he would have had to change or brush his teeth. Instead, he was still in the giant sweatshirt he'd thrown on for school as he tried to ignore Dee's voice in his head. "Stop being a weenie, Luke" it said, and he scowled.

Brain-Dee was an ass.

With her voice in his ear, he couldn't ignore how long it had been since Marcos had last come over. He used to practically live at Luke's house, in his room, on his bed. They used to lie on top of the covers and stare at the ceiling for hours. Marcos would make up stories about how Luke's drawings were fighting to the death, and Luke would let the words wash over his skin.

It had been months since things had been that simple, and everything was fine, but he texted Marcos anyway.

While he waited, Luke contemplated the designs on the ceiling. He started at a profile of a Marvel character Dee fell in love with last year and made his way around a sketchy echo of his own hand, until his pulse stopped beating in his ears. As he moved to *Batgirl*, the door creaked and a weight settled into the open space beside him on the bed.

Hi. I missed you.

"The door was open, and I didn't think you'd mind. I said hi to your mom," Marcos said from the other side of the comforter, and Luke heard the smile. He hummed under his breath and warmth settled in his chest. It was nice to know that she probably said hi back.

"You didn't need to come over."

Marcos didn't bother turning his head. "Yes, I did." He held up his phone so Luke could see his own text on the screen. "You busy?" it read, and Luke's neck burned. For anyone else, at eleven o'clock, that would have been a booty call, but this was Marcos. He knew Luke needed him, so he came. It was as easy as that.

Except it wasn't.

Marcos pointed at the ceiling. "You added new drawings since last time. I don't remember Batgirl before."

"She wasn't as interesting before the new series. I added our Audrey II design," Luke said and pointed to a pencil sketch near the wall. "It's not done yet."

"But it's cool. Every time I come here it feels more like the Sistine Chapel." He nudged Luke's side. "Maybe you could add droids in honor of *The Return of the Jedi* or something for Eddie's audition? I guess he might like the droids too."

"Maybe," Luke said. "I could." This was when he was supposed to smile and nudge back. He didn't say that Eddie was already all over his ceiling, in the sketches of Marcus Chigozie, a superhero from a Nigerian webcomic, and Mercutio from Baz Luhrmann's *Romeo and Juliet*. Marcos was there too. He didn't need to draw their faces to put them in the picture. But even if he could draw them, it didn't mean he understood what he was looking at. "Would you really want me to draw *Star Wars* stuff?" he asked the ceiling. He stared at the white space between the drawings. None of them touched.

"Why not?"

"I don't know," he said. "It's stupid." He didn't know how to say, *I thought that might hurt you. I might be hurting you right now.*

Marcos sighed, not sadly, but as though Luke were young and needed to learn about crossing the street. "You know how every time we watch *Star Wars*, I have a different favorite scene?" he said. It wasn't a question. "I don't think I told you which one was my favorite that time."

"Marcos—"

"Just listen, okay?" Luke nodded. Marcos settled into his pillow and spoke to the ceiling. "Last time, I was all about the big battle with Luke and Vader and the Emperor. Emperor Palpatine rocks the lightning fingers, and I think maybe Luke will say screw it and go to the dark side."

Luke tried for an affirmative, but it came out as a hiccup. That scene put Marcos on the edge of his seat every time. Luke had stopped reminding him that they knew how it would end.

"Last time, I got distracted." He leaned on the last word and elbowed Luke in the side. "When I was paying attention to the movie, though, I liked different parts. Like, do you ever pay attention to how Leia reacts when Luke says she's his sister? It's wild."

Luke wasn't sure if it was a real question, so he waited, and Marcos answered himself. "She's weirdly cool about the whole thing," he said, as if he could see the scene. "She's surprised, but not shocked, and I never thought about that before. That's so low key."

Marcos rolled onto his side until he was inches from the side of Luke's face. He said, "It's weird, right? She should be freaked out that the guy who fought to make out with her is her twin, but she isn't. I guess some part of her already knew. Luke confirmed it, but Leia already figured it out and she was just waiting for her *idiot brother* to get on board." He gave Luke a pointed smile and raised his eyebrows as if to say, *what about it, dumbass?*

Luke could have kissed him. *Or not. No, probably not.* "So, we're Luke and Leia?" he asked. Marcos shrugged, but he was smiling. "And I went on a date with my brother?"

Marcos pressed his lips together, and they twitched. "To be fair, the relationship isn't biological. I think that makes it better."

"Sure, but you also called me an idiot."

"Siblings are allowed to do that," he said with a grin. "We get nicknames, harassment, wedgies." Luke thought about how Lizzy had laughed when he got hurt. The accuracy was real and sweet like rhubarb: sugary with a tart finish.

"What if we already do that stuff?" he asked.

"Then you probably should have figured it out sooner," Marcos said. He laughed until Luke pulled the pillow from under the comforter and smacked him over the head. Then he squeaked. Marcos could have fought back, pillow for pillow, but he just lay there giggling while the pillow shook over his face. "I'm not wrong."

"Shut up," Luke said, and he peeked under the pillow. It wasn't his fault he was a little slow when it came to feelings and friends. He ducked under the pillow until it sat over both of their heads, like a tiny fort. "Tell me if I'm beating a dead horse, okay?" he asked. Marcos cringed, but he nodded. "After the movie, I got confused 'cause it seemed like you changed fast. One minute there was the, you know—" He pointed to his mouth and Marcos smiled. "Then the next minute you were all Zen. Was that because we're basically related?"

Luke was sure he sounded like a fifth-grader trying to teach himself sex ed, but Marcos didn't laugh. "Yes," he said, "and no?" He rolled back on to his back and hugged their fort-pillow to his chest. For the first time in the conversation, Marcos looked as if he wanted to be somewhere else. "This might not make sense to you, but I don't get crushes on people. I just don't."

"Not ever?" Luke asked. He didn't want to sound rude, but that didn't seem possible. He thought back to middle school when he'd liked Marcos and Dee had liked Marcos and Marcos had liked … no one? He came up blank, and it was the same for ninth grade and for tenth. Even when Dee moved on to other people, and Luke just stopped talking about it, Marcos never got stupidly hormonal about anyone. Not ever.

Marcus hugged the pillow closer. "Nope. Sorry," he said, and Luke couldn't imagine what he was apologizing for. "Anyway, when you stopped showing up for rehearsal, after everything that happened, I got worried. I wanted to make sure you were okay and I thought that was maybe what a crush was supposed to feel like." He frowned, as though he'd done something *wrong*, and Luke was keenly aware of all the things in the world he didn't know. "I was pretty sure you liked me, or at least I thought you did, and I got excited 'cause I thought I finally liked you back. It was going to be so easy, but then the movie happened, and when I figured out that you liked someone else, I didn't get mad. I felt like I was supposed to hate Eddie or you but, mostly, I was relieved."

Luke waited for him to go on, but he stopped and stared at the ceiling with his chin tucked over the pillow and his hands clasped around his own wrists. He didn't look scared, exactly, more anxious, as though he'd jumped out of a plane and had to believe the parachute was going to work. Luke wanted to hide under the bed, but not if it left Marcos behind.

"You dodged a bullet there," he said, with care. "I mean with me, obviously. You think it would have been easy, because we're awesome, but relationships are totally different. You would have hated me after five minutes; I would have made fun of your music collection."

"And then there's the part where we're related."

Luke nodded. "There would have been hell to pay at the next family reunion."

Marcos giggled. He actually giggled like a little kid, and Luke's heart started beating again. That was the only sound Marcos was ever supposed to make. "So." He started, slowly, when they'd relaxed back into the silence. "Does this mean you're Ace or Aro?" He wasn't sure he completely understood the difference, but he was pretty sure one meant no sex. "It's cool if you don't want to answer that, though."

"Nah." Marcos still had a little smile as though he couldn't remember how to do anything else. "I don't know. I think I'm both, but I'm also kind of into not knowing for sure. It's my mystery." He scooted over on the bed to bump his head against Luke's shoulder and then left it there, touching. The angle had to be hell for Marcos's neck, but Luke hoped he wouldn't move.

He nudged Marcos's head with his and pointed him back to the ceiling. "Okay. Well, I'm definitely putting *Star Wars* on the ceiling, right under Ms. Marvel. But no droids," he said, before Marcos could ask. "I'm going draw a thing with just the twins."

"You're going to use that poster where she has her arms all the way up his leg, aren't you?"

"Of course. It's about *family*." Luke grinned and he was ready when Marcos thwacked a pillow over his head. He laughed until breath was tight in his chest, and tears left track-stains on his cheeks.

A long time later, after a Marcus-tour through the ceiling and a lot of happy silence, Marcos fell asleep on his shoulder. Luke sent Eddie a selfie. It wasn't a special occasion or anything. It had happened before; it would happen again, and that was probably his favorite thing about the whole night. Marcos hummed in his sleep and the low vibration melted into the space heater buzz until he couldn't mark where one sound ended and another began.

CHAPTER TWENTY-FIVE

LATER THAT WEEK, LUKE FOUND Eddie waiting at First and Thirty-third with his back against an elm tree and his eyes on the sky. He was an easy find. With the exception of a dog walker on the other side of First, he was alone on the street, but that wasn't why he was so easy to find.

It was his posture, or better yet, his grace. Even after a full day of school, Eddie stood with his back straight and his shoulders back, as though he'd found his natural balance between the earth and the sky. Luke could have picked him out of the crowd leaving the downtown bus station at rush hour. He was also exactly where he'd said he would be, but when Luke first got the directions, he hadn't believed that Eddie really wanted to meet in front of Wes and Dee's house.

As Luke got closer, it became apparent that Eddie hadn't been looking at the sky so much as the upper floors of the Corelli house. Luke waved, and a sheepish smile lit across Eddie's face. "You were serious," he called. "I hope you checked for Dee's mom, because I don't think she's ready for a group potluck." He tried for casual, but Margo Corelli could have looked out the window at any time and wondered why Eddie was loitering on her lawn. Dee might have given up blaming Eddie for her brother's concussion, but her mother averted her eyes in the parking lot.

Eddie shrugged. "Her car's gone. Don't worry so much," he said and beckoned for Luke to join him against the tree. He nudged Luke's shoulder, but his eyes stayed unfocused, as if he'd lost himself in his own head. "Is it stupid that I want to go in there?" He pointed at the second floor, where they knew Wes would be. He laughed without humor. "Don't answer that question. I, I know. I keep having these fantasies where we talk and he gets it. He looks into my face, one-on-one, and says he's sorry, like we dropped into a Hallmark movie." He turned and swallowed hard through his smile. "I blame Dee. She's given me unrealistic expectations about people who used to hate me."

"Dee didn't hate you; she didn't know you."

"Neither does he."

Luke nodded and stared at Wes's window. Dee was different, but he didn't need to say that. Since the day at the station, Dee hadn't left Eddie alone. He hadn't entirely believed her when she'd said she wanted to be his friend, so she'd invited him out for coffee every single day. Eventually, he'd accepted an invitation and then another. Dee thought they were fine, even better friends for their mistakes, but Luke knew better. They were friendly, but she got Eddie's "I'm friends with everyone" face, and Luke wasn't sure that would ever change.

For a long time, Luke wasn't sure he deserved any better. By Eddie's count, Luke said he was sorry thirty-two times. He said it after every hug and put Post-its in his notebooks until Eddie started charging him for every apology. He earned five-fifty before Luke got it. Eddie had already forgiven him in a way he might never forgive Dee, and Luke didn't have to understand why.

"Some people need more time," Luke said close to Eddie's shoulder. "Dee tried making him read the new *Black Panther* comics, but it didn't take." Luke tugged on his hand, and Eddie allowed himself to be led down the sidewalk toward the coffee shop on Thirty-third.

"You know she got me an audition this Friday," Eddie said, as much to himself as to Luke. He sounded as though he was still getting used to the idea. "She wouldn't tell me how it happened, but I think she badgered the artistic director at the Continuum Theater Company until she said I could read for their touring cast. They mostly perform in high schools and for community centers, but the material is really strong."

Luke squeezed Eddie's hand. *This boy.* "Will they let me come and watch?" He heard the pride in his voice, and it definitely wasn't for Dee. After the work he'd put in, Eddie deserved sixteen perfect auditions and a puppy.

"I don't know," he said. His voice was calm, but his eyes shone with excitement. "They actually might. There were a million students from other high schools in the building when I took the tour, but most of the actors were Somali and Oromo. You'll stand out."

"And that'll be new," Luke said. "I'm going with you. Afterward, you can take me to that place across from the movie theater." He grinned, happy and shameless. They'd had goat there on their first real date, and he was pretty sure the meal was a message from God.

"Sure," said Eddie, and rolled his eyes, "but we can't go the same day as the audition because—and I can't believe I'm saying this—my parents would like to cordially invite you to their home for dinner." He turned to drop into a bow as if he were thinking about taking Luke to the ball. "And you have to tell your parents. They're invited too, and my mom will put the blame on my head if they don't come. I think she's already cooking."

Luke sputtered into his hand and then down at the top of his boyfriend's head. He'd had thoughts, many of them, but they all flew away at that bow. Of course, thinking would also be easier if Eddie stopped laughing. "I, I, um. When did you—?"

"Yesterday." Eddie righted himself and smiled, as proud as anything. "I told them that I had a boy in my life that I liked very much and I hoped they would like him too. Easy as that." Something behind his eyes suggested it hadn't been so easy. If acting made his parents worry about his safety, Luke couldn't imagine how they'd respond to boys. But if Eddie wanted to skip that story, Luke would let him, and Eddie was almost wiggling with amusement. "My father is trying to be cool about it. I think he's read everything online about bisexuality, and he keeps asking questions. It's a lot better than my uncles. They would have said I was 'sweet' and not in a good way."

Luke squinted at the "questions" until Eddie laughed. "Captain America. He wanted to know if kids these days think Captain America is bisexual, and I just said yes. So, you should probably get ready to talk about that."

"Noted," Luke said with a snort. "But you know it doesn't matter what he says. He could be wearing a Captain America costume, and it wouldn't be as awkward as my parents."

"They were fine." Eddie said lightly and kept walking. "They were very polite, and I was *fantastic*."

"You were a *menace*. We walk into the house and you're all, 'Hi, my name is Edward Sankawulo, and I really, really like your son,'" he said in his best impersonation, and if fake-Eddie's eye-contact was a little more intense than the real thing, it was nothing less than he deserved. Luke's dad almost had a heart attack.

Eddie just about died laughing at the memory. "Don't even lie." He smiled. "They love me. It's a perfectly easy equation. You like me, and they love you. Therefore…" He trailed off, and Luke rolled his eyes. He couldn't let Eddie get so smug, but he also couldn't deny the logic. His father might have been struck dumb when Eddie made his *declaration*, but he'd been blatantly curious about "this boy" ever since. He swore, some days his dad cared more about whether he called Eddie than he did.

"What was it your mother said again?" Eddie turned and walked backward down the sidewalk. And now he was practically crowing. "I think it was something about feeling *so much better*. It must be that magical rejuvenation that comes from seeing your son with a good boyfriend. It's the only explanation that makes sense." That and the therapy, the medication and the time, but Eddie knew all of that. He also liked making Luke swat at him. "You're welcome." Eddie smiled, and Luke tugged on his hand.

"Come on, miracle-worker." He pulled Eddie between the houses, until they emerged in a tiny circle of trees. It was the Dakota Street Garden or, as it was officially known, the Anita N. Gutierrez Memorial Green Space. They'd been here before. Once they'd come by accident, when Eddie had been looking for a shortcut to the bus stop, and one other time with more intention. This time, Luke backed Eddie up against the wide oak that blocked the garden from the street, and Eddie's pulse quickened under his hands. "And what if I said you were right?" he asked.

"Right about what?" Eddie's arms slipped around Luke's waist until he could clasp them and press his thumbs into the small of Luke's back. "Are you saying I really gave your mother a new zest for life? That's adorable." He smirked, but his eyes had already blown from brown to black.

Luke cocked his head and smirked back. "Not exactly, but you might be magic."

Eddie grinned hard enough to show off all his teeth, but when Luke bent toward him, he ducked away. "Wait," he said. "Can you do the thing where you—you know?" He pursed his lips and flushed up to his ears.

Luke held back the urge to laugh into Eddie's shoulder.

Oh, he knew. Two weeks before, Eddie had asked Luke to try the Hold when they were hanging out in Luke's bedroom. Then they'd kissed, and things had spiraled from there. Of course, it had been great for Luke because he'd been *kissing Eddie Sankawulo*, and he was fairly certain his brain would never stop putting that in italics, but it was nothing compared to what it had been like for Eddie. Three hours after Luke let the Hold drop, Eddie had still been awake and texting strings of exclamation points.

In his own words, it was like making out in slow motion, as if his mind started dreaming while his body was wide awake. He couldn't describe it without something nearing awe or without making Luke warm down to his toes. Still, Luke had his reservations.

"Should I?" he asked. "What if the Hold turns out to be like, like a drug?" Eddie dropped his head back against the tree and snorted. "You laugh, but while I'm trying to feel up my boyfriend, I could be accidentally turning you into a superpower junkie."

"Captain—"

"Next thing I know, you're going to be knocking on my window at midnight looking for a fix. Nobody wants that."

"Luke." Luke stopped and grinned into Eddie's stop-screwing-with-me stare. Eddie added, "Don't worry. If I get addicted, it will have nothing to do with the *Hold*."

His boyfriend kissed the way he spoke, all heat and focus and with more intensity than most people knew in their whole lives. If their first kiss rushed into a crash, this one slid into a languid dance. Eddie's lips pulled, soft and warm, and he hummed as Luke cradled the back of his head in his hands. Beyond the trees, the road stood frozen, and, above his head, the leaves were still, but on the ground, Luke vibrated with life. His blood thrummed to the beat under Eddie's skin. Luke kissed his cheek and throat and each fluttering eyelid. He kissed like a prayer to life and motion.

And him.

And him.

And him.

ON FRIDAY, LUKE KEPT HIS head up.

His phone buzzed as he pushed through the school doors, and he itched to check his messages, but he had to watch for the boy of the hour. He was actually the man of the hour. Boys didn't get auditions for professional internships, but calling Eddie "the boy of the hour" made him squirm. He took compliments well enough, but all the encouragement Dee, Marcos and Luke piled on left him perpetually flushed.

"Morning, Captain."

Luke turned as Eddie stepped into place at his side. "Morning, yourself." Luke smiled. "Are you excited, or am I not allowed to talk about that?"

Eddie rolled his eyes. "You're allowed," he muttered, "but just you. If Dee gives me one more note about breath technique, I can't be held responsible for my actions. She means well, but—"

"Who means well?" Dee appeared at Eddie's other side, and Marcos was just behind her. They fell into step and wouldn't shut up about Eddie's audition until they got to Luke's locker. Actually, Marcos wouldn't shut up. One word from Eddie, and Dee stopped cold. It wasn't the first time she'd listened, and it wouldn't be the last.

Marcos didn't notice. He bounced on his toes and told Eddie about the songs he'd collected for the occasion. "Someone had to celebrate our Mystique's audition," he said, and Luke almost fell into his locker. *Mystique?* "From X-Men," Marcos clarified, as if recognition were the problem. He leaned against the next locker door. "I'm trying it out. She's a shapeshifter; Eddie's an actor. So, on an existential level they have similar powers. It's a work in progress."

Eddie's eyebrows were almost at his hairline, and his lips were pinched closed. "Thanks," he said. "I like the idea, but it would be nice to have a name that wasn't evil. No offense."

Dee patted him on the back. "Sorry, Boo Boo. No can do. All the shapeshifters are evil."

Just like everyone who can stop time. We were both supposed to be bad.

Luke nudged Eddie with his shoulder. "Welcome to the evil league of evil," he said quietly. "I'll get you an official jacket after school."

Dee snorted into her hand and waved to Marcos as he disappeared into the junior commons. Luke pretended that she wasn't laughing at him.

"I should go too," Eddie said and jerked his head toward his hallway. At some point, he'd started tapping his hand against his leg, and Luke felt a wave of *once upon a time.*

"We're meeting you after the audition?" It wasn't really a question, but Eddie hummed in agreement and let Luke take his hands. "You're going to break all the legs and then we're going to give you enough sugar to kill a bear, okay?" Eddie laughed and kissed him on the side of the mouth, right there in the middle of the hallway. He'd been doing that for a week, just laying one on him when Luke wasn't ready, and it never stopped feeling like a miracle.

"Yes, Captain. Absolutely," he said quietly and turned to go before Luke could do more than stare at his back. He used to hate that nickname, but damn if he could remember why.

Dee watched him go, too. "You ready for this?" she asked.

"For what?" Luke turned back to his locker and reached for his English folder under the mess. Eddie was too far away to see now, just one head in the crowd, but if Dee weren't there, he'd have watched for him anyway. "I don't have to do anything but cheer him on."

"I know," she said. "But it'll change everything."

Luke wanted to say no. But she was right. He could play the game of whether Eddie would or wouldn't get cast, and it would be pointless. Eddie had to get the part. They couldn't turn him away if they tried, and everything would change all over again.

No more audition rehearsals. No more theater classroom. Eddie would have practice across town while Marcos and Dee did the tech for *Little Shop of Horrors*. Maybe Luke would be backstage, too. He'd thought about jumping back into the rhythm if Madam Stage Manager would have him. After weekend rehearsals, they would call Eddie and meet at a diner: a booth full of tired, disgusting theater dorks drinking pop and sharing a single plate of four-dollar fries until the waitress guilted them into paying for their space.

He'd have to go home after school. His parents had checked on him again. They wanted to know how his tests went and if he had time to help clean out Lizzy's room. They hadn't started packing it up yet. His mom had bought boxes and let them live in the hallway outside her door. Eventually, they'd put her things in the basement with the baby clothes and the old magazines. Eddie wouldn't make that happen, but he'd help put away the boxes and keep Luke from putting himself away at their side. He wouldn't be in the room of a million German posters, but he'd be in Luke's room and at his locker. He'd call from rehearsals or show Luke how to make fufu and jollof rice at home.

It'll change everything. Luke would change everything. He closed the door. Luke would change. He breathed. Butterflies rose in his chest, and he took a breath.

He couldn't wait.

ACKNOWLEDGMENTS

I AM MADE OF LOVE for the remarkable community that made this book possible. They say it takes a village to raise a child, and Hold has never felt more like a little book-human than when I consider the gorgeous people that brought it into the world. For every name I mention, please imagine another page of emojis and loving, derpy gifs.

To Jebeh Edmunds, Ryan Dickerson, Mark O'Brien, Dale Cameron Lowry, Mabelle Caamano, Brooks Benjamin, and Leah Pope: You were some of my first readers and some of my last. Thank you for bringing your brilliance and expertise to these pages. You thought with me, got excited with me, and gave me the chance to do my characters justice.

To Georgie, Faina, Lissa, and the rest of the remarkable Interlude Press family: Thank you for your emotional support on this bookish roller coaster. You supported me when I wanted to throw the computer across the room and take up woodworking. Thanks for talking me back to the page.

To Wesaun, Teagle, Jessie Gurd, CB Lee, and FT Lukens: Thank you for showing me the way, for providing advice, and pointing me toward the people I'd need on my path. You all got to be the wizard at the crossroads, and you didn't steer me wrong.

To Caroline Hanlin, Nicole Rowlinson, Leah Misemer, Cass, and Claire: I don't even know where to start. Thank you for reading and commenting and making this book better, but most of all thank you for your belief. You believed in this project (and my ability to bring these kids to life) in some cases before I did. Thank you for feedback that made me laugh and gave me perspective just when I needed it most.

Thank you to Interlude Press for getting excited about my weird little proposal and for creating a cover that fit the story better than I could have possibly imagined. Thank you to my English teachers: Sandra, Laurie, Susan, Connie, Susan, and again Susan for letting me get credit for playing with words. Thank you to all of my fandom friends for making me think that maybe I could try to write.

To Max: You're my prince. Thank you for loving my masochistic little self, and for always being the best part of my day.

To my mom and dad: There are no words. Thank you for always being my best friends and my biggest fans. Thank you for reading drafts so rough they hardly deserved the name, and for constantly retreading the line between fiction and your own lives. I'd say it again, but thank you isn't enough.

To Michael: I miss you, buddy. Just give me the chance and I'll trip over something to make you smile.

NOTE TO **READERS**

I HOPE THAT YOU ENJOYED your time with Luke, Eddie, Marcos, and Dee. This story is dear to my heart, and I'm so glad you had the opportunity to share it with me.

Now that you're done, I hope you'll consider taking a moment to share your thoughts about *Hold* on Goodreads, Amazon, and other website. Reviews are an invaluable resource for other readers. If you'd like to know more about the book, other LGBTQ young adult fiction, or what I'm working on next, please join me on social media. I love hearing from readers! You can find me on Tumblr at Racheldavidsonleigh.com; on Twitter at @RDavidsonLeigh; and on Facebook at facebook.com/rdavidsonleigh.

Thanks again for reading!

ABOUT THE AUTHOR

RACHEL DAVIDSON LEIGH IS A teacher, a writer and an avid fan of young adult LGBTQ fiction. Her hobbies include overanalyzing television shows and playing matchmaker with book recommendations. Currently, she lives in Wisconsin with her family and two neurotic little dogs. *Hold* is her debut novel. Her short story "Beautiful Monsters" was featured in *Summer Love*, a collection of short stories published by Duet Books, the young adult imprint of Interlude Press.

One **story**
can change **everything**.

an imprint of interlude **press**

@duet**books**

Twitter | Tumblr

*For a reader's guide to **Hold** and*
book club prompts, please visit duetbooks.com.

also from **duet.**

Seven Tears at High Tide by C.B. Lee

Kevin Luong walks to the ocean's edge with a broken heart. Remembering a legend his mother told him, he lets seven tears fall into the sea. "I just want one summer—one summer to be happy and in love." Instead, he finds himself saving a mysterious boy from the Pacific—a boy who later shows up on his doorstep professing his love. What he doesn't know is that Morgan is a selkie, drawn to answer Kevin's wish. As they grow close, Morgan is caught between the dangers of the human world and his legacy in the selkie community to which he must return at summer's end.

ISBN (print) 978-1-941530-47-4 | (eBook) 978-1-941530-48-1

The Star Host by F.T. Lukens

Ren grew up listening to his mother tell stories about the Star Hosts—mythical people possessed by the power of the stars. Captured by a nefarious Baron, Ren discovers he may be something out of his mother's stories. He befriends Asher, a member of the Phoenix Corps. Together, they must master Ren's growing power, and try to save their friends while navigating the growing attraction between them.

ISBN (print) 978-1-941530-72-6 | (eBook) 978-1-941530-73-3

The Rules of Ever After by Killian B. Brewer

The royal rules have governed the kingdoms of Clarameer for centuries, but princes Phillip and Daniel know that these rules don't apply to them. In a quest to find their own Happily Ever After, they encounter meddlesome fairies, an ambitious stepmother, disgruntled princesses and vengeful kings as they learn about life, love, friendship and family—and learn to write their own rules of ever after.

ISBN (print) 978-1-941530-35-1 | (eBook) 978-1-941530-42-9

CPSIA information can be obtained
at www.ICGtesting.com
Printed in the USA
LVOW07s0716250417
532016LV00001B/1/P